DIGUR

DIGOR

In fighting the truth will out

ROBERT HATTON

THE CHOIR PRESS

First published in the United Kingdom in 2023 by
The Choir Press

ISBN 978-1-78963-406-8

Dedication

To Sharon: You showed me levels of kindness have no bounds. You taught me love. To Mum for giving me the strength to never give up. To my girls for filling me with pride. To my Grandsons for fuelling my dreams.

In memory of Gary Wilson and John Putt

Contents

Foreword

Hundreds upon millions of swimmers are bound on a mission of the purest intent. It's not like they have a choice; they can't go back from where they were rather excitedly squirted. Following the pull of a chemical signal, they swim. To have any chance of success they will have to overcome staggering death-defying odds, along their way facing off with real weapons of mass destruction. To facilitate such transit and avoid being killed by burning acid, it will help their cause greatly to get close and friendly with any clear streams of secreted mucus that comes their way. The stronger ones who find themselves still in the race will be met by a heavily guarded fortress where merciless white blood cells will try and beat the elite swimmers into ultimate surrender. The last hurrah will see the leading pack fiercely compete against one another because when they do finally arrive at the egg party, they discover there's only room for one, siblings aside. Which by the miraculous and chaotic end means everyone else has perished or will do so soon, except you. Well done and congratulations!

It should be of little surprise then that when we are born into this world, our default programming is set for fighting. Some will continue their fight for survival facing impossible odds. Some will find the fight for their just cause, others will go on and fight professionally; some of them will enjoy it, and then there are those who will never raise so much as a clenched fist in the entirety of their existence. After such a tumultuous start who could blame them, but make no mistake, we are all fighting something.

This story, just like the one about the sperm hinted at earlier, started with its own struggle, not the least of which was how to pitch it. Fiction won. It was a close call. In making that decision, the battle lines blurred, but the story that compelled me to write remains intact. Some boys want to drive trains when they grow up; some want to fight. Thankfully, though, it is not all about physical fighting. The fight is the heartbeat of the story, the goddam fight.

A cursory glance on the internet provides front-seat access to the myriad fighting styles that are around today. You can wonder at those from a bygone age; a click of the mouse and you're steering along the superhighway, dazzled by promotions from clubs all around the world. The comments that follow are the stuff of playground taunts – my dad's bigger than your dad. Thumbs up or down, there's always someone with an axe to grind. People judge, people argue, and people definitely fight. Some are so bloody good at it. And some are so disgusting that the deaths of children won't stop them from doing it.

Mixed martial arts changed the game. Arriving on the scene in spectacular fashion, MMA has a voice that booms real and far. The internet and social media have given us a window to look through and witness this tsunami. So popular has been the spread of MMA that stadiums around the world are packed out for tournaments – clubs can expand into world organisations in a short time. But there is a price to pay … there's always a price to pay.

From somewhere among the echelons of fighters, I will try my best to show you what it's like to be at the bottom looking up, to pick yourself up from the dusty floor and make an ascent, and share with you my story inspired by true events along the way to a simple yet profound discovery. For some there will be nothing new; the answers still lie in the time-honoured traditions of the past. For the inquisitive mind, dangers lie ahead.

I thought social studies were for academics to pick apart, but I found myself embroiled in one. Come with me on a journey and see what you think. Are we in for a fight?

Customer quality guarantee – my promise to you for taking the plunge. You should become a better fighter after reading this and, if I may be so bold, a little wiser. With a good wind in your sails, it could take you to a level you never thought possible, and at the least it should help shine a light to a better path. If you are not completely satisfied with the quality of this product, please write to customer care, or better still read my next book. That one will show you how to recoup your money, and possibly make more than you could ever imagine.

For the dreamers and grasshoppers, a cautionary tale.

Acknowledgements

Special thanks to:

Andrew at the Writers College.

My former editor Lesley for wielding her sharp axe.

Rachel at The Choir Press Publishers.

My friend Terry Mitchell for planting the seed, and everyone else in between who helped shape this story.

Your Truly,

Bobby

Chapter 1

Growing up slowly

Norbert Jennings faked a move left and shimmied to the right with the nimbleness of a hummingbird. He was now free and into open space. He swung his right foot, and a scuffed plimsole launched the heavy plastic ball into the afternoon air. Only then did he look up, open-mouthed and still, fear and dread clung in the widening whites of his eyes. The gods cursed, cramming all the certainties in the entire world into his young nine-year-old mind, and they all sang an unequivocal truth. There was absolutely nothing that was going to stop that ball from hitting its mark. Shame that it transpired not to be the small metal-framed goal at the other end of the playground at which he had taken aim. All he could do was watch his absolute worst nightmare play out. Time stood still; the other children who had frozen into temporary stillness were light years behind Norbert's realisation. Thwack. It stung into the face of the school bully with not a bit to spare.

Between the tragedy and joy of life's spectrum, it is a rare thing indeed that such a random act could pinpoint a place in time for monumental changes that would shape someone's life and later reveal something extraordinary. Yet there it was.

Norbert was an only child. When his jealousy got the better of him, he told anyone who asked he had five brothers and five sisters. He never knew his dad, but that never tethered him down, and besides, his mum, Rosemary, plugged any gaps with strong love and a fierce determination. Norbert adored his grandparents, but they had long since stopped adoring each other. Nan Sophie was hooked up with Fred, Norbert's fiery, petulant step-granddad, who took a shine to the youngster, despite loathing his mum. Rosemary defiantly squared up to Fred if he dared to threaten Sophie – the vacuum cleaner still bore a kink in its metal tubing as evidence. Granddad Fred was an angry man and if he returned from the post office without waving his walking stick in someone's face and telling them to fuck off, he was having an unusual day. Think Alf Garnet with extra snarl and you are there.

Enticing the elders across the road was a traditional working-class pub with black and white features snuggled next to the local fire station. Those dressed smartly could enter the saloon bar with carpet underfoot; for the working man it was the public bar, a game of darts perhaps. Either way, it was smoke-filled, noisy, and lively, the heartbeat of the community.

Norbert was tucked up in bed early evening, shielded from the harsher realities of life, his bright blue eyes missing the moments of madness such as his grandparents trying to kill each other when filled with alcohol.

Norbert's stepdad was kind but cold. He was there, strictly speaking only at weekends and holidays, but he never reached out with a cuddle or comfort; it just wasn't in his nature. Norbert had many aunts, uncles, and cousins who lived far and wide, but were tight-knit and met often. His playgrounds were the earth he trod amidst the vast council estates and derelict warehouses overlooking Old Father Thames in a pocket of South East London. Long after the last barges emptied and the job losses bit, the smell of the spices lingered. Remnants of a lost time still blew through the empty warehouses onto the narrow streets, and collecting at the sides of the kerbs were particles of tea, coffee, and exotic colourful spices.

Bermondsey wasn't a fashionable area back in the early seventies; most people were there by circumstance, not choice. Norbert was a happy slum dog. Their comfortable two-bedroomed first-floor council flat had large sash windows. Norbert's bedroom overlooked a courtyard, the layout of paving stones arranged across the ground in neat patterns of squares. It was perfect for playing games like hopscotch or tag. Inside there was the odd twist of having the bath beneath the kitchen worktop. When the cold winter came, and breath was visible, he snuggled in front of the coal fire. Upstairs, beyond the upper floor and spread across the entire top tier, was a washing room. Norbert couldn't resist spinning the old mangle that mums used to wring out their wet clothes. Life on the Dickens Estate was a magical place to explore.

Norbert was born into an age where children made their own fun and amusement away from a hard drive. They had to be resourceful; on his own all he needed was a ball and a good wall. Sometimes the streets were flooded with kids playing bulldog on the grass, racing go-carts.

'It's Joe the ice-cream man,' Mark Dulligan would scream. Norbert would run over and stand beneath his windows, and after a sharp intake of breath shout 'Muuum.' She'd have heard the chimes and would throw out some change. He'd race to join the long queue.

No matter the hardship, food was always on the table. 'Fetch me an errand from the baker's, Norbert,' Nan would ask, 'tell him to put it on the tab.' There he was, thinking the baker was so kind, giving him warm crusty loaves of bread and the most humongous custard tarts as a treat with no money changing hands.

When he was eight, the family moved a short distance on the same council estate. It felt like an exciting upgrade, to be up on the top floor. Having a lift was a welcome luxury even with the constant smell of stale piss in it. School was Riverside Primary, an enormous, imposing school with a haunting-looking bell tower perched on the middle of its roof. From Norbert's balcony, he could see the river Thames sweeping up from behind the school, meandering from Greenwich towards Tower Bridge. School was easy; teachers cared. During school holidays he longed to be back.

Most days his friend Billy Walker would come knocking, and after a short play with his train set, they would set off to school early, seeking out the headmaster for the football to kick about in the playground before anyone else arrived. Most parents never had a car and would walk their kids in all weathers from the neighbouring areas; slowly but surely, they would arrive and split into one of two playgrounds. Football was allowed in one for the older kids and before long there would be a match – every morning and afternoon – always football.

Chapter 2

Idiopathic craniofacial erythema

Back to that fateful moment, the afternoon when he kicked the ball and had an out-of-body experience. He watched it on its inevitable path, hitting Mark Grippa plum in the face, a real stinger. Anyone else and there would not have been a problem, but him …

'Oh fuck,' he's mad at you,' Billy swore. Norbert's heart sank like a lead weight. *Oh, shit.* Grippa raged towards Norbert, eyes watering, anger screaming out of his puffy face. Grippa's fists clenched tight, white of knuckle bursting out of his brown hands. Fight or flight, the choice monumental, Norbert swallowed hard, his heels rooted to the ground. His very first fight was upon him.

Grippa swung and Norbert intuitively reacted. Windmill arms spun and clashed, adrenalin took over and numbed the blows. A second or two later and it was all over. Grippa turned and ran away. Billy strutted around the circle of kids that had gathered.

'Woo, he had that coming – did you see that?' And of course, they did.

Norbert had survived unscathed. Unbelievably, he had just beaten up the gobbiest, toughest kid in school. Afterwards he definitely walked a little taller. He was unsure how he'd won – he put it down to all the play-fighting and wrestling with one of his best friends. Whatever it was, he had something. Maybe luck, but definitely something.

School may have been innocent and carefree, but other fights followed. Trouble had a knack of finding him.

'Norbert Jennings, come here,' Mum ordered. 'I've just had

Lee Deleslie's mum on the phone telling me you beat up her son.'

'Mum, he started it, honest to God.'

'I don't bloody care, get round there and say sorry. Now!' she shouted.

Lee and Norbert shook hands and made up, and Norbert was invited along to a local judo club. Lee's dad was a jeweller. He had the most amazing car; it was American, and it bleeped when you didn't wear your seatbelt. Back in 1977 that was truly jaw-dropping. Norbert stared out of the window when the car accelerated away, his small back pressed into the cream upholstered seat.

In a rundown building off the Old Kent Road was Tokei, a family-run judo club. The floorboards creaked as they walked in. Norbert was tingling with goosebumps, the tiniest strands of fair blond hair standing to attention on his arms, his eyes drawn like a magnet to the different coloured belts of the class: white, yellow, orange, green, blue, purple, brown – and, of course, black. The instructor wore black. 'Ichi, ni, san, shi,' he shouted, his voice echoing around the walls, filling the dojo with authority. Norbert and Lee were mesmerised. This was to be Norbert's first taste of martial arts, and he quickly blossomed.

One time, Norbert was practising with another lad who wasn't taking it seriously, too much fooling around. Norbert seized the moment. He turned in, sweeping his arm beneath the lad's armpit, using it as a lever. Norbert hoisted him onto his back, and with a flick of his hips and a thrust up the boy was airborne and thrown flat onto his back. The startled boy looked up, disorientated.

'Ippon,' Norbert hailed.

On his last day of primary school, Norbert walked home alone, clutching a book on bomber aeroplanes, a leaving gift from the teachers he loved. He didn't especially care for war stuff; it was only chosen because the title was the same as his nickname, Bomber. A fishing or a football book would have made a far better choice, but it was too late now. Heartbroken, he wasn't ready to leave. After tea and a cuddle from Mum, he lay on his bed sobbing, until little Bomber fell asleep.

Secondary school beckoned – Bacon's, a local mixed comprehensive with a strict reputation enhanced by a stern-looking headmaster, Mr Ing, who dressed in a black gown complemented by a mortarboard. He fervently believed in handing out a good old-fashioned thrashing, caning many an unruly child for intolerable behaviour like throwing a snowball when it was banned. With predominantly local working-class kids from the neighbouring areas of South East London, the school was notable for its bold uniform of reflex blue blazer, and a cricket-type cap embroidered with an emblem of a golden lion proudly declaring the Latin term *Gloria in Excelsis Deo*. This was South (spoken as-Sarf) London, not leafy Richmond or posh Chelsea. Norbert wore the ridiculous get-up, but the first chance he got he would hurriedly remove his cap and stuff it in his pocket. Bacon's pupils were visible prime targets for kids from the rougher neighbouring schools.

From the first day of big school, a seismic change took hold of Norbert. Something inside altered and he felt off-kilter; his self-confidence made way for trepidation and persistent curdling embarrassments. The sheer number of other children didn't help. After the safety net of primary school where in the last years he liked to believe he ruled the roost, he was now uncontrollably apprehensive, timid in a way he hadn't recognised before. He developed the involuntary reflex of blushing at the most random of things – someone calling his name, a look from a girl. The more conscious of it he was, the worse it became. Gradually he moved from centre stage to the shadows, and there he quietly stayed, peeping his head out occasionally like a tortoise.

'David, how did you get your muscles that size? Is it weights?' asked Norbert, dead jealous of gentle giant David.

'No, I drink a pint of milk every day.' David Mortimer offered up his bicep for Norbert to squeeze. 'They are big though, aren't they?' Both he and Norbert looked at them, dewy eyed.

'Massive, mate, Popeye would be proud of them.'

As soon as Norbert got home, he guzzled some milk;

quickly bloated he let out the most disgusting smelly burp. A few days later he chose his moment to speak again to David. He was always one of the last to get changed after PE; he would know what to do.

David must have sensed him stalling. 'What's up, Norbert, is the milk thing working yet?'

Norbert changed direction. 'Why do I continually blush, David, what's wrong with me?'

David Mortimer stood up and his towel fell to the floor. Norbert saw a man cock, the size of a baby's arm holding an orange. Full pubic hair.

'Fuck sake, David.'

'Sorry, Norbert. See, I don't care about anything – nothing bothers me and nor should it you. Stop worrying about everything.'

Norbert left red-faced, traumatised, with no muscles, and no man cock. Being a late developer was a torment, and he willed his willy to catch up.

Daily bizarre episodes hemmed him in, some recurring, like bad dreams.

Miss Farrah was the most attractive science teacher. After football practice one time, some of the boys saw her bending over in her tennis whites fetching something from the boot of her small sports car. The scene instantly became a go-to fantasy in Norbert's kaleidoscopic mind. He borrowed from it frequently. It never helped in the slightest in class; he could never relax.

'What makes the noble gases unique, Norbert?' Miss Farrah asked.

Norbert's eyes glazed over. *Why me, every time – why do you always ask me?* His face lit up like a crimson light bulb. Some of the other pupils laughed.

'Come on now, Norbert, give me something – anything.'

What Norbert wanted to give was vastly inappropriate. Instead, all he could pathetically mumble was, 'I don't know, miss.' He was drowning in a sea of redness. *Right now I could barely answer my name, let alone stupid gases, Newton's law, or whatever the fuck you always ask*. This continual baiting of hers kept Ms Farrah amused in every class for years.

Football and sport saved him. When busy doing something active, preferably outside, his inner demons loosened their grip and, in these moments, he found some respite. Norbert was drafted into the first-year football team, and a couple of weeks later played his first match. The howling wind blew his jersey, which was so big on him his shorts underneath were barely visible.

'Have we drawn the right team?' he asked his teammate. 'Look at them – they look ginormous.' The battle was lost before the game started; it was a rout, as if they were standing in the way of a juggernaut. They were walloped 13-1, despite his teammate scoring arguably the best lonely goal he'd ever seen. Norbert was shocked through to the core. What fighting spirit Norbert had deserted him. His beleaguered soul had left the building, and it looked like it wasn't coming back any time soon.

Chapter 3

Just fabulous

Paul Sanderson was the bully sent from hell, smart clever, street clever, with a fast mouth, but boy did he have a chip on his shoulder. A walking ticking bomb primed to explode at the faintest of touches. Who knew where his wrath came from; was he starved of a cuddle? The truth was something only he knew and no one would be stupid enough to ask. Norbert wanted to like him; he genuinely empathised seeing him go through adolescence suffering with the most terrible acne.

'Oi, Sanders,' one of the older lads shouted, 'the spots are queueing up on your neck to get onto your face.'

'Yeah, my spots will go one day. But you'll always be ugly,' Sanders replied, sharp as sand.

Sanders had an answer like that for everything; he was ready to fire back a put-down like a cobra spitting poison into someone's eye. Even the older boys were wary and gave him a wide berth. All Norbert and his friends had was the now, the daily living nightmare of Paul's aggression and anger. It made everyone around him fearful and uncomfortable. He was a powerful bully, his fighting prowess improving with every victory he chalked up, his ego burgeoning with it. Sanders didn't fear anyone. Norbert was dead jealous of that. Nor did he have any real friends – he scared them all off, apart from one other slightly less mad boy, Kenny Brown.

Norbert and a few friends were playing at the local park when Sanders and Kenny arrived. Looking menacing as ever, they were out for trouble and sure enough Sanders declared he wanted to fight Bomber.

'Run, Norbert, run,' a friend told him. But like a stupid fool, he accepted the challenge. Norbert ambled behind Sanders to the gallows. *I'm going to lose so I may as well just take the punishment, get it over and done with,* he told himself. In a clearing on the grass, Sanders floored Norbert with a single punch, quickly straddling him, his tree-trunk thighs pinning Norbert's torso to the ground as he rained more punches down on Norbert's pitiful face. At each blow, Norbert shrieked in pain and hoped that Sanders would take pity and stop; eventually it worked.

Norbert never threw a single punch. He was no David outwitting this Goliath. Afterwards Norbert didn't know where to look. He sat on a swing staring at his feet. The humiliation of being crushed in front of his friends weighed heavy. The sky was the clearest blue – it should have been a good day to be outside playing.

As uncomfortable as Norbert was in his own skin, he tried to not let it stop him from having some fun. There was always sport and, once the first end-of-year school party broke the ice, there were girls to kiss, lots of pretty girls. Drinking alcohol gave Norbert a protective layer – inhibition was temporarily pushed aside, allowing him some room to breathe.

Being in the top set at school meant shitloads of homework. But there were the youth clubs to break the monotony of study; London's Bermondsey was awash with them. Norbert could have easily gone to hang out at a different one each night of the week. His favourite by far was Millpond boys' club, set up by a maverick dad who was always looking for a deal. Big Dave punched the club way above its weight. There were many trips out to the seaside, and further afield, to Germany, no less. Dave even secured a visit from the Duke of Edinburgh.

Norbert and co relished the chance to practise and hone their skills: football, obviously, but also pool, darts, table tennis, and badminton, which Norbert took to like a duck to water. It kick-started him into playing badminton seriously at another local club where he excelled. Shaking hands after a badders match, drinking squash and nibbling biscuits was much more congenial than running for one's life back to the safety of the changing rooms on some ghoulish common after playing yet another rabid local school footie team.

Norbert and his buddies were good kids; the youth clubs got them off the streets and kept them out of trouble, period. Norbert would save his pocket money all week till Friday night or Saturday came around when one of the older-looking lads would pluck up the courage to try and get some cans of lager from the local off-licence, then together they would find a plot somewhere on the streets or nestled in one of the council estates. There they would drink and fool about into the night, and these new experiences they shared until they were old enough to get into the pubs and play grown-ups for real.

Norbert was a sheep following the trend of the herd. If someone was wearing a smart pair of trainers, he would copy them and have the same. A new diamond Pringle jumper, Lois faded jeans, a faux leather jacket; he found refuge in conformity. He reasoned that if he looked the same and acted the same, the path would be less bumpy and safer. Being a follower was not such a bad thing.

In the midst were the natural-born leaders, the rainmakers; they made exciting things happen. Norbert followed loyally. There were a couple, but one of them stood out head and shoulders. Nathan Wilkes was one year older at school but years ahead in life terms. He was smart and damned good-looking; he attracted girls like a magnet. He had a knack of telling a story, and was engaging and funny without trying; he was cool beyond belief. If Norbert and his friends downed three cans of lager, Wilkes would drink four – his little way of showing his authority. They were happy for him to play his part as unelected leader.

Nathan was seeing a girl. She was attractive, funny, different to his usual fodder. Pamela lived in the same block as Norbert. Norbert didn't know where to look when he bumped into them kissing in the stairwell.

'You alright, Norbert?' Pamela asked.

'Hi guys.' Norbert tried to skip past them both to the stairs, which would be quicker than waiting eternally for the lift.

'Not so fast, Norbert,' said Nathan. 'How you doing, mate?' Nathan put his arm around Norbert's shoulder, looking extremely pleased with himself. 'Ain't seen you for a while. You got five minutes?'

'Yes, but you guys look busy.'

'Always got time for me pals,' Nathan said.

They talked, they all laughed, and Norbert lost some of his uneasiness.

'I've asked her to marry me.'

Norbert laughed. 'Seriously?'

'He has,' Pamela said. 'Told him I need time to think about it.'

'I don't know what to say,' Norbert said. 'Obviously I hope it works out for you both.'

'Cheers, pal,' Nathan said.

Chapter 4

An hour will kill

The ordeal of school came and went, and Norbert left with dry eyes and few qualifications. Luckily, though, time was on his side. Aged sixteen it was easy to find work. Jobs were plentiful – all he had to do was put his feelers out. He got a whisper that there was a job going in the city as a barristers' clerk. After a phone call and following a short, rushed interview, he was given his first job.

Mum took him out and bought two suits. Thankfully there was no cap to wear this time around. The following Monday was his maiden voyage, discovering the pleasures of the bus and Tube in the rush hour.

'Excuse me,' a woman said. Norbert looked up. 'Would you mind opening the window?'

Norbert's nervous fingers fumbled around with the catch until it released some air into the carriage. His face is so flushed, he sees the entire carriage looking at him, he exits stage left at the next station to get some relief and another train to continue his onward journey.

It was just like being back at school – he was overwhelmed and apprehensive and the blushing was continuous. When he got to South Place, Gray's Inn, he was stunned to discover that there would be four of them crammed into a tiny office the size of his bedroom.

The senior clerk, Mr Pelan, chain-smoked and buzzed around as far as the phone leash would let him. He was on it constantly, trying to placate solicitors and barristers alike. It was left to the second in command, Keith, to fill Norbert's day.

'Here you go,' Keith said, dumping a stack of files on the desk, 'Tina will show you what to do with those.'

Tina was the typist and gossip queen of the chambers. 'Keith's gay,' she whispered to Norbert. She tutted. 'Such a waste.'

14

'How d'you know?'

'All his friends are girls, that's how I know. Besides, Norbert, all the best ones are.'

It appeared some things were a little complicated inside the office, but one thing wasn't. Tina hated having to leave the office womb for anything, which was great news for Norbert. Much of his time was spent as the errand boy, walking down Chancery Lane to the Royal Courts of Justice, or squirrelling out a chambers in the Temple for a barrister's urgently needed papers, or picking up lunch for the busy barristers. He relished the escapes, the moments to daydream. He'd have walked up Kilimanjaro to get out of that stifling office.

Watching the lawyers in chambers and observing them confidently strut their stuff in court only served to highlight his anxieties. Norbert questioned himself – *Was it public school that gave them this air of confidence? I wish it came in tablet form. If it did, I'd surely overdose.*

At five o'clock he would stare longingly out of the window, watching the workers head for home. He finished at six – how cruel – and by the time he got back home and finished supper, his teenage battery was utterly depleted. *Is this how it's supposed to be? What sadistic bastard thought those hours up and how come the working week is so long while the weekend goes in the blink of an eye?*

Nearby was a constant reminder of his schooldays in the shape of the Sir Francis Bacon statue in Gray's Inn. In an instant he could be temporarily transported back to those often painful schooldays. *Get me back there now, he wished. As bad it was, it was still miles better than this.*

Norbert endured six months of self-inflicted hell until with a heavy heart he handed in his notice. On his last day, they thanked him and presented him with a book, *Rumpole of the Bailey*. 'They were so nice, Mum, I felt so guilty leaving.'

'Those suits and shirts I bought you, what a bloody waste,' she said.

However, the scent of freedom in his nostrils was too strong for any last change of sentiment. But it was the words of a portly QC, Mr Addezio, who was cock-a-hoop since Italy had recently won the World Cup, that stuck with him: 'This won't be the last time we see your face, young man.' Bomber understood and blushed, naturally.

Norbert had secured himself a position as a trainee printer in a small factory close to Millwall's Old Den home ground, a near half-hour walk from home. No suit, no commuters' eyes to avoid, and the hours were 8.00 a.m. to 3.30 p.m., giving him some of his precious life back. Norbert had to pinch himself; he couldn't quite believe his turn of fortune. The caged bird had flapped its wings and taken flight to a big open machine floor. Banter with the lads, no girls to set his pulse racing, a radio, and once again Norbert was back in his comfort zone.

One cold December night, at the age of seventeen, Norbert and his friend Chris went to the pictures to see *Jaws*, and the evening left an indelible mark on him. He swore afterwards that if he ever went swimming in the sea, no matter where in the world he might be, he would hear that dull, gripping tuba, the intense music, *dun*, *dun*, *dun*, *dun*, quicker and quicker. His heart would race and he would be convinced a fucking great white shark was going to come up from below the waters and tear him apart.

Chris suggested they go for a drink, and they randomly popped into a local bar on the way back from the picture house. The pub was quiet, but soon they struck up a conversation with two girls. They both knew Louise from school, but the other girl Norbert had never seen. He liked her straight away. Norbert's mum was out for the night and Chris, with all the confidence in the world and the gift of the gab, persuaded the girls to join them. The first time Norbert kissed Meara, he sneaked open his eyes to check if she was real. He asked her out and to his utter surprise she agreed, becoming his first proper girlfriend.

Life was sweet, working in a new job, going out with friends, and enjoying a drink to dampen his insecurities, seeing Meara whenever he could. He fell head over heels in love.

Chapter 5

Butterfly

At the local baths, ten-year-old Norbert sat poolside next to his mate Phil for the annual gala as part of the Riverside Primary School swimming team. It was crowded, every local school represented. Noisy excitable kids sat huddled together on the cold tiled floor beneath their respective school banners, cheering on their friends during the races. Furled bunting around the sides of the hall added to the party atmosphere. Proud mums and dads packed the upstairs gallery. Looking across at the swimmers standing at the front of the lanes ready for their race, Norbert picked out the tall skinny kid in the middle lane.

'Betcha he wins,' he said to Phil, who slowly shook his head. Phil's mum helped with the swimming team and secretly shared glucose sweets with some kids when the teachers weren't looking.

'He will win,' Phil declared, pointing at a shorter fat boy.

Norbert laughed. 'No chance,' he said. They played this game all day, and Phil crushed Norbert with an almost hundred per cent winning streak. Weakened by their game, Norbert pleaded, 'How do you know who is going to win?'

Phil stuck out his orange tongue then looked to the ceiling, shrugging his bony shoulders. When he was done teasing, he explained. 'Simple, I just picked whoever was wearing the black and gold swimming trunks.'

'Why, what's so special about them?'

'Because they're the colours of the local swimming club. Pete Wilson runs the club, and they're the colours of his team, Wolverhampton Wanderers.'

Norbert was already a splendid swimmer, but under Pete's strict no-nonsense instruction he became bloody good. By eleven he could swim three and a half miles and did more tumble turns than the average washing machine. His greatest success in races was swimming backstroke, his least favourite, with water backwashing up his nose and a continual fear of smacking into the wall. The thing he was most proud of, though, was being able to swim butterfly because it took him so long to learn. With diligence, his weak flailing arms and breathless gulping of chlorinated pissy water eventually transitioned to the sinusoid wave motion of a dolphin. He managed a school record at senior school when he just pipped one of his best mates in a very closely fought race.

Fast forward to age eighteen, Norbert and Meara were at the travel agent's.

'Why don't we go there?' she said, indicating a poster of the Grand Palace of Bangkok, Thailand. Norbert stared intrigued at the shining gold spires; he was more than happy to follow in Meara's slipstream.

'You can mix it up with a break from the city to the coast – the beaches are gorgeous,' the travel agent told them. She expertly flicked through the pages of a glossy magazine to a double spread that she clearly knew would lure them in.

In 1985, Thailand was not mainstream. This was a big deal, and once the ordeal of getting vaccinated was out the way, they were good to go.

Bangkok was everything they imagined it to be – vibrant, noisy, chaotic, hot and humid. Riding around on tuk-tuks, Norbert's polo shirt stuck to his slender frame, but it couldn't dampen his delight. After sightseeing it was back to their city hotel to cool off in the rooftop pool where Meara's wet hair only served to make her look more desirable.

When they reached Pattaya and stepped out into the night it took their breath away – the lights, the bars, and of course the girls. Most were impoverished, unlike the tourists who flocked there to avail themselves of this cheap commodity.

Norbert and Meara found a bar they settled into every night. He drank a cold beer, and her emerald eyes watched her favourite cocktail being made. The locals took a shine to them. They struck up friendships in their short visits, and the guys from the bars took them out after working their shifts. One girl fancied the pants off Meara and was so desperate to have her she offered money for the experience.

'It could be fun,' Norbert said in hope. Meara gave him a look. End of story.

On their last night of the most fantastic holiday, they said their goodbyes in the same bar. Meara had a fit of giggles when her long blonde hair was touched playfully, while one girl warmly held Norbert's hand – he was enjoying the attention. An older girl noticed and shouted to Norbert, 'You butterfly,' and motioned with her fingers how it would flit from one place to another. She had hit the nail on the head with absolute precision.

Norbert had an affinity with butterflies.

Chapter 6

Slice of pie, anyone?

Steven was an older trainee printer working alongside Norbert, a burly lad with a firm tongue mostly rooted to the ass of Roger the overseer. Steven revelled in his sexual fiendishness. He left porno mags in the changing room and the toilet walls were plastered with his favourite page threes. He had no problem saying whatever was on his perverted mind.

'Last night, Norbert, I came all over her face.' Emily, his girlfriend was the lucky recipient. 'Why do you look like that Norbert? It's fucking great, I love it.'

Batons were used to manipulate stacks of paper; they could be fed into the machines much faster when they were straight. Steven found another use for them. He launched one at Norbert, who didn't even realise – he thought it had been dropped by mistake until another thumped him in the back. Norbert picked it up and threw it back where it came from but was not even close. He turned back to work. Another came harder, hitting him in the rear, then another.

'For fuck's sake, Steven.' Norbert threw another back. Batons went like arrows back and forth as quickly as they both could reload but with more severity, spiteful. Steven picked up a bunch, throwing them in quick succession like machine-gunfire and stepping towards Norbert. Norbert tried to return the compliment.

'Do you want some, you little cunt?' Steven's arm reached out and grabbed Norbert by the throat, holding him up against the wall.

Roger came running over as fast as his fat belly allowed. 'Lads, lads, calm down.'

Steven came to his senses but Norbert's were scrambled.

He was trembling. *Where the fuck did that come from?* Steven dusted himself down and returned to work, cleaning Roger's ass as if nothing happened.

At home, later, Norbert's mum said, 'I've run you a nice bath. Go and wash all that smelly ink stuff off your hands and I'll make some dinner.' It was like she had a sixth sense sometimes.

The next day Steven marched up to Norbert whose heart skipped a beat. 'Sorry about yesterday, Norbert, I was bang out of order.' They shook hands.

It was a big dollop of luck and relief when Norbert changed jobs, still in the print business but nearer home. Vitesse offered him more money and an amazing continental-style three-day week. It was very old school, primitive, thirty or forty of the nutters at their busiest. Everyone was given a nickname, from the obvious to the absurdly ridiculous. All it needed was a connection; it might be loose, but it was there somewhere.

To name a few, there were: Wolfie (he was hairy), Wolf-Cub (son of Wolfie), Shoody Elbow (Bob Carolgees lookalike), Ridgeback (he was South African), Fossil (he was old) and Hodgie Pie. Hodgie was a poker player (cheat), golfer (big cheat), and well-off (sort of cheating, his wife had a well-paid job). Hodgie Pie was a tormentor, that was how he got his kicks; he wound the bosses up no end. Someone had been flooding the offices below by blocking the upstairs toilets with bog rolls. Every time someone flushed, the water cascaded down, creating havoc. Norbert knew it was Hodgie; he climbed the stairs as quietly as a mouse and saw him doing it. Norbert was faced with a choice; in an instant he tiptoed away – his pee could wait. Norbert admired Hodgie's daring.

The camaraderie was constant and the banter brutal, but things were kept in check by the two bosses, who were both strict and wealthy when the print business was thriving. It was staggering therefore that one director, Mr Pritchet, a loathsome slippery eel of a man, never smiled, always appearing to be unhappy with his lot and bitter about anyone who was doing well, or better than him, particularly Hodgie Pie.

Norbert was riding high and earning well. With overtime, some machine operators pulled in an incredible £800-plus a week, far outstripping most skilled trades back in the late eighties, but the beauty was that he had so much time off he could almost fool himself that he never worked. There were many visits to the local pubs after shift, and at weekends with any old excuse. There were some serious drinkers among the older lads. One in particular, Bumper, had the looks and angriness of Harold Shand in *The Long Good Friday*. He drank like a fish – the beer never touched the sides. In Bumper's company the beers came thick and fast, and Norbert and his pals would be pissed before their night had time to get going.

They were lucky; going out in Bermondsey in the eighties was special. Bermondsey was the in place, red hot, and people would come from afar to visit. Pubs were busy, and there were lots of them to choose from in the sweet spot. Norbert's favourites were the Royal Oak, the Lilliput Arms, the World Turned Upside Down, and the Rising Sun.

In this heady atmosphere of teenagers, drinks and girls, some fighting was inevitable. The bouncers would intervene and snuff most trouble out. Mostly it was handbags at dawn; sometimes, however, it got serious.

One night his old mucker Nathan Wilkes waved across a crowded bar. 'See you later, Southsides,' he said. Norbert gave a thumbs up. Norbert's little group of pals ventured off into the night somewhere else. By now, the circle of friends had fragmented, and Norbert's inner circle comprised close friends who just enjoyed the drinking. Nathan's close friends drank but they were involved with drugs – nothing serious, mostly smoking joints, but that was enough to put a little distance between the groups. Norbert dabbled, having an occasional line of Charlie or the odd ecstasy tablet when they first arrived on the scene, but they were drinkers. Cannabis was out – it sent him into a fit of coughing and splurging, much to the delight of his friends.

To Norbert and his close friends, Nathan was charismatic

and popular. But to another particular lad, he was an irritant, a thorn in his side, a 'fucking mouthy cunt' that was to get his 'comeuppance'. That night, in the packed bar of Southsides, this idiot strode in and, lurching from behind, shoved a knife into Nathan's neck. Nathan never stood a chance, and died before the light of day.

Predictably there were no witnesses. 'No one grasses to the filth, do they?'

So a killer stayed free, basking in his notoriety. Free to supply drugs, free to carve a way unhindered, seeing as how he had what most wannabe gangsters craved, a hard reputation; it didn't matter that his act was carried out in cowardice.

The father of a lad that had been fucked up by the killer's drugs a short time later wasn't buying into that. For supplying the drugs and messing up his son, he sought him out. Revenge came quickly and was exacted by knife; the killer was stabbed and killed. He had lived by the sword and died by the sword; some would call it poetic justice. There was no denying it did have a bleak symmetry about it. In the aftermath, the family and loved ones left behind carried the wounds. Nathan left behind a big hole. The Waterboys got it right – some people do see the whole of the moon.

Chapter 7

Come and have a go if you think you're hard enough

On this particular afternoon, a smaller group of kids from another manor were casing the estate, seeking answers after an earlier altercation. They were of a different skin colour, which was not a good omen. Bitter words were exchanged, and Norbert's friend sprang off a bench and chinned their leader. Things kicked right off. In a red mist, the strangers were chased away by foamy-mouthed boys. Norbert's adrenalin was pumping; he ran with the chasing pack but made sure he kept a safe distance.

Fist fights like those revealed who could fight and how. Some lads had boxing training but there were a couple who were natural fighters. Norbert's friend Paul (not Sanders) was one of them – he was a little older, brave, strong, and could punch absolute howitzers – he never had a lesson in his life. He was raised by a dad who believed you stood up to everything: 'The harder they are, the bigger they fall' was etched onto his mind. If Norbert hit a punchbag in the gym, he would yelp at the pain agonisingly reverberating along his arm; when Paul hit it there was a deep dull thud. His fists had slain many a foe.

The madness of fighting could be seen at football matches. Millwall and their fans had a reputation. Some of Norbert's friends gravitated towards their firm 'The Bushwhackers' for kicks, literally. After many ventures, the lads would tell their stories of how sometimes, even though outnumbered, they stuck together as a defiant unit to triumph in the face of adversity. Fighting the likes of Crystal Palace, Portsmouth, and their fiercest rivals West Ham with their own 'Intercity' firm.

Norbert didn't have to hear about it. When Luton Town hosted Millwall at Kenilworth Road on Wednesday 13 March 1985, in the sixth round of the FA Cup, national television and the newspapers reported the carnage as 'Arguably the worst football hooliganism seen for years.' Norbert was stunned to see friends on a TV loop running riot, ripping out seats, running battles with the police. For every tough fighter there were the idiots, mentalists who couldn't fight but were safe in numbers, out stirring trouble. They threw coins at players and abused rival fans – when they were far away from any repercussions, of course. The trouble would often start way before kick-off. On away games, the special trains were vandalised, people were abused; everyone was fair game, especially trainspotters. Coachloads of travelling fans could quickly overrun a pub, doing whatever they wanted, living the mantra 'No one likes us, we don't care.'

Was Norbert tempted to cut his cloth, roll up his sleeves, and have some tear-ups? Hell, no. Norbert might have lapped the wild stories up, but although intrigued by the fighting, he was not about to join in the melee. Another incident reinforced his neutral stance. It was autumn and somewhere in one of the many London parks that on a Sunday hosted football matches, Norbert and his friends had come to watch and support the older Bermondsey lads play a game. They stood on the touchline, waiting for the game to begin.

Norbert was fooling around with two of his besties.

'Bomber, there's Haystacks,' said Keith. 'Didn't he used to work at Vitesse?'

'He left before I started.'

Paul intervened. 'He was sacked when I was there. The manager had these fancy new lockers installed for everyone and he,' he said, looking at Haystacks, eyebrows raised, 'left a shit in one, crazy fucker.'

Then right on cue Haystacks yelled, his words splitting the atmosphere like a bolt of lightning: 'Come on, Seaney, let's do these black cunts.'

'This could kick right off,' Keith said, 'look at them, they're fuming.'

Paul said, 'We can't fuck off now, can we, it'll look like we're bottling it.'

'I fucking am,' Norbert mumbled under his breath. Some people laughed out of embarrassment, and some just pretended they never heard it, but they did. Thankfully, once the game started, everyone settled down. Norbert breathed a heavy sigh of relief, and Haystacks? He didn't bat an eyelid. He didn't care if there was a reaction, and unzipped his fly to piss downwind on the side of the football pitch.

Sensing trouble, Norbert and his pals made their excuses soon after and left. Some of those older lads were dinosaurs; they would never change.

Chapter 8

Football v sequins

Imagine everyone's surprise when, while on a stag weekend in Majorca, a pal rushed back to the poolside. 'You'll never guess who I've just clocked in reception!'

There was stone-faced silence until Biscuit (because with girls he wouldn't leave a crumb) sarcastically asked, 'Was it Jimmy Savile?'

'Yeah, he was with Gary Glitter, you fucking dope,' said Tony.

Turned out their beloved Millwall team was staying in the same hotel. It didn't take long for them to all get acquainted. For one balmy sunny week, Norbert, his friends, and the stars of the pitch rubbed shoulders.

'What goes on tour stays on tour,' one player said.

'Well, he would say that, wouldn't he,' Norbert whispered to a friend.

'Not everything stays here though, does it?' his friend replied.

'What are you talking about?' asked Norbert.

'Let's just say some of them clinics are busier than Clapham Junction in rush hour.'

Norbert scrunched his face.

Binge drinking had taken hold stealthily, and it tightened its grip on trips away.

Back home, with help from Mum, Norbert acquired a small ground-floor studio flat overlooking the Albion Canal. In summer he watched lovers walk by hand in hand on the canal path and brave coots nesting in the middle. By winter, the birds had made way for shopping trolleys entombed in ice, jutting downwards like mini-*Titanic*s. His new independence was life changing with the sudden realisation he could do whatever he wanted whenever he chose. And for a while he lived the dream, going out drinking with friends and earning well at work. Meara and he hopped off around the world, east and west, anywhere they desired.

Meara applied her make-up and finished her darker than usual highlighted hair, neatly and tightly held away from her attractive face. Dressed in ballroom splendour with waxed legs and oiled soles, she fandangoed in dance halls up and down the country.

Norbert came back to football, better late then never. He changed into his kit and laced his boots, strong and ready to lock horns with the opposition. Rather than be a shrinking violet, he seized his chance and improved. Like all good teams, theirs had a mix of young and old, skilful and strong. Norbert was one whose duties were found in the trenches, and with a rabid centre forward, some seriously skilled artisans and a gifted man mountain in goal, they gelled into quite some team. Dartech Sports FC were on an upward trajectory – they managed a season of playing unbeaten. Cieran, a towering defender, coined them the Invincibles of the Kent Suburban League and, in the summer of 1997, they won a closely fought cup final to boot. The following season, chance aimed an arrow and fired it into their lives when they had been drawn to play Grove FC in a cup game.

Sandwiched between grey cold industrial units was a pitch that couldn't have looked unfriendlier beneath the cloud-covered sky. One of Dartech's lead players, Kevin Jones, who let's say chose an alternative career path, recognised the opposing team instantly; it consisted of staff from nearby HM Prison Belmarsh and local police officers. And worse – they recognised him.

Jonesy, a pumped fist finding his teammates one by one, glared into their eyes. 'Come on, let's give it to these cunts.'

Norbert's posture shrank. He lowered his head and looked at the stud-holed ground. Vicious insults flew around from both teams. Grove were just as aggressive, and more than ready. Barely had the game started when the referee was forced to abandon play. Sporadic fights were happening in almost every direction among both players and supporters. Norbert had no axe to grind. Police cars were on the scene in seconds and Jonesy was off on foot. He was, with practice, rather good at this, having once single-handed outwitted an entire police station in Valkenburg, Holland on a football tour. When the administrators threw Dartech out of the league, Norbert's football career was over.

Determined not to let his relationship go the same way, he and Meara tied the knot soon after. They were both twenty-four. It was a picture-perfect day – proud parents, relatives, and friends cooed at them in the sunshine. The nervous bride looked stunning, and Norbert cut a dashing figure in his pastel suit. The preparations for the big day had galvanised them together, and for a while, they briefly walked on the moon. Yet even at those dizzying heights there were niggles; they had spoken about it, the odds of lasting from childhood sweethearts through to old age. It was a fight they both took on, even with their doubts.

The marriage from the start was beset by constant trivial, niggling arguments. Sex for Meara becomes a chore; married life was wading through treacle, mentally draining. They tried clutching on to something they once had rather than forging a future together, both selfish and pulling in different directions as it slowly began to messily unravel.

On life continued, Norbert going out getting drunk on a Friday with friends, working and rowing, and as the years marched on their love turned septic. A trial split became the last nail in the coffin. While Norbert overthought ways to save and sacrifices to offer, Meara saw the light elsewhere. The damage had been done, cut by a thousand stripes. She put the relationship out of its misery.

'You'll thank me one day,' she said.

Norbert, choking on his tears, said, 'Tell me you don't love me.' *If she does, I'm done. I'll give up the fight.* Except he couldn't give up; his resolve was off the scale.

'I'm not in love with you anymore, but I'll always love you, Norbert.'

'Is that meant to make me feel any better?'

The coldness of separation hit Norbert like an arctic chill – alone in his flat, every song, every photo, all the memories, all that raw pain. Meara mourned, then brushed herself down and attacked life with renewed zest. Energised and cut loose, her dancing feet found their busy way and they would barely rest again; not a second would she waste. Her shining blaze left behind charred embers. The first cut was the deepest, and it was also going to be the longest. The demise of their marriage marked the beginning of a dark period for Norbert.

Chapter 9

How to make hurt

Norbert took off in his car, not knowing where he was going. As the light faded, he made a snap decision and headed to the red-light district of King's Cross. A magnet was pulling him, drawing him away from his dull, empty, newly single world. His heartbeat quickened; he would just look, be close and amongst it – a secret spy, voyeuristic, excited at the sight of those girls on the pavements. An hour passed and as he slowed at a pedestrian crossing, a street hooker saw her moment. She stepped towards the car. 'Do you want business?'

'Yes,' he replied. She got in and directed him to a local backstreet away from any prying eyes. His hands trembled on the steering wheel. He raised the window and felt overcome by the stink of cheap perfume and sex.

She broke the ice. 'I was getting close to calling it a night – it's dead out there.'

'It's my first time,' Norbert spluttered.

She spelled out her list of services; what she didn't do, he didn't want to do. Norbert gave her thirty quid and her head disappeared from view. Norbert's hand found a breast, the other tried to stroke her hair, but it was too greasy. For the next few minutes, he was distracted from his faltering world in which the girl he loved just didn't love him anymore. The physical pleasure was a million miles away from the real thing.

The seeds had been blown and sown. Norbert would have his cake and eat it; if at the end of a night out he got lucky, then great. If not, he knew exactly where to find a willing girl to give him his fix. What started as a slightly warped remedy for his troubles overrode his rationale. *I'm not doing anything wrong, not hurting anyone, just enjoying the thrill, flirting with danger*. The non-commitment and ease was intoxicating for someone intoxicated, and in his numbed brain it somehow all made sense. He became addicted.

Most of the girls were fighting drug addictions. During one encounter he caught one girl trying to rob him; with his pants around his ankles and her mouth busy, her hands were rifling through his pockets, multitasking with all the skill of a plate-spinning artist. That was the nature of the beast.

There was an unusually high police presence one night. It was making Norbert more nervous. He spotted a girl he recognised on the corner, one leg raised against the wall, her long black coat tantalising what was underneath. He needed to move fast. Approaching in his car, he lowered the window. 'Dawn, isn't it? Quick, get in.'

'I remember you,' she said. She opened the passenger door and slid in. 'You're the one who likes to watch me smoke.'

He was flattered she remembered. 'I swear I've never seen so many old bill. Would you come back to my place? I'll make sure you get back.'

'It'll cost you extra.'

They agreed on a price, and he relaxed a little as they headed away from the hotspot.

'It's a visual thing, the smoking, that is. I'm not sure why it turns me on – I don't even like it. Naughty girls smoke, right? Okay, you busted me – I'm a pervert.'

'All men are perverts,' Dawn reminded him.

'I guess we are.' He had no defence, not then, perhaps not ever. 'I'm sure you've been asked to do weirder stuff.' She nodded matter-of-factly. He wasn't going to let it go; he wanted to know. 'Go on then, what's the rudest thing you've been asked to do?'

Dawn took up the challenge, and it didn't take her a moment to pull something out, literally. 'Well, there's one old man who asks me to shit in a bag for him.'

'What the fuck, seriously?'

'Yup.'

'What does he do, I mean—'

32

'Who knows, he can have a mud bath in it for all I care.'

Norbert was disgusted. 'Serves me right for asking,' he murmured.

They had arrived at his flat. He now needed to get her inside without being seen. He walked ahead quickly and thought he had got away with it – except for Margaret from the next floor up, who locked eyes with him. She had seen everything.

'This is a nice place Norbert, very clean.'

'Thank you.' Norbert meant it – he was proud of his place. They got down to business, and Dawn helped Norbert paint lurid colours in his mind.

When he ran her back, the conversation changed to more mundane topics. She had no pimp, which was a good thing and a bad thing. She told Norbert her plan to buy her house outright, that she was working on a strict time frame to achieve her dream. Norbert was happy to help; it gave him some justification for the choices he was making. With Dawn, it felt a bit closer to the real thing, but most of the time the sex was pretty uneventful, on a timer – *wham bam, thank you mam*. This sex could never satiate; it was cheating and all it achieved was to perpetuate the cycle of trying to make things better but making them worse.

The police were never far away – for them it was a hunting ground. They knew the girls; in fact, as Dawn could testify, some of them used the girls. It was a constant game of cat and mouse. It all added to the heady adrenalin rush of which Norbert needed his fill. It was only a matter of time before he was pulled over and questioned; they never suspected him of kerb crawling – he was just another routine, random stop. A breathalyser was produced, and he stood there forlorn in the night alongside the police vehicle flashing its blue warning sign alerting passers-by. Some gave him daggers, some were relieved. It flagged up *fail*.

Norbert was escorted to the nearby police station and arrested for drink-driving. Going through the rigmarole of fingerprints and DNA swabs took an age. This night, which was now becoming the early morning, the police were

33

stretched for numbers. All manner of shit was kicking off and keeping them frantically running around. Norbert's cell was needed for another more serious incumbent, which probably explained why he was given another breathalyser test a couple of hours later. This time he passed; the delay had given his body enough time to recover. The damage, however, had been done.

It was time to go home and lick his wounds. A few weeks later, in the City of London magistrates' court, he was handed a fine and a year's ban. He was given some first-time leniency, but this was a serious warning. Being without a car was a minor inconvenience; Norbert got by without one just fine. The new Jubilee Line extension had recently opened and a station was practically on his doorstep. He could be in the West End in ten minutes to pick up something nice for his tea. His car sat motionless in his allocated car park space. Looking at it was such a tease, but for once common sense overrode any desire to drive it. He could walk to work in half an hour. He daydreamed most of the next year away and the ban passed quickly. He was soon back on the road. It was a relief and for a time all was calm.

Chapter 10

Love thy neighbour

Norbert routinely checked the post in his mailbox in the communal hall. One morning, he stopped for a brief chat with Margaret from upstairs, a nice lady, who knew everyone's business. 'How are you, Norbert?' she asked.

'I'm good thanks, Margaret,' he replied. They chatted for a while. She told him she was going to buy another flat – she was an estate agent and was very upbeat about the area. As Norbert said goodbye he sifted through the usual junk mail; an official-looking envelope stood out. He tore an opening, pulled out a letter, and his finger traced the gold-embossed heading of McCullough's solicitors. He read the divorce petition and started to shake uncontrollably. Seeing it all laid out in black and white was killing him.

He closed his front door and crumpled to the floor, bleary eyed. His body was empty of his usual hunger pangs; he had no voice, no reason. Only hurt. He got through the rest of the day numb to the touch.

Work eroded time and gave him a reason to pick himself up and move forward. Friends would try and pull him around. 'Try looking at it another way,' his bestie Paul said, 'you're young free and single now, you can go out whenever you want, see whoever you like.'

Norbert smiled back, unconvinced. 'This is like one of the recurring nightmares I have whenever I'm on holiday abroad. For some unknown reason I manage in my dream to be back in England far away from wherever I am, and all I want to do is get back. The harder I try, the more frustrated I get and the further away I remain. She made my heart sing.'

'Bomber,' Paul said, 'sort yourself out, man.'

Mum provided a shoulder to cry on, but every waking

moment was more reason to think about Meara. Norbert tried going out with other girls, but, weighed down by the heaviest emotional baggage, he just wasn't ready for other relationships. Some girls he found it easy to sleep with, others impossible. If he wanted sex, it was much easier to find a hooker.

Binge drinking at the weekends made it easier to normalise the choices of thrill-seeking and respite from his sad existence. He was stuck on autopilot, heading straight for the mountains. Something had to give, and give it did when the mouse was caught again. Norbert tried stalling and refusing the breathalyser, believing he could buy himself some more time and pass the test later as he had before. All rational thinking had left his mind. Panicking, all he managed to do was to magnify and worsen the situation. Arrested for drink-driving again, his double life of respectability on one side and an absolute reckless desire to push the boundaries on the other side came into sharp focus when thirty-four days later he stood alone in the Thames Magistrates' Court.

They handed him a large fine and a three-year ban, and warned him that if they ever saw his sorry face again, he would go to prison. Could things possibly get any worse? He should have known the answer when Margaret from upstairs called out from her balcony on his return. Norbert was trying to work it out and surmised that she had seen him that morning going out dressed in a suit. *Can't resist the nose ointment.*

'Oh, Norbert, I'm so sorry to tell you, you've been burgled. I heard a loud thumping and came downstairs – the communal side door was hanging off its hinges and your front door was wide open. I called out to you. Then he rushed past me. I was so scared – he had a big bag over his shoulder, nearly knocked me flying.'

'Did you recognise who it was?' Norbert asked.

'Never seen his face before.' She looked around, then whispered, 'He was brown though. The police gave me this.' She handed him a note with a crime reference number and a contact to call.

'Thanks, Margaret,' Norbert said. When she finally left, he crossed the threshold to his flat. It had been ransacked, cash and credit cards stolen. *What a fucking mess, what a fucking day*.

He sat down unable to move, seized by the gravity of the situation and the ridiculousness of it all. He said aloud, 'What a shitstorm – where are you when I need you, Meara?' The silence was killing him.

Eventually he picked himself up. He phoned the banks, cancelling his cards, and then called the police sergeant, who, possibly feeling sorry for him, lets slip accidentally on purpose the name of the suspect. It turned out to be Maxwell Anton.

Maxwell was a rogue, a scoundrel. Against the advice of some of his friends, Norbert hung out with him on and off for many years. Norbert was never bothered by the colour of someone's skin; he thought they were solid. This all changed with immediate effect when Maxwell was caught red-handed; the stupid fuck had tried to use one of Norbert's cards in a local bank, messed up, and created enough of a scene to arouse the suspicion of the branch security. They called the police. He offered no excuse as to why he was in possession of Norbert Jennings' cards.

Norbert was going to put Maxwell's fingers into a sharp steel blender when he caught up with him. It did nothing for race relations. Then again, not much did at that time and place. There was no getting away from it – Bermondsey was seen by many as one of the last frontiers of whiteness. Norbert was blinkered, swept along in the current, growing up indoctrinated, told by some family and peers that other colours were different, not to be trusted, they come over here ...

Sometimes you need a catalyst for your eyes to be truly opened. His was coming. Now, though, the stakes had been raised, so what would an ordinary person in these circumstances do? Perhaps they would retreat to some corner, reassess the situation and conclude something was going badly wrong, apologise to family for the umpteenth time with pathetic excuses, and bloody well change.

Chapter 11

Ding-ding, all change

With a forced change to his modus operandi, Norbert went shopping for a bicycle, settling on a mid-range silver mountain bike which he rode home from the local discount shop. As a youngster he had practically lived on his red Raleigh Chopper. At first, he was a bit wobbly, but it soon kicked back in. He smiled to himself, thrilled to be back in the saddle after so long. However, three long years of his driving ban awaited, which would be a lot of cursed weather, but he had three years to pedal a change and come good.

His work colleague Gibbo asked, 'Norbert, fancy doing some casual work? Sudrick' – who had frequent tidemarks around his neck – 'told me there's a firm in East London looking for printers, £150 a day.' They both were eager to check it out.

After a month, Dave, one of the directors, formerly invited them on board full time. Gibbo and Norbert had no hesitation in accepting, leaving Vitesse and joining Caspian, a new start-up.

Caspian, like the galloping horse it was named after, was set to go places. There were three directors, all driven and all dipped in the most engaging source of energy. The first year had Norbert and his mucker Gibbo practically chained to their lithographic press working all the hours under the sun and through the night, turning out anything from pizza leaflets to corporate accounts for blue-chip companies. Suffice to say, it kept Norbert busy and out of harm's way, so it was a blessing in disguise. The business ballooned a couple of years in. Things became so hectic on the shop floor that they had to draft in some of their former work colleagues to help.

One of them, Wizz, had short, thick, bristly hair. Norbert teased him and rubbed the back of his head as if searching for the Action Man toggle switch to move his eyes.

Norbert cycled to work through the Rotherhithe tunnel, which had a pathway he could freewheel down. From the middle it was a slow leg-burning slope up and out into somewhat less stifling conditions. The traffic noise inside was deafening, and he had no way of knowing Wizz and his passenger Animal, a long-haired caveman-type creature had slowed to a crawl in the car behind him.

Apparently they could hardly contain themselves as, once within earshot, Wizz lowered his window. 'Sex case,' he bellowed, blasting the horn.

'Cunts,' Norbert screamed. It had scared the bejesus out of him, and he wobbled and brushed into the grimy tiled wall so his arm was smeared with all the disgusting residue.

They played their silly little game whenever they could. Norbert got his own back one particular evening. After the usual abuse had faded, he watched them turn a corner and hit a wall of traffic. He caught up and tapped on the passenger window.

'Bomber, you look like Darth Vader in that mask,' Wizz said.

'May the force be with you, knobhead,' Norbert said. Oh, how he laughed as he merrily rode on, wankering them with an outstretched hand. He found out the next day they were stuck there for nearly two hours.

The banter flowed from the top down, especially from Steve, one very madcap director who took great pleasure in sneaking up behind everyone and pulling their shorts down. There was one sales rep who dressed smartly in a suit. Steve would hide in waiting, like Kato, then leap out with scissors ready and cut his tie crudely across the middle. It was a miracle he never gave him a heart attack. It was bedlam, but as long as the presses were rolling along, the directors didn't care. Everyone was fair game except one of the night-minders, Geoff. He was solid, strong, and good-humoured; no one could get the better of him. Lord knows, Steve tried, but he couldn't get him and it infuriated him incessantly. Geoff despatched Steve away like his namesake Geoffrey Boycott in the crease.

Chapter 12

Penguin erector

Time had marched on. Norbert was approaching thirty, had a good job, money, and time off. On the outside he looked dandy, but those close to him knew that inside he was broken; he needed therapy. Instead he got a change of scenery. When two of the lads at work arranged to meet up for a day of golf and a night out in Kent, he grabbed the chance to join them. For a city mouse, the Kent marshes were a breath of fresh air. Norbert inhaled it deeply. There was a connection from the chaos of London to this sparse Constable-like vista; Norbert was enraptured. They later partied into the night.

Standing at the side of the bar was an angel, glittering in silver and dark blue.

Norbert plucked up some Dutch courage. 'You look a little lost.'

'Had to get away from upstairs – all that house music does my head in.' Dexy's 'Come on Eileen' was belting out in the bar.

Norbert said, 'Yeah, this is so much better. I'm Norbert – what's your name?'

'Nikki Christie,' she replied.

Wizz was at the bar with Spike, his right-hand man and all-round good guy.

Spike shouted, 'Bomber, beer? Does your friend want one?'

Nikki accepted a JD and Coke and they formed a little circle. 'Thank you – so what do you all do?' she asked.

Wizz spoke up. 'In the summer I'm a deep-sea pearl diver.' He says it so straight-faced every time.

Nikki fell into the trap. 'What do you do in winter then?'

Spike looked on, engaged; he and Norbert must have heard it a thousand times but it still creased them up. Besides, they genuinely didn't know what Wizz would conjure up. The fantasy jobs alternated, anything from penguin erectors in London Zoo (they fell over when looking at the planes flying overhead) to ...

'In the winter I put chocolate on digestives.'

She almost spat her drink out. She and Norbert talked like old friends; they probed, they laughed, and at the end of the night, they kissed. After that kiss and looking into her warm hazel eyes, there was no way on God's earth they weren't going to be lovers.

Nikki introduced Norbert to the countryside. They would stroll across the big green opposite her cosy village house and walk hand in hand by the orchards to the local pub.

'There's something about this place, Nikki. It cracks me up that passers-by say good morning.'

'I can tell – you're like a little boy, aren't you?' She tickled him in the ribs. 'There is a downside – it doesn't take long for everyone to know your business around these parts.' She finished in a mock country accent.

Her down-to-earth family welcomed him with open arms. That night they were looking after Nikki's young daughter, Casey. Nikki made nibbles; everything she did was with a skilful touch. They drank some wine and gradually the full story of her ex came to light.

'At first Richard was brilliant – he does have the nicest blue eyes – but after we had Casey, well. The signs were there before, thinking about it, but what can you do. I gave him time, for Casey's sake. It was a nightmare though, he's mental. He showered us with money, would think nothing of buying expensive toys for Casey. It was all for show. Deep down he was rotten. Do you know on Casey's first day of school he told her he was going to kill me, that I wouldn't be there when she finished?'

'What? That's disgusting.'

There were tears in her eyes.

OMG, she's such a delicate flower. It was the cruellest thing Norbert had ever heard; he couldn't believe what he was hearing.

41

'The school phoned. I had to go and get her, she'd peed herself in class. Her first day.'

'The poor kid – how did that go down with your dad?' asked Norbert.

'My dad hated him, but he never knew the half of it. I thought about killing Richard, to end it all – apparently there are these poisonous frogs, deadly and untraceable.'

OMG, she's a Venus flytrap! 'Not sure if you can get those down Pets at Home.'

'Seriously, if I could have, I would have. What he put me through.' Her head bowed. Then she looked up at Norbert, tears in her eyes. 'Casey loves him – she's still so young and blindsided. My brother lived here with us when I finished with him. Richard took it badly. We never knew what he might do, but luckily, he's more mouth than bite. But he's still her father and as long as she wants to see him, as long as he never lays a hand on her, I have to try and do the right thing. Casey is hard work, battle scarred. I'm telling you this because I want you to know what you're getting yourself into.'

Norbert was in. He wouldn't dump on Nikki; after the shit she'd been through, she deserved better. Casey was slowly introduced to the relationship. Was Norbert a stepdad? Not quite, not while Casey was still seeing her so-called real dad at weekends. It worked out great for a while, leaving Norbert and Nikki free to enjoy most weekends together, a situation made even better when Norbert successfully appealed his driving ban and was back on the road. Norbert would stay out of the way when Richard picked up or dropped young Casey back home. It was much easier that way. But hearing all those stories of bullying and what a narcissistic cunt Richard was gnawed away at him.

A fortnight later, Norbert could hear the familiar voices arguing at the front door. His curiosity getting the better of him, he approached to see what was going on. Nikki was trying to placate Richard at the porch, and Casey was still happily hopping around the small front garden blissfully unaware.

Richard was mouthing off. 'Why don't you tell that college

boy cunt of a boyfriend to move his car somewhere else.' Norbert had heard enough. Rushing through the hallway he confronted the shit, outside by the front door. Richard swung at him but Norbert lunged first, getting a headbutt in.

They wrestled until the pandemonium was broken by Nikki screaming, 'Look what you're doing to Casey.' They broke and looked. Casey was sobbing; Richard blamed Norbert.

'Just go, Richard,' Nikki pleaded.

'Don't fucking worry, I am.' He jumped in his car and started the engine. Lowering the window, he called, 'Don't cry, darling, Daddy loves you.' He roared the car away like a madman.

Nikki held Casey's hand and led her back indoors to sanctuary. Norbert apologised.

'Twat-man deserves it,' she said, 'but still, you can't make things worse.'

'I had to put down a marker, a line in the sand – he left me no choice. I know it was pathetic.' Norbert shuddered. 'Can you imagine if I'd lost? Hey, you were right about his eyes though – fucking crystal blue.'

After that episode, things settled down for a while, until Nikki stopped Norbert in his tracks almost two years on. She was pregnant. Norbert asked for some time and space for the bombshell to sink in. He walked over to the church in the village and sat on a corner wall behind the cemetery as the full weight hit home. *What the fuck am I going to do?* He looked to the heavens for answers. His inner voice spoke: *You always wanted kids one day, expected to with Meara – maybe now the time is right.* A thrill washed over him, and he sprinted back to see Nikki, apologising for his rash unenthusiastic handling of the news. They cuddled and decided that this was going to happen.

After the fiasco with Richard, this was all the motivation Norbert needed to get serious about learning to fight; now he would have his own family to protect from the psychopaths lurking out there in the shadows.

Chapter 13

And for my next trick

Next time Norbert was in London he phoned the Docklands Centre, it had an impressive modern building overlooking the inky mirrored waters of the local docks. Its clientele were white-collar workers during the week; evenings attracted the locals and weekends saw the youngsters come in. As well as all the usual aquatic activities they had a smorgasbord of different fighting classes on their timetable. The receptionist told him he was welcome to come down and have a look at any of the classes.

With some trepidation, Norbert first looked in on a judo lesson. The class was small and the instructor was big – big as in fat sumo big – and he began by putting the class through its warm-up routine. Norbert sat at the back on a low school bench. Fifteen minutes into the class, they were still jogging around the dojo doing star jumps, burpees, changing direction, repeating, then press-ups. After half an hour, the instructor was still barking instructions from a chair barely big enough to hold his arse. Norbert was exhausted just watching them; it was stifling hot and there were no windows. The air was damp, filled with the smell of raw sweat.

Incredibly, an hour and a half later they were still at it; not once had the lazy git got up and joined in. Norbert watched through gritted teeth, his hands in mock prayer covering his face, his blood simmering. The class was fatigued; all the fun had long been sucked out like a vacuum. One girl's facial expression changed, twisted. He genuinely couldn't help himself. 'For fuck's sake, man,' he shouted. All eyes were on Norbert. He was blushing, uncomfortable, but defiantly held his ground and gazed. Before the instructor had a chance to voice his disapproval, the girl fell to the floor, convulsing in an epileptic fit. Norbert looked around for clues as to what the fuck was going on. Miracles abound; finally the instructor nonchalantly got up and sat beside her on the mat. He used his towel to fan some smelly air into her face, and after what seemed an age, she came round. Norbert had seen enough, and glared at the instructor as he left. He cursed to himself all the way back out to the street. *What a fucking disgrace – how that cunt even had the nerve to call it judo …*

Norbert was undeterred and determined to persevere, so a fortnight later he was back at the same venue at a different time observing a different class, praying he wouldn't have to squeeze past the fat instructor. He was there to watch a Ju-Jitsu class.

What a difference. This instructor was in his late forties and had a northern accent. He was fit, clean-shaven, and impeccable in his gi, calm and engaged with his class, showing his techniques for the class to practise. Norbert didn't make a peep; he had seen enough and when invited to join in, he jumped at the chance. Borrowing an old gi from the club and trying his best to tie the white belt around his slender body, he hastily removed his shoes, bowed his head, and followed the class out onto the mat for the first time. After practising various breakfalls for a while, he was ready to go. Angus would show a move: a punch glided in, which he parried to one side, simultaneously dropping to one knee. His other hand would grab a lower trouser leg, and with grace and forward momentum he would effortlessly take the opponent down to the mat where he would manoeuvre them into an armlock so taut they couldn't move. It looked easy.

Norbert tried, making a complete hash of it. He looked at Angus. 'Wow, this is going to take some time.'

'Nah, only thirty years, give or take.' Angus smiled a lot; when the white belts messed up it made him laugh, kindly. 'Don't worry, we've all been there. Rome wasn't built in a day.'

Norbert learned to fall a lot, getting thrown around like a stuntman on a movie set. Over the next couple of months, he made slow progress, but the excitement was waning. Inside he wasn't convinced by it; it felt a little too choreographed. As effective as the moves looked, there was no reality check – not for nothing was it called the gentle art. He limped on with the class, keeping his reservations to himself.

Things at work were getting crazier by the hour. Busier meant overtime. In the morning, on the shift changeover, Norbert would briefly chat with Geoff. He mentioned his training and how he was doubting it. 'What happens if someone comes at you with a knife?' Norbert said holding a biro in mimicry. 'I'm not that stupid to think I could use one of my airy-fairy moves.'

'Try to stab me with that,' Geoff told Norbert.

Norbert's eyes shifted from Geoff to the pen and back. He paused, then lunged forward with the pretend weapon. He heard the slap on his arm, then an instant tingling numbing sensation as the pen spiralled into the air.

'Fucking hell – that was amazing, like magic!'

Geoff laughed and walked away, leaving Norbert open-mouthed.

Chapter 14

Small ads

Norbert naturally wanted to get into the nuts and bolts of what Geoff did. He didn't have to wait long; Norbert was scheduled to work a night's overtime with Geoff the following Saturday – a twelve-hour shift laid on for one city corporate accounts job, which commanded top fees for the speed of turnaround expected.

Six o'clock and Norbert finished loading the last of his food and drink into his rucksack. He had had for once a quite uneventful Friday night and a lazy day watching the box. He needed the exercise, so he wheeled his bike outside and straddled up for the commute. Riding through the tunnel without the usual abuse being yelled at him made for a pleasant change. It was still light as he plotted his way through E14. The last road was long. Staring down from the east side were rows of council flats, block after block. He was hard pushed to find a single clean set of curtain nets amongst them all.

The locals had set upon one lad not a month before in a racially motivated attack like a pack of wolves, hurling their belt buckles into him as he fought them off. He had made it back to work bloodied and bruised but not done. Knowing where they hung and particularly what cars they drove, he exacted revenge by torching one of their cars. Everyone had since been on a state of high alert. Norbert clicked the gears up a notch and finished the last leg with a sprint Bradley Wiggins would be proud of. Pulling into the industrial unit on the other side of the road, he saw Geoff's car and reassured, relaxed somewhat.

An hour in and the press was loaded ready with paper and ink. Norbert climbed the steps to the plate-making department to get an ETA for the job, but Frankie hadn't heard anything. Norbert tried some small talk, but Frankie was too busy with other jobs. Noticing Frankie's psoriasis around his elbows were looking flakier than parmesan cheese, Norbert made his excuses and left, scratching himself. Geoff and Norbert sat in two chairs in front of their machine. Looking down at them from the grey breeze-block wall were a bevy of naked poster girls, and the radio was playing. Norbert dived straight in. 'Is it kung fu, you know, the stuff that you do?'

Having been asked about his favourite topic, ever eager, Geoff did not waste this moment, and being quite the history buff, he went in with the long answer. 'Yes, mate, kung fu from Ancient China to good old East London. The Chinese, you see, fought so many wars, but they were slaughtered more often than a rafter of Bernard Matthews turkeys. It's why they're so secretive, mistrusting – and racist, it has to be said. Look at the Terracotta Army, you know about that, right?'

'Of course.' Norbert nodded, knowing next to nothing.

'Well, what you might not know is how one of their emperors buried his soldier workers alive, to be ready to fight even in the afterlife.'

'Why would they let foreigners have it then, their fighting secrets?' Norbert shook his head slowly.

Geoff rubbed his fingers and thumb together as if he was caressing a nipple. 'What's the one thing they love more than anything else? Money!' He smiled. 'Lucky for us.'

Norbert smiled back; he appreciated the *us*. The sight of big John limping along momentarily interrupted them. One of his legs was swollen and looked like a donner kebab. He wore shorts all the time, whatever the weather, for better circulation, but it didn't seem to do any good. On his way back from the toilets he caught Geoff in full lecture mode, going through a chronological history of China and then on to Chairman Mao, talking about how millions were killed in poverty and wretched conditions while his hands were on the steering wheel. 'Sounds like a right cunt,' John said with impeccable timing, on his way back to his department.

'Is it any wonder, after all those miserable defeats and

massive death tolls at the hands of despotic rulers, that fighting systems would rise from the ashes? To survive, son,' Geoff pumped his chin out four times, 'you have to survive.'

Norbert's mind edged into song and he hummed GG's tune, 'I Will Survive'. He didn't get far before Geoff declared, 'Let's get some pizza.' Norbert didn't have the heart or bollocks to refuse.

Geoff popped outside for a cheeky spliff. Drugs helped calm him down – his energy was like constantly fizzy pop. Norbert asked around to see if anyone else wanted pizza, but they all declined. 'I could see Geoff bending your ear from up here,' Frankie said.

'Yeah, I'm getting a history lesson tonight.'

'Let me guess,' Frankie said, holding his hands up to mimic kung fu knives. It turned out they'd all had the same lesson. Still with no news on the job, Frankie said, 'You better get back to your class.'

Munching through their Hawaiian dustbin-lid-sized dinner gave a brief respite, but Norbert wanted to know about Geoff's kung fu. 'What sort of kung fu do you do?' he asked.

'I'll do better than that, son,' Geoff said. Producing his phone, he showed a blurry video image of his instructor taking a class, way out east, in Leytonstone. The students were blindfolded. Norbert watched them bounce off each other in full kick-ass mode, like flies bouncing off a windowpane. Norbert's Ju-Jitsu looked pale in comparison.

'If only your class was a bit nearer,' Norbert said. It looks awesome – what's it called?'

'Wing chun. A woman created it.' Geoff delved further into the mystique. Apparently, a fugitive abbess, Ng Mui, observed a fight between a snake and a crane, and combining her observations with her knowledge of Shaolin kung fu, she then supposedly crafted this amazing fighting system. 'Yeah, right load of bollocks if I've ever heard some. Seriously, though, the art passed down through the generations, making legends along the way. The famous Yip Man and his many students, Bruce Lee, and have you heard about Wong Shun Leung? Let me tell ya about that guy.

'Back in the day, different kung fu schools met secretly with each other for challenge matches. Wong was said to have faced opponents from many disciplines of every style of martial art in the colony. Defeated them all. They used to 'ave it on the rooftops.'

'Wow, fucking hell, is it dangerous?' Norbert asked.

'Well, it can get a bit naughty when I spar with a karate black belt mate of mine, but no, it's all controlled, Norbs.' Geoff was getting really friendly now as if he was about to welcome a newcomer into the fold.

Frankie shouted, 'Job's here.' Norbert flew out of the chair but Frankie hooted with laughter. 'Sorry, mate, had you there for a moment. Just heard it won't be arriving till late morning.'

Back to the chairs and Geoff held Norbert under his spell once more. They travelled right around the world, along the Silk Road, where the different religions and cultures came together, all adding something into the mix. Geoff eulogised about different masters, different systems. 'Be a magpie, Norbert. If it's shiny and it works, use it. Disregard the rest.'

He had Norbert hook, line, and sinker, hanging on Geoff's every word.

History lesson complete, Geoff offered a lift home, which Norbert gratefully accepted, mentally fatigued as he was. They folded down the back seats of Geoff's Beemer to accommodate the bike and turned the radio on; they were all out of talk. A short while later, Norbert was back home, his head spinning from all the information he was still trying to process. 'Can't thank you enough, Geoff, that's gotta be the best shift I've ever not worked.' They both laughed and it was hard to tell who was more pleased.

Norbert remembered Geoff explaining the meaning of kung fu; apparently, it meant working hard with merit, something that was not lost on him now – money for old rope that night. To cap it off, he had a copy of *Combat* magazine that Geoff had finished reading. Inside was a display box advertising a local wing chun class, up the road in Greenwich.

The next day Norbert called and left a message. When he

returned home, he saw that the answering machine was flashing its green luminous light. On playback, a softly spoken guy introduced himself as Larry, informing Norbert that he was welcome to come and have a look at his wing chun class and confirming the time and address.

Chapter 15

Larry

Maurice Blake understood what a camshaft was supposed to do. He could tell what was wrong with an engine from the sound it made or from the silence it tried to steal. He was one to stroke the whiskers and make them purr. Home used to be a small ramshackle plantation in Trinidad until he and his wife, Rose, with their two young children, Cecil and Alice, boarded a ship bound for England, the mother country. He was twenty-four years old when he arrived, and within twenty-four hours the scales had fallen from his eyes.

The biting cold and rain never helped. They had set foot in post-war Britain, to an insanely monochrome place. Pubs and accommodation were free to declare no Irish, no dogs, no blacks. There simply was no room for any hierarchal movement through shade or pigmentocracy. If you were black, the struggle felt keener. Their strong Catholic faith would be tested to the limits, but with a fortitude so typical of their generation, with sleeves rolled up, they dug in and carved a life from granite, or Deptford to be precise.

Recruited by London Transport, Maurice helped keep the buses running in nearby Camberwell. Supervisor Mr White (the irony was not lost on Maurice Blake) said, 'Blackey, make sure you clean down the forecourt when you've done.' Maurice was sure he heard him whisper *fucking jungle bunny* as he walked away. Maurice stood tall; where others stumbled, he smiled and carried on. Water off a duck's back.

He would talk to the other drivers and conductors, realising he was lucky to be out of the firing line. Some told how they had been spat at, suffering racial abuse daily. It was not how he imagined it would be, but he figured it out, why people were so abusive. They were scared, scared of losing the little they had, losing their houses and jobs to the foreigners. Within a year, Rose and the kids would be joined by another – young Lawrence. It was touch and go whether the tot would make it onto this mortal coil being so premature, but Rose had given birth to a fighter who had already shown a glimpse of his future pedigree.

The eldest kids were surviving through school rather than thriving. It was always going to be trickier for them; when they looked around, theirs were two of very few black faces. Alice and Cecil were walking home from school one day. When they got in, Cecil couldn't keep it in any longer. He burst out crying, tears streaming down his soft face.

'What on earth is the matter, my love?' Rose instinctively put an arm around his shoulders.

'The other boys have been calling me names all day.'

'I'm hungry,' Alice said.

'Never mind that – are these horrible bullies picking on you as well?' she asks Alice.

'No, but I am really hungry.'

Rose turned her attention back to Cecil. 'What are they saying, boy, what things?'

He sniffled and cleared his throat. 'They call me Cecil Blake the chocolate flake, all day. Even my teacher, Mr Anderson, he heard them.'

Maurice heard this and roared with laughter. He looked at Cecil who saw his father's smile leave his face. 'Go and sit with your young brother in the sitting room. You too, Alice,' Maurice said. Rose followed them all in; she knew. Gentle Maurice, a quiet man; when he had something to say it was generally worth listening to. They all squeezed onto the sofa while Dad stood.

'Do you think that your mother and I left Trinidad to come all the way here to Great Britain to be upset by fools who know no better? The world is full of bad, nasty people. They're everywhere. I read in the paper last week that in another neighbourhood somebody discovered a young teenage boy discarded like rubbish and left in some alleyway.'

Rose's eyes widened. 'You trying to give them damn nightmares, Maurice Blake?'

'It won't. They caught the monster responsible. They need to know, because as bad as you might think this place is, it is not even close to the horrors we left behind. Do you think that Trinidad was all warm sunshine, blue seas, and mangos? We left behind a ghetto plagued by robbers and murderers, parents who beat their children, husbands who beat their wives. I swore it would be better for all of us, and it will if you rise above this nonsense.' He held Cecil's hand and said the magic words, 'We love you.' That was all that mattered.

'Tell them fools that it's true, you are a flake, beautiful and delicious.' Rose squeezed Cecil so hard he almost died.

'Never let them see you're hurt,' Dad proclaimed, 'sticks and bones may break your bones ...' Young Lawrence sat quietly, watching the melodrama unfold, a fire bubbling away deep inside.

They lived on the first floor of an old Victorian house, the back garden out of bounds except to the Rawlings family on the ground floor who let the weeds run riot. It was a constant moot point; Rose could have made so much of the small space and the kids would have enjoyed playing outside. The window boxes she kept glared out a will of defiance to the greyness. The blood-red scarlets and luminous pinks of the pelargoniums would give the finest chaconia back home a run for their money. Together they nurtured, watered, fed, and cared, as the years melted away like the snow they laughed at when they touched it for the first time.

Both elder siblings knuckled down in secondary school. Maybe to stave off her constant hungriness, Alice found Home Economics. She became a wonderful cook, fusing many of the Caribbean influences passed down by Mum. Cecil followed Dad into the world of the automobile. Together their skilled hands would repair back to life many of the cars in the neighbourhood. Cecil would have his own garage. Maurice stayed with London Transport despite Mr White's idiocy; he was faithful like that. Whatever was thrown at him, he whistled away; you can't get to someone who can't be got at.

Lawrence was a distinct entity. One day a scrawny scrote hurled some abuse his way and called him a stupid n——— before a punch squashed his nose back into his unwashed face. He couldn't have been older than thirteen. Teachers reprimanded both boys, and they excluded Lawrence from his favourite lessons. It was a pattern of disruption that continued. He was vocal, ready, and able to raise his hands, and the teachers didn't know how to handle him. Some thought most black kids were educationally challenged, under-achievers.

It was left to an older teacher, Mr Hoskins, to deal with the mess. 'Son, why are you always here on detention?' he said as he handed out paper for the naughty kids to write their lines. Week after week, both parents were called into the school for talks. Neither could explain it. No matter what they said or did, they couldn't break the cycle until Lawrence reached his fourth year. That was the year his options kicked in and he chose technical drawing, taught by none other than his old guard, Mr Hoskins.

The tide turned immediately. Where other kids saw muddle, Lawrence saw clean sharp lines and neat angles; dissecting linear shapes with precision, he excelled. With a set square, a T-Square, and fiddling the knurled end of his pencil-lead compass, he engaged. One day the class got their homework back. 'Wrong, wrong, wrong,' said Mr H, handing them back. He was going to have to go over it all again on the blackboard. Chalk in one hand duster in the other, banging the board as he drew, he said, 'Pay attention, everyone, everyone except brilliant Larry.' He turned and winked at Lawrence.

For Lawrence already knew from the gold star shining on his work that he had passed muster, and he stood ten feet tall with a throbbing heart. Mr Hoskins rarely saw Lawrence in detention again. He didn't want to let him down now there was this bond, and from that moment on people started calling him Larry. Lawrence liked that.

Chapter 16

Two for one and one for all

First, we had Cole Williams, shaven brown head, standing six foot two and looking like he could be part of the American Harlem Globetrotters. He was athletic, with hands so big they could probably wrap around one side of a basketball, and he sauntered along seemingly without a care in the world. Smiling and sociable, he also fitted some black stereotyping perfectly because he could dance like you wouldn't believe, and he knew the movement and mechanics of the body intimately like a trained physio. Cole's journey into martial arts had seen him on a merry dance of fruitless endeavours, especially around Chinatown, where the late-night showings of classical kung fu films thrilled audiences from far and wide.

Cole was awestruck by the trailblazing Bruce Lee and the prowess of Jackie Chan. Seduced by the sight of red lanterns, golden dragons, and bathed in the glorious aromas of dim sum leaking out from every restaurant, Cole immersed himself in the culture, where he began to build his dream of finding then learning kung fu. But just like the brightly lit casinos of Las Vegas, the charlatan teachers knew best how to part you from your money. Martial art schools in Chinatown gave nothing of substance away, and most definitely not for free.

Cole's attention turned to a local karate class. What he saw was a bullying instructor bulldozing his way through techniques, beating his students black and blue with all the finesse of a baby giraffe. He was an instructor with the scent of blood in his nostrils. Talking to two lads afterwards who had suffered some beatings, Cole got a whisper of a new kung fu class they were going to try out, and he persuaded them to take him along. 'I've got nothing to lose,' he said.

When Cole arrived at this class, he thought he had arrived at the finest Savile Row tailor's. Nico, the instructor, was showing effective kung fu techniques with skill the like of which he hadn't seen outside the movies. This was what he had patiently been searching for, real kung fu. His hopes of finding a teacher, a sifu who could show him the way, unlocking the key to a secretive society, non-Western, were finally realised. The first moment he saw Nico Attila at the 'cave', he knew in his heart that this was right on the money.

Then we had our Larry Blake. At fifteen, he too was drawn into the world of martial arts. David Carradine's television series *Kung Fu* saw to that, watching the Shaolin monk Kwai Chang Caine walk the rice paper and brand himself with dragons from the scalding cauldron. It had a massive appeal to those who harboured dreams of being able to fight effortlessly, good overcoming evil, championing justice and sticking up for the weaker man, upholding moral values with honour and integrity. Intrigued by this philosophy, Larry started his journey.

All paths eventually led to Chinatown. Simon Vardigans looked the part, Chinese with jet-black hair and the tiniest moustache, slim build. He wore his kung fu traditional uniform; black frog buttons neatly secured his black top with the sleeves rolled back revealing their white ends. The slippers he wore on his feet let him glide around with an air of arrogance. The style of kung fu he taught was wing chun, the year was 1984, and he ran a popular class that attracted many people but no Chinese. That should have raised the alarm. He told his students the Chinese were too big-headed and above themselves to learn from him. He talked a lot and the little he did, he did well. Any information was drip-fed slowly. Larry never questioned things, embracing the class and everything Simon said.

These two young men, complete strangers, were essentially searching for the same thing but on different paths. But here they were, sitting opposite each other on a train heading out of London.

Cole noticed something straight away and couldn't help himself. 'What's that film you got there, is it Jackie Chan's latest?'

Larry looked up and revealed the VHS cassette. 'Yeah, fearless hyena, have you seen it?'

'No, the last one I saw was . . .'

'Snake in the Eagle's Shadow,' they said in unison.

'That's the one, lousy plot, crazy dubbing, but the fighting was epic,' said Cole, looking at the shiny gold trophy nestled next to Larry. 'Nice, what's that for? Kung fu?'

'Oh, it's nothing – freestyle kick-boxing competition, brawling, not much kung fu. Not like this guy.' He admired the ripped cover picture of a youngish Mr Chan.

Cole liked his humble manner and they continued to chat. By the time Cole got off fifteen minutes later, they'd swapped numbers and he was the one clutching the new JC film.

They soon became better acquainted, inevitably talking martial arts, and Larry explained to Cole the slow progress he was making under Simon Vardigans of Chinatown fame. 'Thing is, one week he tells you to do one thing and then a short while later you are told to do something else. It changes all the time, Cole.'

They met up the following week. 'Why you still walking around with that trophy?' Cole asked.

He returned the film as Larry shot him a look and explained the absurdity. 'This,' he declared, 'is another trophy, not the same one. Another win.'

Now Cole was really intrigued; he simply had to see what this young man's fighting ability was all about. He invited him to have a little spar at a small church hall close to where he lived. When Larry turned up a day or two later, they sparred and Cole pinned him up using the flavour of wing chun that he was being taught by Nico – pinned him up and locked him out. Using carefully positioned technique, he nullified Larry's every movement. 'Medals won't give you that.'

Larry's lack of technique had nowhere to hide. His standard was exposed as ineffective against the more experienced Cole Williams. And then, to make matters worse, Cole revealed that Larry's teacher Simon Vardigans had an identical twin brother, Randall.

'Yeah, I had been talking to my teacher, Nico. Apparently, it's well known in their circles that Simon lets Randall take his classes while he goes off chasing the ladies, and Randall don't know kung fu. Plus he likes the boys – you know, too touchy feely?'

'What, one of them's gay?' Larry asked.

'The only time you'll likely see Simon is if there's a pretty girl in the class. You see, no one knows who's which. Impossible to tell them apart unless you see them together, and that's rarer than the sight of the Loch Ness monster.'

Larry was lost for words. His fighting skills had been exposed as poor, and the only thing that made any sense right now was why his class had confused him so much. *Those sneaky Vardigans switching cardigans. Greedy parasites.*

Larry came to turn with the obvious and asked Cole if he would take him to his class. Cole could have brushed him off, but returned Larry's trust and agreed to take Larry with him to Nico's.

A small sign outside ushered them into a nondescript downstairs space that was home to an elusive world. The cave lacked any modern comforts such as windows or air-conditioning; it was basic and honest, and this was very much reflected in the training. There were no uniforms or coloured belts. Larry was the youngest student at the time and with his lack of technique, he spent most of the early years defending himself against all and sundry; in hindsight this wasn't a bad thing for a student. However, that being said, the class mentality was to defend by attack; they were to martial arts what Brazil or Barcelona were to football – attack, and the rest will take care of itself.

Chapter 17

Seekers

It was a rite of passage for the top students at the cave to be invited to Hong Kong to train with Nico's teacher (Si Gun), Grandmaster Wong Shun Leung, or Si bak (Wong's senior student), Li Wei. To seek the experience of the masters, a pilgrimage to their Mecca, you had to have a letter of introduction. You couldn't just rock up to a class; it was by invitation only. If they permitted you and allowed the visit (although, of course, they did; they scammed everyone one way or another) this by no means guaranteed a joyous experience.

Robin Gerhard was the best senior student at the cave and his time had come; he had saved up his hard-earned and the formalities had been dealt with. This was to be the icing on the cake for the keenest of students. But Robin had some qualities that were more of a hindrance than an edge. First, he was big, impressively muscular, and second, he was emotionally unprepared for the experience; being black didn't help him either. Bounding about on the streets of Hong Kong, he received constant uncomfortable stares and telling looks from the locals. Chinese whispers about the heiren swept through the class. Nobody spoke a word of English to him, and he hit a brick wall. Self-preservation was entrenched in the Chinese mentality; Wong wasn't about to show his techniques to Nico's much stronger student. He never made it to Li Wei's school, and cutting short his miserable stay, he left with his tail between his legs.

Undeterred by Robin Gerhard's experience, Larry, now aged twenty-three, was on a plane heading to Hong Kong. A three-month stay was scheduled including a plan to seek and train with both masters. But the teachers were not speaking to each other; they had quarrelled and fallen out over something trivial. Not wanting to offend either teacher, Larry decided in his wisdom to train with and visit them both but not tell either about the other. Once in Hong Kong, Larry alternated his time between the two teachers, attending both day and night classes. His humble and cunning began to unlock some of the secrets. As for the looks from the locals, the nudging, the finger pointing, he didn't care; he was feasting at the table and it was proving to be some banquet.

Halfway through his stay he called Cole. The phone box was swallowing coins quicker than a mother can feed her hungry chicks – Cole liked to chat, but Larry dispensed with any waffle.

'Wong's class is good, but most of the time he's sitting down drinking, gambling – he loves the horse racing on television,' Larry said.

'I guess he's earned the right to take his foot off the ped—'

Before Cole had a chance to finish, Larry continued. 'His students though are switched on, really rough and aggressive. Wong encourages them to fight. The old bugger still obviously likes a scrap, and if you're weak in his class, they will get you. However, once I made it to Li Wei's class, things were so different.'

'In what way?'

'What stood out straight from the start was his class was so much more about the technical side. I mean, don't get me wrong, they can scrap as well, but their moves are far superior. I'm staying in the new territory, quite a way from Li Wei's class, but I always make sure I get there early, every time.'

'I bet Li Wei loves that.'

'Yep, he gets to his class for a smoke before he starts and he talks to me, shows me stuff.'

'God, he must like you. To Li Wei it's the ultimate compliment that you sought him out and not his teacher Wong.'

'I think it's more they don't see me as a threat. I mean, I don't attack, I defend.'

'Clever.'

'Listen, I have to go before my money runs out. I'm extending my stay for a couple of months – why don't you come and join me?'

'Definitely.'

Larry ends the call, and imagines Cole doing a little jig.

Cole saved up and made it for the last month. Dumbfounded by Larry's metamorphic transformation, he could see that the new techniques were there but not fully absorbed yet. He saw the flavour of the flower, rather than the full bloom; he was stunned but humbled by Larry's ability. When Cole finally met and trained under Li Wei, he was in for a disconcerting reality check.

Li Wei said, 'How long you been training?'

'Ten years.'

'Wrong.' Li Wei held Cole's elbow and pushed it into Cole's own ribs. 'Through the middle, not out. Watch Larry. Your feet are open. This foot' – he kicked it inward – 'should be here.'

'Thank you, sifu,' Cole said.

'Why you bother? It's not for everyone, you know. Easier to give up than be bad.'

'Thank you, sifu,' he said through gritted teeth.

Li Wei's class continued in this vein. Larry didn't mind; through Cole's relearning he was understanding the techniques even better. Another night in class, nearing the end of their time, Cole was being passed around like a mobile punchbag. The older students in particular were giving him a real beating. Cole had to politely say thank you to them all afterwards.

At the end, Li Wei had them all stand in a circle.

Li Wei was centre stage. Cole was sweating, bruised, and battered. Li Wei walked over. Cole thought he was coming over to give him a pat on the back, a well done for all his hard work. Li Wei's hand reached out to touch Cole's shoulder. 'You know there is no shame in giving up.'

Li Wei turned icily away, his attention on Larry. 'I know you been seeing Wong.' You could have heard a pin drop. Larry had been busted; it was an age before Li Wei broke the awkwardness. 'It's okay I understand. Back in the day, I did the same thing. Wong, however, he's very upset, he takes things personally. Come join us for dinner Friday – you too, Cole.'

Both sifus had manoeuvred Larry and Cole out for dinner, one last dance. When the guys turned up and saw the teachers sitting at an enormous round table with their burgeoning families, they took a deep gulp of air. The sifus were full of praise for both young men, raising their glasses and toasting their success. How they kept a straight face when the young pretenders were presented with the bill is another story.

When they returned home to Blighty, much improved but substantially shorter of money, they found that training back at the cave had changed. For a start, Nico had gone and was eagerly chasing fame and fortune in America. The seniors left in charge at the cave were told by Nico that Larry and Cole had been met by the usual wall of silence regarding information. They had been shown nothing of substance, they were no threat. Some found out the hard way that that was not the case.

Cole said afterwards, 'I saw Robin try to run through you like a bull tonight.'

'All he can do is chain punch. The second I changed it up, he froze like a rabbit in headlights. He's lucky all he got was a busted nose,' Larry said.

'There was blood spilled tonight. Everyone was watching you beat him up. You're younger, and he's a lot bigger. It was embarrassing.'

'He wasn't interested in learning – he just wanted to win.'

'Boy, did he lose. I'm telling you, that sent a shockwave through the class. I mean – Robin is their best.'

'Not anymore.'

Two days later, Larry phoned Cole. 'Hi, Cole, who do you think called me up last night?'

'Nico, I told you. What did he say?'

Larry explained. 'I thought he was going to have a go, but get this – he says they needed taking down a peg or two, getting too big for their boots. A big ego is a big problem, he told me. He wants us to venture out and teach his style to promote the cave. He still wants paying, though.'

'Is he asking us or telling us to leave?'

'Both, I think. Anyway, it's time. I've looked around and found a place to teach nearby in Greenwich, South London.'

It was a new start; Larry would rip up the Nico rule book and start teaching and practising the way of Li Wei from his time in Hong Kong. Larry sought counsel from Li Wei on paying Nico. Li Wei explained that was not how things were done; out of respect for his sifu, Li Wei would give Wong a large red packet every Chinese New Year, but it was from him, not his students.

Cole warned Larry to expect a backlash from Nico. And, indeed, once the money stopped, Larry was told in no uncertain terms he would not be welcome back at the cave. They had split somewhat acrimoniously.

In time, the cave fizzled out but left behind an almost mythical, legendary status. For now, though, Larry was free to develop and build his style of teaching wing chun. He was the one that got away with the crown jewels; going underground away from any interference, he was to set about polishing them so they sparkled bright.

Cole was smart, grateful he had a part, and let Larry assume the ascendancy, knowing shooting stars never stop.

Chapter 18

Norbert, meet Norbert

Tucked on the corner of a quiet street, away from the bookshops, bars, and bustle of Greenwich High Road was a rather bland church and community centre. The class had already started when Norbert arrived. He made his way through the glass doors of the reception; noises emanated from the other side of the deep blue door to the right side of the waiting area. He heard laughing and several voices in conversation, but no loud *ouss* sounds or karate *hi ya* noises, which encouraged him further. Pausing briefly to settle, his heart beating wildly, he pushed the door open. This revealed a sizeable, well-lit, L-shaped hall, with an old parquet wooden floor, the sort you might have sat on as a child in school assembly. There was a small row of chairs near the door and a group of some twenty or more men dispersed around the hall engaged in various forms of practice, and some going through their stretching routines. A man walked over, offered his hand, and introduced himself as Larry Blake. 'Norbert?'

Norbert nodded.

'Take a seat and we'll talk after.'

Norbert took a seat; the clock on the wall showed 8.12 p.m. *Who does Larry remind me of? Eddie Murphy, that's it, but bulkier.* Larry was dressed in a casual black tracksuit and T-shirt; everyone was dressed in black. Most people in the class were black. *It feels like I shouldn't be here,* Norbert thought. *If some of my friends could see me now.* His eyes darted around the class as if he was a lizard looking for a tasty morsel, not knowing who to look at, who to focus on. His gaze kept coming back to Larry Blake.

Watching him move with speed and grace, with purpose and intensity, he could see the respect the others showed. This wasn't like the choreography of the Ju-Jitsu class he had previously taken part in. There were no belts, no guards; it was controlled fighting. He saw hands and arms interlocked, shapes like a swan's wing reaching into the air, people in harmony with each other, moving around. They look so accomplished, but it was Larry who ran the show, pulling the strings, setting the pace and rhythm. What set him apart was how effortless he made it look. Like anyone on top of their game, he made it look ridiculously easy.

I remember that chess grandmaster on TV moving from chair to chair, simultaneously playing many opponents under the pressure of time, analysing the game and perfecting a move to end it or set up a finish in an instant. It's the same thing in front of my eyes here. Speed chess. Fucking hell, this looks serious. He was salivating at the prospect of learning, but something else was happening. Inside his busy mind, past prejudices and stereotypes were being awoken. Over two hours in, and he was still sitting in that damn plastic chair. *I'm not moving, not even for a piss. This feels like a test.*

The class eventually finished at 10.30 p.m. and all the participants made their way slowly towards the chairs where Norbert was sitting, sweat pouring off some, all looking energised and pleased with themselves. The silence towards him finally broke when someone asked, 'Well, what do you think?'

'Yeah, it looks great – is there a beginner's class?' There was laughter.

'This is the beginner's class,' a man called Cole Williams proclaimed, 'we're all in it together.'

Larry spoke. 'It will take about three years of training before you will be allowed to spar. It takes patience and time to learn the various forms and the ability to apply them. The fees are sixty pounds for the month, but you can come and train all three classes a week.'

'Great,' Norbert said, 'I'll see you next week.' He prised his numb ass and tingly feet away from the plastic chair that now felt like he was wearing it.

Chapter 19

Baby steps

The following week Norbert started over, and after a couple of hip circles that cracked and neck turns that scrunched in a meagre stretching routine, his bones felt relieved. One of the younger students explained that he was going to demonstrate the first form in wing chun – si lim tao. The first form was quite static – from standing, hand and arm movements flow forth, changing positions, both sides moving continuously. It was quite long but physically not too challenging. *Doesn't look too difficult.*

'Your turn,' said the student.

All the moves Norbert had just seen evaporated away. He couldn't remember where to start; he was stuck. 'This isn't getting off to a good start, damn. Sorry, I need to pay more attention.'

The guy laughed. 'Don't worry, it's quite long. I'll show you again.'

When he did, Norbert was able, with a little nudging, to copy some of the movements. Norbert was officially on his way, along the same path that Geoff, Larry, and the masters before him had trod.

Norbert was a stickler for time; he had an inbuilt clock, hated tardiness, and more often than not he would be first there, daydreaming, waiting for Larry to arrive and open up. Once inside, it was his duty as the newbie to put the chairs out, assemble the wooden dummy inside a door frame, and in one corner place a tall standing mirror that perched on a chair. For the first year, at every class he would be found standing in front of said mirror, practising the first form, checking the reflection had him square. *It's not about admiring your pretty self in the mirror, Norbert!*

The moves were empty of substance if you didn't know how or when to use them, but slowly, over time, these details were explained, and he was given specific drills to practise, both on his own and with a partner. Most of the other students were so helpful, especially the seniors who would correct his positions and explain the differences between the right way and the wrong. This theme continued right across the class, Larry explaining frequently that they would all improve together. There was no favouritism. Everyone got all the techniques when and only they felt they were ready.

Larry's finger was on the pulse of the class. If someone tried to steal a technique before being vetted, they would be found out. Punishment was probably taking some choice digs from Larry, *ouch*. After the six-month threshold had passed, if someone did a move wrong, their partner had licence to hit them. Sometimes it would hurt, but taking a few digs, a cut and a bruise, the occasional thick lip, was all part of the package. Time with Larry in the early days was precious. He shared his time around with everyone, so it was spread thin. If you got five minutes one-to-one with him you were lucky, but when you did it was worth it. It was one thing to watch someone and admire them from a distance, but when you engage, you open up to new sensations.

Back at Mum's, Norbert was lying on his bed, digesting the information from class when Larry had spoken about the importance of awareness and feel. Norbert had a black notebook for all things wing chun. Every drill, technique, and idea went in there. On the first page was the date of his first lesson – 12 May 1999 – and above it the family tree ascended from Norbert to Larry, to Li Wei, then to Wong, and lastly to Yip Man. Four grandiose steps away from greatness, there was his name set among some of the greatest in the pantheon of kung fu protagonists ever.

Norbert, deep in thought, cast his mind back: *I'm standing outside in a queue on a swelteringly hot summer's day waiting impatiently for people to exit the local lido. As someone left, another could enter through the turnstiles in quid pro quo sequence. The noise inside was from a deafening riot of activity that made me desperate to get in there and join in the fun. Trunks rolled up in a towel under my arm, through the gaps in the turnstiles I could glimpse the paradise on the other side. Over a thousand people must have passed through on a fine summer's day.*

The first time Norbert entered he was taken aback at just how big it was. The pool was huge; the light blue colour dazzled and reflected the glare of the shimmering sun. Along the sides were changing rooms, the doors reminiscent of pastel-coloured seaside houses. They gave you a brief chance to escape the crowds, which towards the far end grew denser. There was a café with a queue that stretched forever. And there in the centre of the grounds stood the wedding-cake-style fountain, water pouring out from the top and cascading down. It was like a magnet drawing your gaze. The day was a picture postcard of summer, and it gave the local people an oasis to escape the weather when it was at its most intense. The shallow end was a buzz of excitable kids and families splashing around in the water, but in the deep end there was no one; something was not right. Water, water everywhere, but not a soul to swim. He dipped a toe in and realised the rumours that some had died from heart attacks in those icy waters might be bloody true.

Norbert thought, *Awareness – no one was swimming, and Feel, it was unbelievably fucking freezing.*

Yeah, it might be silly, but Larry told us that being in tune with your senses could save your life – it deserved a big asterisk next to it. Norbert finished his notes, lesson complete.

At the next class, Larry called Norbert over to the centre of the hall. Larry told him to punch twice. Norbert stood still and did as instructed.

'Step forwards and do it.'

Norbert did as he was asked.

'Again, do it again. Faster. Again. Harder, with meaning.'

When Larry had Norbert doing it how he wanted, he stepped in to meet the first punch. Larry glided at a slight angle, deflecting Norbert's second punch, and then turned in and released three punches from hell, rapid fire, that stopped a shard away from Norbert's face. 'Don't flinch. Do it again.'

He did it again.

'Don't move.'

Fucking easy for you to say. Every nerve of his body instinctively wanted him to get out of the way.

'Face the horror,' Larry said.

At that moment the penny dropped – why people wanted to go into a cage submerged in the sea to get up close and personal with a shark. You knew you were in the presence of something with the potential to hurt or kill, but you wanted to be as close as possible, to enjoy the ride. The adrenalin came from the potential and through the closeness came the respect, and with this knowledge, the ego accepted it. It had to.

Norbert faced the horror.

Chapter 20

Band of brothers

A steady trickle of new people was joining the class. Norbert partnered up with Steve, British-born with a mix of Chinese and Vietnamese ethnicity; they were both as keen as mustard. Steve had a soft air of confidence about him, bordering on arrogance. It was clear he was a natural. They were going to be good for each other, both hitting the trail together at an excellent time. Eventually, the cream would rise to the top, and Steve was one of those fast improvers, making it look far easier than it was. Norbert seemed to suffer from 'white men can't dance' syndrome at times. He struggled to find a technique. Either his hips were not turning or his back was not straight, head up and down, feet wrong, elbows out; he made every mistake in the book, to be frank. Big Cole would point out how Steve was doing it correctly. 'Look how he moves, fluid,' he would say. Norbert hated Steve, of course, the bastard – kindly, but jealously.

But Steve and Norbert become friends. Sometimes they would pop to a restaurant for some crispy squid and sizzling beef, washed down with a cold refreshing drink.

'What is it you do, Steve?' Norbert asked.

'It's Cuong.'

'Come again?'

'It's Cuong, Norbert. My name, it's Cuong.'

'Well, why the fuck does everyone call you Steve, you fraud?'

'It's easier.'

'Cuong?'

'Yes, as in King Kong. And I fix people's teeth, sort of. I'm a cosmetic dentist.'

Norbert almost choked on a noodle. 'Let me get this right,

Cuong – you try to knock people's teeth out in class, and then you'll fix them up.'

'Exactly.'

While Norbert struggled and fought to earn, the pound notes just flooded into Cuong's wallet effortlessly. He wasn't flash, and Norbert really liked him. Their chat came right back, and they enthused about Digor.

Students called Larry, *Digor* (pronounced Die-gor) rather than sifu. He reasoned that the master symbolised someone who had attained such a level they could become complacent and stop striving to improve, satisfied with their level. Digor kind of meant big brother, and it had a twofold purpose: first, it bridged the gap between teacher and student, taking away any stigma of unattachment, making you feel you were fighting alongside your ally in the trenches; and second, it reminded Larry that he would always be a student and that he could never master wing chun. Whatever the reasoning, it worked, and although there was no bowing to the teacher hand over fist, his students had nothing but the utmost respect for him.

The seniors would ensure that would remain the case. One time, a guy came into class and tried to claim Digor's chair. The clue should have been that all the others were positioned slightly behind in a row, and this was the biggest. Not stopping to think, the guy threw his stuff down on the chair, the way halfwits go about claiming a sunbed with their towel on holiday. This act of mindlessness was quickly pointed out and he sheepishly removed his belongings. He was given a word of advice – try not to piss the teacher off just before class.

Likewise, if they all went out for dinner, Digor would get the best seat and Digor would start eating first. Digor would always play down his position as the head. 'Don't wait for me, get stuck in,' he would say. It was always about being respectful to everyone. In Norbert's mind, it singled him out as a unique teacher and person.

Attending three classes a week, Norbert was bonding socially with people from different ethnicities and making new friends. The shackles of the Bermondsey mindset took far too long to let go, but he had passed a point of no return. The class experience and the mix of people rubbed off on him, changing him; prejudice had been a stubborn beast and now it was being tamed. He was learning about life and getting a close look through other people's eyes. Sometimes the silliest trivial things tickled him.

One of the students was asking Digor about a movie. 'Where did you watch it, in Catford?' he asked.

'Listen, when I want to watch a film in peace I go where the white people go.'

'Make you right, Digor,' Cole chipped in.

'Black people are a nightmare – they scream out the plot, always spoil it, too loud.'

Norbert was listening, absolutely intrigued.

Working in a print shop on long twelve-hour shifts was exhausting, but Norbert always dragged himself to class. Punching and letting off some energy was a therapeutic release from the stresses of the day. No matter how tired he was, Norbert always left the class content, and a little wiser. On a social level, having his eyes opened to new experiences and friends was rewarding, but there was another tangible feel-good factor that had him hooked. It was fun.

Even before entering class, he could hear Digor. His voice carried and laughter was never far away – during class, as well. It was a strange, slightly weird phenomenon that when he was in the middle of an onslaught, being outmanoeuvred and beaten by Digor, it was not unusual for Norbert to burst into a fit of giggles. You couldn't fight back with anger, or you'll just get more of the same beating; you could cry and break down out of frustration, but it was better to just laugh it off. Laughter and positivity sat comfortably alongside the teachers' other strengths of humility and enthusiasm. In the early years, it was rare that Norbert missed a class, and if he did, he wanted to know what he had missed. This was the right attitude and, with a fantastic teacher, the result was that his wing chun was fast improving.

Norbert and Cuong were joined by Johnny, a drummer with elastic arms, and Jason, a plumber with heavy arms. Both loved a good scrap. This small band of brothers clicked, training hard and often. Together they collectively pushed on, riding on the coat-tails of the seniors. Sometimes they chilled in the pub after class.

Digor's level continued to confound them all. 'Could we be that good?' asked Johnny.

Cuong shot them down. 'Never. He lives it, breathes it, it's his life, man. There's not enough time left for us to catch him up, even if he stopped now. Maybe if we'd started at seventeen, but you know that's when you start discovering girls.'

'And music,' said Johnny.

'And drugs.' Jason rolled up his sleeves.

Johnny was always tapping or drumming something, his fingers beating the table.

Jason's arms were bruised, the fresh hue of blueish purple.

'Thought you'd been injecting some shit – you need some ice, ice baby.'

Jason said, 'I swear to God, if I didn't know better, I'd think Digor's arms were square. It was like an iron girder cutting into me.'

Wise owl Cuong spoke. 'Years spent training on the wooden dummy hardens your bones. The other week he hit me with the body bag on – I almost died.'

'Yeah, I had the pleasure of that one,' Johnny added. 'Quiet tonight, Norbert.'

Norbert said, 'Jack's pissing me right off.' Jack was one of the seniors, supposedly the best. 'Every time I finished our drill tonight he shoved me aside like I was shit on his shoe. Three times. I mean, why couldn't he just tell me what I was doing wrong?'

Cuong said, 'That's mean, man. I mean seriously, that's cruel.'

'He winds me up – you know he's fucking racist. Have you noticed he never partners up with anyone white, seriously,' Norbert said.

'Trust me, guys, in a couple of years, we'll be giving the seniors a run for their money,' said Cuong.

Johnny winked at Norbert. 'Never trust a Chinaman.'

'Can't fucking wait,' Jason said. He was clearly looking forward to it.

'Ditto,' said Norbert. They all clinked their glasses.

Chapter 21

Lush baby Simpkins

Norbert was stumbling along through life watching his pregnant girlfriend Nikki's belly slowly get bigger when something quite unexpected, weird, and wonderful happened. He'd been waiting patiently for it for so many years.

He had always been on the lookout for ways of making some extra crust. He must have been around sixteen when he first started scouring the newspapers for jobs and ideas. Flicking the pages over, reading from the back, the colourful page spread of jockeys and racehorses stopped him in his tracks, but he knew next to nothing about the gee-gees, couldn't even write a betting slip. He pondered over a way to back some winners, coming up with a Baldrick plan of action. Following the tipsters, and seeing there were three, all he had to do was pick out a horse whenever more than one tipster selected it. If the tipsters agreed or were unanimous, well, they couldn't all be wrong, could they? *World of Sport* was hosted by Dickie Davies, and interspersed between cliff divers in Mexico, speedway Bravehearts, and madcap wrestlers, was a full programme of horseracing. He'd watch the races unfold on television to see if there was any money to be made.

After the first favourite was beaten out of sight, he quickly lost interest, his great plan foiled at the first hurdle. He went back to poring over the paper. Next, he scanned the financials for the share prices, some up, some down. This world was unapologetically all about the money, and judging by the size of the directors' pay and bonuses, those in the game were making bucketloads of the stuff.

Day turned to night; he had got nowhere fast with his extra-money-making plans, but he started reading the financials on a much more regular basis. If he wanted to join this elite group, he better try to learn, figure out the figures. Companies outperforming others, dividends rising, acquisitions, mergers, takeovers, it captured his imagination; he was looking outside into a world of rich players that he desperately wanted to be a part of. At first, it meant nothing, but slowly over time he began to understand the jargon and caught the drift.

He was still in his teens when another small piece of the jigsaw jiggled into place. One of his mum's best friends, Pam, had invited the family to join them for the day. It was a hot sunny day, and the lure of their swimming pool was good enough reason to tempt young Norbert and Meara, his girlfriend at the time, to come along. Pam and Brian were lovely people, warm hosts. Grabbing a bite to eat inside, Norbert spoke with Brian.

'You're so fortunate to have a swimming pool, Brian.'

'Yes, we are, especially as we didn't pay for it.'

'Are you serious?'

'Deadly, Norbert. You want a beer to go with that?'

'Are you having one?'

'Shame not to, hey.'

The others soon left to go back to their sun worshipping. Norbert prodded a little more. It turned out that Brian had been buying into every share privatisation that came along.

'When the shares double, I take out my original investment. In for nothing, I sit back and watch the rest make me more money. Time after time they all paid off handsomely, giving me extra cash for holidays, pools, and anything else.'

Fucking hell, this is it, the missing piece. All I have to do is copy this fucking genius. They talked for ages, Brian sharing his pearls of wisdom about buying into forthcoming privatisations, what magazines to read, finding a stockbroker and becoming a shareholder. Norbert started applying for shares in all the upcoming privatisations, of which there were many. The Tories had committed themselves to a bout of de-nationalisation in the troubled unionised industrial seventies, and what started as a trickle led to a downpour.

They sold most of the country's silver – a nation of Sids actively encouraged to buy into the dream.

He ventured into buying other shares. 'Don't buy following recommendations in the papers, Norbert,' Brian told him. 'Here's the thing – when you're buying off a recommendation, especially in the popular newspapers, you're being snared. The conniving bastards already own these shares, and when the gullible public buys in, they are selling.' Norbert was careful, sometimes making a few quid, more often than not losing. Millwall, the local team, seemed cheap to buy, and as soon as Norbert bought in, they became a whole lot cheaper.

Back to the present day. Norbert's wages had improved, but his desire to extract more from the well never waned. He was treading water with the investing, still reading the financials when he happened upon a technology newsletter. He took out a subscription on the simple basis that the newsletter's recommendations were given out before the securities were added to their portfolios, which seemed a much fairer playing field. The newsletter's holdings were flying, producing mind-boggling returns. Month after month he would gawp in awe at their steadily rising shares until he eventually took the plunge and bought £5,000-worth of shares in a company called Cedar Group. He liked trees. Working at Caspian gave him a good wage with guaranteed overtime, and he could afford the risk. Yet still in the pit of his stomach there remained a nagging doubt that he could lose the lot.

A couple of weeks later, Norbert read that Cedar Group had a rights issue to raise some more money for growth, and they strongly advised investors to take up the offer. It meant shelling out another three grand. He was in for a total of £8,000. He tried not to dwell on it too much, but the thought of it all blowing up at a time when Nikki was swelling bigger by the day scared him shitless. The shares cost a pound each. All he could do was wait. Luckily there was more than enough going on to divert his mind; work was busy, he had his training, he was still managing the odd night out at weekends with friends, and, best of all, time with his darling Nikki. *Thank heaven for shift work!*

Nothing could prepare him for what was about to happen. By sheer coincidence, he had drifted right into the eye of a storm. It was 1997, the new age of the Internet. Those new technologies were going to shake up and change the world. Everything ending in .com was being snapped up in a frenzy of buying activity; shares were being massively valued, with future earnings projections measured in millions and perhaps billions. Some companies had never made a profit, but that trivial piece of information didn't matter; everyone wanted to own a piece of the future action. People were scrambling to board this runaway train, and there Norbert was, sitting on board, having got in at the starting terminal, feet up and holding a big fat ticket.

The newspapers were full of tech mania day after day, doling out how life was transforming and how everyone needed these new important technologies to survive. Norbert phoned his broker weekly from the telephone that hung on the wall at the end of the machine he was working on. 'Two pounds to buy, sir,' the broker informed him on a Monday morning. The next week it was £3-something; at this rate his holding was increasing by about eight grand a week. Adding his wages, was he possibly the highest-earning printer in London, or the world? He was positively buoyed by the idea. A couple of weeks later and, far from running out of steam, things were gathering some serious momentum. The wider public was being lured in. Everyone from the man in the corner shop to the errand boys at work who knew little about investing was talking of becoming rich on the back of their shareholdings. Anyone could have randomly picked out any technology share and watch it soar away like an eagle.

But even with Norbert's limited knowledge of investing, he knew they would not go up indefinitely. The shares were now £5-something, so he phoned his broker and sold a tranche, and a few days later twenty grand was sloshing around in his bank account. *Oh, techno, you beauty*. On and on they climbed every day. Eventually, he panicked and cashed them all in. Adding some of his other smaller holdings, he was good for about seventy grand. Happy days? Not quite.

First, if he'd known what he was doing, had the time to read a chart, or had an astute broker, he could have gotten a lot more out of the share run. They eventually topped out at about £15.00, when as sure as night follows day, the bubble did burst in spectacular style. He could have grabbed two hundred and fifty grand if he'd known what he was doing, but he was not greedy. Late momentum players are rarely rewarded in the markets, and work pals and those who joined in at the death stage of the cycle were punished.

Norbert, on the other hand, was now in a place where he could go to town. And go to town he did – Nikki's place was transformed with lush carpets and magnificent baby stuff he never knew he would need. Shopping sprees to buy expensive designer clothes without looking at the price tags, and next, a new car. A brand spanking new Mercedes, silver. The thrill he got when he drove it out of the showroom onto the nearest main road, headed towards Rochester for no particular reason, coasting along on cruise control, the smell of *new* filling the car and he could see the three-pointed star sitting proudly at the front of the bonnet; everything was wonderful.

He had arrived, and was now in the big time, his head spinning, intoxicated by his new-found wealth. On a whim he bought a picture from an art gallery that had snuck up at the local shopping mall. He was not exactly the wolf of Wall Street, more like the fox cub of Surrey Quays. He was convinced that this was just the start of his investment career, and more riches would follow. He contemplated for a time buying back into the technology market, which had by now been hammered but decided on a different turn. Big mistake, a *Pretty-Woman*-style fucking huge mistake. He pushed on and ventured out by opening up a spread betting account with a popular broker. He never really understood options trading, forex, the currency stuff, but he knew about the main indices – the Dax, FTSE, Nikkei, and the daddy of them all, the Dow.

He lobbed a few grand in and then phoned his broker with

a sell order of ten pounds a point to short the Dow. A day or two later, Norbert got a margin call at work from the broker, telling him he needed to add some more money to the account. 'Why?' he asked like a supreme novice.

'Because, sir,' came the reply, 'the market has turned against you and you are down.'

'Well, can you close out the position and instead of selling the Dow, reopen with a buy.' The brokers loved it, all that tasty commission.

Norbert did not have the faintest clue that most investors blew up their accounts in the first few months. He was caught in the mix of professional market makers who moved the markets around to shake weak players like him out of their positions. And didn't it work a treat? He lost ten grand in two weeks, and he called the market right.

He was still sure big times were coming.

Chapter 22

Tipping point

It didn't get any bigger than when in the early hours of mid-October 1999, Nikki gave birth to their daughter. Norbert was there, reduced to tears and helplessness at Nikki's amazing ability to shrug off the pain and wretchedness of childbirth. Nikki, after just a couple of hours, demanded to go home. They returned to her pretty little house where the rest of the family later gathered, marvelling in the joy of welcoming in their newborn. The house was comfortable for two, but now there were four, and soon the rooms would overflow with baby stuff.

Casey was mostly the stepdaughter from hell. There was definitely something wrong; at the flick of a switch she would lose her temper, crying a small river every single day. She couldn't let go once on to something, harassing Nikki for hours about the tiniest detail of their day. There was talking and there was Casey. Her chatter was constant and one way. She was unable to converse, words falling from her like a waterfall. Her mood swings were infamous; they could darken the brightest day.

'There's only so much you can blame on her father and her childhood, Nikki,' Norbert said.

'I know. I sit down with her and try to explain. She says sorry and then the next day, we go through it all over again.'

Nikki was exhausted by her but valiantly tried to smooth over the cracks before Casey tore everyone apart. Norbert didn't have the foggiest how to handle the red-hot potato that Casey was. *She'll never change,* he told himself. At her severest he thought of packing his bags for good, to be rid of her, to save his sanity. Instead, he sought refuge in his work and flat in London. When alone in his single world, it was easy to tell himself that it was just one last hurrah every time he went out before settling down; it wouldn't hurt anyone, would it? There was a reckless part that couldn't resist pushing to the limit. He had all but stopped going out into the night looking for thrills in the red lights, but when fuelled by drink, he had the money and he could do what he liked. Eventually, his spread betting would pay off. Living on the edge was what he was all about.

On 5 August 2000, the day after the night before, he was on his way to work, called in at short notice to cover someone, when the police randomly pulled him over. Perhaps not so random – they saw someone they assumed was too young to be driving a big fuck-off new Merc. He failed the inevitable breathalyser. Arrested again, he desperately tried to hide his past record and gave a false name. Of course, it just delayed the inevitable. When the police officer went through his credit cards he was bemused and angry.

'Who the hell owns these then, dickhead?'

'They're mine.' It was all over.

Norbert's lies caught up with him and his world came crashing down on his sorry head. The indignity of another court summons. How the hell was he going to explain this one to Nikki and his mum? For a long time, Mum had made Norbert the focus of her life. Dad had pissed off and Mum had single-handedly brought him up and been a constant rock throughout, helping him out financially at all the important junctions in his life, being there whenever it mattered; and this was his way of repaying everybody.

He needed to sort his shit out fast, do some serious back-pedalling. Norbert had a meeting with the bosses at Caspian and told them the situation – he was facing a sentence – and to their absolute credit, they promised him his job would be there on his return. They had their differences, but even before all this business they were by a long chalk his favourite employers; it was about his only relief. Next, he put his beloved flat up for sale to stop him from acting like a twat and to commit to Nikki; he intended to get them all a place where they could live as a family. It was only two days until a lady put an offer forward for the full amount.

By the end of the month, he was up before Thames Magistrates. He walked to court alone dressed in a sombre suit and tie complete with smart black brogues. It was a fine summer's day. Savouring his last moments, his thoughts flowed fast and free, surveying and taking in the surroundings, old buildings, that huge former Victorian asylum the Royal London hospital. *Was that where the Elephant Man was once held?* He was trying to divert his mind; he knew the fate that was about to befall him. As expected, following his previous cautions and warnings, the magistrate sent him down: three months in Her Majesty's Prison, Pentonville, the salubrious environs of the Caledonian Road, N7.

He was taken to a holding cell in the back of the court, where there would be plenty of time to acclimatise to his new captivity. Later on, joined by the other suckers, he was driven – handcuffed – in the adapted transport vans used for ferrying prisoners around. Small blacked-out one-way windows enabled Norbert to watch people going about their daily lives. They were oblivious. He remembered as a small child on holiday being driven past Dartmoor prison, Mum explaining how bad people went in there and they couldn't get out. That thought had scared the young Norbert to death, imagining what it must be like in that cold, grey shadowy place. *Well, Norbert,* he told himself, *you finally got what you wanted. Now you're on the other side you're about to see for yourself.*

And here's the odd thing: part of him wanted it – the prison. He wasn't cursing his luck; he was fully accepting. You do the crime; you do the time. Like a drug addict, he needed to hit rock bottom, to make his way back and make some sense of it all. He was fighting with himself; he wanted it to stop – it had to stop. *What, God forbid, would have become of me if I had hurt or killed someone when driving under the influence?* These thoughts were sobering. *A bit fucking late now, Norbert. A deep breath.* Then the wave of guilt. *How can I do this to my beautiful family? Let down Mum, betray Nikki, the kindest person I've ever met. And what sort of father do I want to be for the girls?*

Chapter 23

Porridge

Once inside, he was stripped, and all belongings handed in. Next came the uniform. His was a dowdy maroon tracksuit. After a night in A-wing, he was taken to his new accommodation. Norbert was paired off with another first-timer, Roy. Norbert chose the bottom bunk of a small cell, en suite – well, a shit-stained toilet in the corner, but at least there was a window which, if he opened it to the couple of inches maximum before it stopped against the outside prison bars, he could just about glimpse some of the outside world – the Caledonian High Road. A room with a view, what a treat. No mini-bar, TV, or white fluffy towels shaped like swans riding the contours of a king-size bed; nothing to take his mind off the cockroaches and straying rats that he had been on the lookout for after hearing other prisoners complaining.

The heavy steel doors slammed shut and the prison warden locked the door and closed the peephole. *Goodnight, Mr Mackay.* Then they talked.

'What you in for?' Norbert asked Roy.

'Assault, you?'

'Drink-driving.' *Seems lame.* 'Got three months.'

'Same.'

And they talked some more. It was night-time. Norbert wanted to settle down and sleep, sleep to forget, and sleep to go to another place. *Anywhere else would be better than here.* His head needed some attention; there was a lot to sort out and straighten out.

Lights down, and then it began. Slowly at first, the cell blocks came alive – lone voices shouting, threats of violence one block to another. 'I'm going to fucking stab you, you cunt,' one geezer screams to another. The insults fly back and forth.

Then there were the drugs. Roy was standing by the window eavesdropping, watching it all and giving a running commentary. 'Fuck me, they're passing them down to each other in a cup on a string, you got to be joking.' The walls were creeping, alive with activity, drugs being passed from cell to cell. The party had started; voices were becoming louder, more people joining in the mindless quarrels and threats. Music, drugs, it was a fucking rave; it was quite funny at first, but then his patience wore thin. Norbert got grumpy when he was tired. Eventually, after an age, it settled down, and he slept.

The next day and he joined the queue for something to eat. Standing in a line for the first time he could see the size of the prison – an open-plan maze ascending to the heavens and down to Satan's hell, a labyrinth of cells, each wing divided into floors and each long floor guarded and served by prison officers, the screws. The food was edible, taken back to his cell to eat, and the doors locked again. The noises become familiar, the lockdown of the doors, the jangling of keys.

Walking along the corridors he saw the nameplates on the outside of each cell and the jail term. Another three months. *Ah,* he thought, *we must all be banged up together, categorised by the same prison sentences. Hang on, what's this? Three years?* The next cell was twelve years, then, *fucking hell,* twenty-five. Everyone was thrown randomly together. The cells were open and people were free to mill about. There was a pool table and table tennis, communal television, but that was it. He tentatively nodded to a couple of people when their eyes met. Some looked fucking scared shitless.

Norbert adapted quickly. He kept himself to himself and played the game; if nothing else, he was a survivor. An hour passed and he was back in the cell again. Very soon it became apparent what prison and the game was all about. Time. Time to do nothing much except think, talk or get stoned. Prison time was done in your head – it was a battle with yourself. Occasionally they were let out in the yard for some outdoor space. It was a welcome relief from the monotony of staring at the cell walls. Walking around, Norbert clocked the other inmates, wearing different jumpsuits – bright yellow and green combinations. Was the idea to look like the fucking Joker from *Batman*? Strolling around in a jaded tracksuit with shiny expensive-looking brogues, he told Roy he felt a right knob.

No one cared. They were just doing their own thing, but it was surprising they weren't trying to kill each other after the talk the previous night. Most of the talk was just idle threats. Then one cool-looking black dude caught his attention; long dreads hung down his muscular back. He had no top on – he wanted everyone to see he was ripped, and there he was looking resplendent going through his karate forms, everyone giving him space and respect. 'Don't fuck with me' was the message he was showboating. *Perhaps I should go over there and ask him if he wants to have a spar,* Norbert thought, but fearing his actions could start a bloody riot, his better judgement took precedence. His heart sank some more when he realised that he would miss his training. He needed to phone Digor to explain the situation.

They put Norbert on work duties as a painter and decorator with cellmate Roy. Any excuse to get out of the cell. The entire work experience was a bit of a joke. The tradespeople who were in charge were like racehorses that had long had their last gallop. Now they were meandering around a field of lowlifes, scoundrels, and knaves. It was an easy number, a cushy little job with very little manual work to do themselves, a sweet ride out until retirement.

Cellmate 'the great Roymondo' was getting stuck in like you wouldn't believe, painting a cell in quick time; anyone would have thought he was getting paid per job on finish. He was just one of those types that loved a good honest day's graft, a couple of jars after work, and go home to have tea and shag the missus. Very affable unless you pissed him off, he was in for assault, so someone pushed his buttons in the wrong order.

Chapter 24

He's had a right touch

Norbert was surplus to requirements seeing as Roy was doing the work of two, so when another tradesman said he was looking for a tool carrier, Norbert seized the opportunity to jump ship. 'I'll give you a hand,' he said, and the guy looked at him, sized him up as the no-trouble kind of type, and said, 'You're on.'

Free from Roy's busting-a-gut work regime, Norbert landed perhaps the best job there ever existed in a prison. He would carry Mike's bag of tools around – a position of trust and honour. He loved it; it got him around the whole prison, where he was able to have a good nosey at all the inmates and their sentences. It was a bit like *Through the Keyhole* – 'now who lives in a cell like this?' Lifers, thieves, career crims, first-timers. He heard stories from Mike, like how Charles Bronson, formerly Michael Peterson, served time in the 'ville. Apparently he was a very charming man who took exception to bad manners.

'Don't turn your back on him,' Mike warned Norbert if they were ever to meet.

'Thanks for the heads up, Mike.'

Mike was up on his history with this place, telling Norbert about past executions, actually pointing out where they once took place on their rounds. But his real forte was making killing time and doing fuck all appear like a precision art form; at this endeavour he was a master. Someone told Mike one day that he needed to get over to C wing because apparently a cell had been smashed up; it was about 10.00 a.m., their first job of the day. 'Right,' Mike said after a long cup of tea, 'let's go have a look.' Norbert motioned to get the tool bag but he was stopped. 'Leave them, for now,' Mike said.

Every damn section of the corridor was separated by a locked door that required someone on the other side to open it up. The screws were weighed down with enough keys to keep a locksmith busy for a hundred years. Get through one door, you soon came to another. The warning sirens went off for the first time, splitting Norbert's ears. Everyone was ushered into the nearest cell, off the landing, while mobs of screws rushed in to calm or beat a prisoner up depending on the situation.

'Don't worry,' Mike said, 'it'll soon pass.' And it did, and they were back to their duties. More locked doors and finally, an hour and a half later, they arrived at the cell where Mike immediately diagnosed that all that was required was a screwdriver to tighten up one of the door hinges. *Damn, if only we had brought the tools!* By the time they got back to the common room it was nearing lunch. 'We'll see to it first thing this afternoon.' What Mike meant was 'If I hang this out all day, as I am sure I can, it will be another day of gravy, sweet and thick.' Unsurprisingly, this was the total of their day's work. The hinge was tightened later that afternoon – another job well done, pats on the back all round. To Mike, it was all in a day's work. Norbert imagined him going home to his other half. 'Hard day, love? You look shattered. Put your feet up and I'll make you a cup of tea.'

A couple of weeks passed, and Norbert's trainers finally arrived. It put a spring in his step. His sweet girlfriend Nikki had sent them in with a little bundle, including some precious photos, which he eagerly stuck on the wall next to his bed. Norbert made a point of kissing his baby girl every night before bed. He made a deal with himself to one day tell her all about it in the hope she could understand and choose a different path for herself. *Shouldn't be too difficult.*

Every night while the monkeys were shouting, he had time for a few home truths. Where did it go wrong? Why did he make those daft choices? Did he need a father figure to sternly point him in the right direction? Had his mum wrapped him up in cotton wool, protected from outside badness, and was he now living the consequence? There were no excuses. He

89

accepted the obvious: he was a dim fuck; he had enjoyed pushing things to the edge to see where it took him; he had taken the ride, and now it was time to get off and start thinking about his responsibilities and others.

Time for some changes. Norbert made a pact to never binge drink again – that seemed a good starting point. Second, he would try to be a better father and partner. He'd go back to following those who were living by good example, and there he was, one of the most balanced, contented individuals he had ever met, looming large in his life, coincidentally the best fighter he had ever seen: Digor.

Work gave him a measly three quid a week prison income, enough to buy some goodies and a phonecard. After catching up with Nikki, his next priority was to call Larry. After a couple of rings he got through.

'Digor.'

'Norbert, that you? How you doing?'

'Getting used to my new surroundings.'

Digor laughed. 'Woah, you okay?'

'Yes. Look, I just wanted you to know that I can't wait to get back to the class,' Norbert said.

'Don't worry – we are there for you, we're not going anywhere.'

Norbert held back tears that wanted to freefall. They small-talked and then Norbert hung up. Norbert headed back to his dreary setting – the brain-numbing existence of lock-up – yet his pride was swollen and steady. Larry would never have known, but it was that day in prison that Norbert fully committed to his training. It was a win-win; he could learn how to fight and be around someone who he believed would influence him to be a better man.

Some people went to prison and found God. Norbert found a father figure and he came to fully appreciate just what fate had bestowed upon him. It was a turning point, no doubt; however, it shone a light on another niggle. Some friends were inherently racist, and that now jarred. He would have to let them go. He was on a roll, having a bit of a cleanse; Norbert had remarkably found some inner peace.

He practised his si lim tao form in his cell and taught Roy to play chess, which along with the new work post made the time go by quicker. A couple of weeks in and he'd bonded with several cons. There were the loners who just chose to be by themselves, the pricks that made all the mouthy shouting threats at night. Then there were the real-deal tough fucking cookies. He recognised those. Norbert comfortably settled in the middle somewhere. Even at this early stage of his wing chun practice he had the confidence that he could fight if needed, so he never took any bollocks and just got along. There was one fella, a big bald West Ham fan with the hammers tattooed proudly on his arms, who strutted around, chest puffed out as if he owned the joint. Norbert watched him one time grab a skank by the neck, pinning him up against the wall. Later they were standing close.

'Watch that slag – I saw him earlier casing Dave's cell. We've got each other's backs down here, Norbert.'

'Yeah, I saw you have a friendly word with him.'

'Too right.' They chatted, and football rivalries aside, Norbert liked him; there was something about Vince. He ran a thriving business, cleaning up after vandalism, did a lot of work for the local councils, and when it was quiet, he paid some tearaways to go and spray a bit of graffiti around the manor. He was sharp, streetwise; he reminded Norbert of his old mate Nathan Wilkes: a leader.

'D'you play football?' Vince asked.

'Yeah, of course,' Norbert replied. No more needed to be said.

Later that night there was a knock on the cell door. 'Norbert, come on, son, you're in the football team,' Vince ordered, and up they went to the rooftop gym to play five-a-side. Norbert was one of the better players. To be fair, most of them were not that good; henceforth he was a regular. Every Tuesday he got to play football and, because they missed dinner, they got theirs later when they returned. It turned out to be a slightly better meal deal finished with sponge and custard. Not bad at all.

Time passed and the daily cycle continued. Weekends of

lockdown inched by painfully slowly. He longed for the Monday to Friday normal week, even if it was with slow Mike. There were people in prison that chose to be in there because their lives were so crap, for the regular meals, a bed, and blankets to keep them warm at night. Many gave up the fight; suicide was more common than it should have been.

Chapter 25

Restart

Release day promised to be a special day – it would definitely be better leaving than going in. The rigmarole of keys opening doors, reclaiming belongings, was irritatingly slow. The desk sergeant worked through the red tape at a snail's pace. *No one hurries in this place, and why would they?* Norbert had to forcibly stop himself from getting up and stuffing the paperwork down the old boy's wrinkly throat. Even though so many days had recently been spent with master time burner Mike, this was different. Norbert's freedom was at the other end of this delay. He tapped his feet and flicked his hair – when he caught it right it made impressive audible clicks.

At long last he got to swap back the ragged-looking trackie for his suit and brogues, Mr Benn style; he looked every inch the respectable business person. Out of the back doors, he hastily walked round to the front and hailed a black cab to the nearest station. He found possibly the grumpiest taxi driver in the city, but it didn't matter; he was wearing the feeling of Christmas Eve. Like someone who bites a doughnut and doesn't hit the jam, he knew it was coming – seeing his little bubba and Nikki.

He watched the people going about their daily grind. Okay, he hadn't served the longest time by any stretch of the imagination, but it was still porridge. A train out to furthest Kent took him through some glorious countryside piercing into the heart of the garden of England. The vista transformed from busy, gritty urban areas around Deptford – railway arches, some hiding juicy secrets, yards with cars perched like Jenga puzzles – to suburbia, smart cars waiting in the stations to carry the bankers, accountants, and solicitors back to their generous piles. Norbert tried to conjure up evidence like a forensic investigator from gardens and house types to imagine the lives going on behind the curtains. The open fields with a sprinkling of oast houses, orchards, woods, and the odd golf course sat seamlessly amid the scenery with their manicured greens, members enjoying their retirement. On the few occasions he made the train journey he never tired of window watching, witnessing the changes of the seasons and daydreaming.

The train soon came to a stop in Ashford.

There she was, standing at the end of the railway concourse, holding his little bundle of joy in her arms. His heart leapt. He kissed Nikki and as he took his little girl into his arms, an uncontrollable soft tear of pure joy trickled from his shiny blue eyes. Grinning as widely as a Cheshire cat, he stepped back to get a better look at Nikki with her newly highlighted hair. 'You look gorgeous – take me home, baby.'

All the way there, he was a touchy-feely monkey with both the girls. With a lot of pride and no doubt tubs of elbow grease, Nikki had her place looking amazing; she had a knack for that sort of thing, and Norbert never remembered it feeling more homely, with a warm soft glow of a strategically placed lamp and the soft deep pile of the carpet enhanced by a perfectly placed rug with an equally luxurious look and feel. *So good to be back.* To be around the family and spend time with his girls. The outlaws, who lived a short drive down the road, popped through, and as ever were supportive and understanding; he couldn't have asked for better. They were very special. Mum was going to be a different proposition, but that awkwardness could wait a little longer. There would be a right time and place to have that heart to heart, but Norbert knew their love would come through. It was unconditional, perhaps impenetrable.

Nikki was now doing all the driving, and she loved it. A nice family VW had replaced the Merc, and because she had only been driving for a relatively short while, the excitement and thrill were still new. Any excuse and Nikki would enthusiastically jump behind the wheel, *vroom, vroom*. It soon became apparent that they were going to need more room, and they started looking around for a bigger place. This being Ashford, they could find an affordable four-bedroom detached house with a small garden nearby on a pretty estate; the girls would each have a bedroom. Nikki got a bigger kitchen (it was the only thing she had complained about in her old house) and an en-suite bathroom, and Norbert got the mortgage. He had only lived in flats before; to have a garden and stairs and three toilets and a dining room – his head was up in the clouds once more.

Chapter 26

Hungry hippos

The work shift was a week-on, week-off arrangement and it worked a treat, staying in London when on shift with Mum and getting around on his trusty Claude Butler steed. Come rain or wind, it kept him fit, and he never missed training when he was in town. To get to class he preferred to weave his way through the backstreets, heading towards Greenwich following the river. The view was better and it was safer away from the major roads. One evening, just as the light was fading into the night, a black sports Mercedes approached from the opposite direction. Norbert was wearing a high-vis jacket and had his lights on, but the driver didn't see him as he made a right turn straight across his path. Norbert hit the corner hard, the impact instantly snapping the mountain bike's sturdy forks and sending him spiralling up onto the bonnet. He rolled over into a sideways position, falling off on the driver's side onto the roadside. All those years spent at judo and Ju-Jitsu practice doing breakfalls had maybe saved his life. The driver leapt out, shouting, 'Look what you've done to my car.'

'Thanks for the concern.' Norbert, still dazed, looked again at the car, engine still running, lights on, straddled in the middle of the road halfway through its turn, and *no fucking indicators*.

'You never indicated, mate – you didn't indicate.'

'I'm not your mate. You cyclists think you own the road, you're scum.' He was now close enough for Norbert to smell alcohol on his breath – strong.

'You've been drinking.'

Norbert watched his manner change instantly – aggressive to passive in the blink of an eye.

'I'm just gonna move the car,' he said.

Norbert was on to him straight away; street sense did that. 'Do not think about driving off,' Norbert told him, but he did just that, with not the slightest remorse.

Norbert, breathless, trembling but focused, kept repeating the number plate over and over. *Keep saying it, don't stop.* Norbert scribbled down the reg in his training notebook. His breathing was painful now as the adrenalin quietened down in his body. The bike was immobilised, and he had no phone. He was a bit of a dinosaur regarding mobiles, saw them more as a hindrance, and he didn't like the fact that they would effectively put him on twenty-four-hour call with work. He regretted that now.

On the opposite side of the road was a smart newish corner block with a large communal intercom. Norbert pressed the first button. No answer. *Fuck, no one ever answers their buzzer, do they. Next one. Nope, same again.* He pressed them all randomly like he was playing a keyboard one-handed.

'Hello?' A voice came through and shook him out of his pattern.

'I've been involved in an accident,' Norbert spluttered, 'and I think I may need an ambulance.'

Sometimes when you think the entire world is against you and nothing seems to go right, one little thing can make all the difference and reinstate your hope for humankind. This was that moment. 'Don't worry,' the voice said, 'we saw everything and have already called one.' Moments later, a couple opened the large electric doors and came outside. Youngish professionals, their heavenly forms were just about the loveliest sight he had clapped his eyes on for a long time. Their balcony and window overlooked the roadside, and they had witnessed everything, especially the part where the driver had left. It had horrified them. They couldn't have been kinder, letting Norbert store his damaged bike in the hallway of the flats. They exchanged details, and before he knew it, the ambulance arrived. The paramedic gave him a brief look over and decided he needed to go to the hospital to get X-rayed. As he lay in the back on the way to St Thomas's, all he could think was *Bugger, I'm going to miss training.*

He sat for hours in the waiting area, fidgeting, restless, unable to get comfortable, feeling like an elephant was leaning into the side of his torso. The X-ray came back and confirmed that he had indeed suffered contusions to the ribs. He would be out of action for at least a week or two. A convicted drink driver, the victim of a hit and run; he could hear the laughs now. *Got a taste of your own medicine.*

Calling the police a couple of hours later was a massive anticlimax. They assigned a police officer who would be in touch. 'Well, can't you find the guy's address on your database and arrest him now while he is still drunk?' Norbert asked.

'I'm sorry, sir, someone will be in touch.'

Norbert guessed correctly that he wasn't exactly a priority for the stretched police service. It was all a numbers game, and his number had snaked its way down to the bottom of the board. A few days later some crime bod called.

'Look,' he said, 'I won't lie to you – there is very little we can do if he doesn't admit to the offence.'

He gave Norbert a reference number. It later transpired that one solitary officer had to deal with the mopping up of about a hundred petty similar cases, so they would much rather you fuck off and sort it out yourself.

Later, at Mum's, he said, 'So much for tough on crime and tough on the causes of crime, hey, Mum.'

'What did you expect, Norbert? A team of Columbos straight on the hunt for the guy?'

His next move was to call one of those ambulance-chasing solicitors, the no-win, no-fee deals that they advertise remorselessly on the radio. Apart from Norbert's word against his, he had an ace up his sleeve. Norbert had a witness, two, to be precise, and they were independent. The formalities began, the paperwork was signed, and it was left with the hungry solicitors for now.

Norbert bought a big expensive bottle of red wine, some indulgent chocolates, and a small bunch of flowers. Luckily, one recipient was in when he called round.

'These are just a little thank you,' Norbert said. 'I am so grateful for your help.'

'Oh, there was no need,' she replied.

'Look, you might be asked to explain what happened when my solicitors get in touch ...' *and I would appreciate it if you tell them what that cunt did to me.* No, that was his head running away. He kept his thoughts restrained. 'If you could answer their questions, I would be grateful,' he said. 'Thank you again.' He left, leaving them to get back to their world in which he hoped they would receive the karma they deserved.

Chapter 27

Sweat, baby, sweat

After spending a few unplanned but very welcome extra days with Nikki and the girls, Norbert was soon back to full speed and the following week resumed training, with a surprise not everyone would be delighted with. Geoff. Curiosity had got the better of him and he had phoned Norbert and asked if he could come along and see his class to see what Norbert was so constantly excited about. A chance perhaps to measure his standard. Geoff picked Norbert up and drove across town.

'Thanks for the lift, mate – it's foul out there tonight. Nothing worse than getting to training with soggy feet and a damp arse.'

'My pleasure, son – thanks for squaring it all up, making sure it's alright. I know how funny some schools can get with park rangers visiting.'

Norbert was puzzled. Sometimes he didn't get the rhyming slang. Geoff was ahead of him. 'Park rangers, strangers. Come on, son, get with the programme.'

Norbert's thoughts were elsewhere. *Fuck, maybe I should have asked Larry.* 'It'll be fine. There isn't a class goes by without Larry telling us if you have the chance to train with someone to go for it. Well, I'm making that possible for all of us.' Norbert looked at the remains of spliffs, roll-ups, and dog-ends fighting for space in the ashtray and wondered how the hell Geoff was so strong and fit. He concluded he was a freak of nature, just like that Spurs footballer who never trained, just turned up on matchdays and produced the goods.

They entered the building, then the hall. One senior had what looked like a torture device of rope attached around his ankle, pulling it through a loop that raised his leg to a taut slow stretch. After a long hard day's work, it was good to eke out those aches and pains.

Norbert felt lost. 'Where's Digor?'

By some miracle, Jack spoke to Norbert. 'He's had to go and take care of some business.'

'Must be serious, he never misses a class.'

'Who's your friend?'

'Oh, guys, this is Geoff. He's the one you can blame for getting me started.' There were a few wry smiles and some suspicious looks.

Most of the seniors were hovering close by. One of them, Donald, offered Geoff a hand. 'You're more than welcome to join in. I'm guessing you've got a good few years under your belt, right?'

'You could say that. Thanks for the offer, I will,' replied Geoff.

Donald turned to Norbert and winked. 'Nah, nothing serious. Digor might call through later. Right, everybody find some space and go through your forms.'

The mood of the class would slip into a quiet reflective mode when going through their forms – one through to seven forms to practise depending on experience, which meant people would finish at different times.

Then you would look for a partner to practise some drills with. Norbert looked to hook up with one of the three musketeers, Cuong, Johnny the drummer, or Jason, all eager as beavers. The starter drills consisted of one person palming towards the other's face, who would block or deflect the strike away. With a slight circle motion of the hand, the positions were reversed, so the person doing the striking would have a go at blocking. Lots of variations to rinse and repeat, all done with one arm in constant contact; it was called *sticky*.

You are meant to feel the movement and tune your sensitivity, keep your structure and use the techniques as they were being taught. It was a slow, defined process of reprogramming one's body to react in a fight situation with control and independence of thought, rather than chasing hands and resorting to mindless brawling. Five or ten minutes of this and then they would change partners. Geoff was being passed around like a new toy; he was politeness personified, shaking everyone's hands, bowing hand over fist before and after every exchange. Some were encouraged; their movements were more precise because they saw errors in his technique.

The class was rhythmically moving along when Digor showed up. He was followed in by Cole and Dave, a colossus of a bloke. They were all dressed smart casual; it was the first time Norbert had seen Digor not wearing a tracksuit. And everything ground to a stop. Norbert stepped forward. 'Hi, Digor, this is Geoff, my mate from work. He's the one who introduced me to you, through the ad.'

Digor swung a mighty arm round, cupping Geoff into a big handshake, pulling him into a warm shoulder embrace. 'Carry on, practise,' he told everybody.

Norbert partnered up with Cuong and practised hard, dreaming of being as good as Digor. Years of those types of sensitivity drills had left him with reflexes and speed of thought that was near impossible to comprehend. 'I'm sure if a fly walked along his arm, he would notice if it had a limp,' Cuong said, and laughed. Up and down the hall they went, Norbert and Cuong, clumsy at first, like ducks waddling around on dry land, and mostly off at a tangent instead of a straight line, but slowly it sank in. Norbert's head was bobbing up and down like a float being tugged under the water by a fish. 'Imagine you have a pint of beer on your head,' Cuong told him, 'now don't spill my beer,' he barked. Gradually the faults were corrected. Everything was for a reason, and when Digor explained it, it all made sense. A little angle of the foot could make all the difference between right and a kick in the balls. Everyone in the class was given the explanations that went with the drills; there was no favouritism, but there were levels.

Digor must have wanted to check out Geoff before he left. He searched him out, beckoned him over. Geoff offered his arms to find Larry's. They locked, they rotated, they moved. Digor smiled as he stepped forwards. Most of the class were looking, watching intently. 'Cole, this is the same as that guy in Honk Kong, student of Lok Bo, same lineage.' The teachers leave a DNA; it's more about their energy. Geoff was concentrating hard but in three short steps, his back was pinned to the wall, unable to move.

'Nice one, man.' Digor released Geoff, who wanted more but was sensible enough to not voice his thoughts. Digor circled around the class with a few greetings, then told everyone to continue to practise as his entourage headed back out.

'Are you here tomorrow, Digor?' someone asked.

'Of course,' he said as he was leaving.

After the warming up and sensitivity drills, you were ready to get into some of the meat of the class. Norbert was still getting his head around some more basic movements. Pac soa, enabling you to make a line of path to strike your opponent. There is a magnificent example of it in *Enter the Dragon* when the irrepressible Bruce Lee snaps a pac soa strike at lightning speed to bamboozle the guy who murdered his sister in one of his many fights. It was about developing your attacking skills, but it was just as important to learn to defend yourself, so practice alternated between striking and counters, the ying to the yang. Then it was the same deal – change partners and repeat.

Time flew that night; the last half hour was upon them, playtime. All drills were cast aside. *Anything goes.* Steve was the first senior to step up with Geoff; in terms of fluidity of movement he was one of the best, until Geoff tipped him over the edge, rough-housed him black and blue. Steve's artistic flow was no match for the brawn of Geoff, he just couldn't handle it, but he was man enough to admit it afterwards when they shook hands. Geoff had a point to prove. Norbert and co were sparring themselves but keeping a close eye on proceedings too.

Next up was Jack. Geoff started pulling him around like a rag doll, forwards, backwards, Jack had no defence against him. There were some concerned looks. Jack was supposedly the best in class, but Geoff was making a mockery of that.

103

Norbert was jumping inside, elated that his nemesis was getting his ass kicked and some. Geoff bulldozed his way through the seniors and then came to Donald. Norbert loved Donald, who was generous to a fault with his time. Just like Geoff, Donald hailed from a rough part of town; both were lions.

They clashed. Close, Geoff headbutted him for crying out loud. Norbert's heart was leaden. Donald pulled away. 'Normally we don't use our heads, but what the heck.' They went again. It was hard, fast, and difficult to tell who was getting the upper hand. Everyone was watching at this point. At 10.30 p.m. the class had to stop; the building had to be locked up for the night. Sweat was pouring out of Geoff, and the look on his face told Norbert he'd loved every second of it. Donald and he shook hands in mutual appreciation.

Johnny called out to Norbert as he was leaving. 'Looks like you brought a hand grenade with you tonight, Norbs.'

Geoff started the car, windows down to release the steam from them both.

'Fucking hell, mate, you destroyed Jack.'

'Which one's Jack?'

'The white skinny one, who's bloody rude to me usually.'

'Look, Norbert, to be fair, I've probably got years on them. In all honesty, a couple of them are pretty decent.'

'What about Donald?'

'The last guy?'

'Yeah.'

'Boy, did he hit me with a couple of shots I know I'm going to feel in the morning. We had a proper scrap.'

'And Digor – Larry?'

'We barely did anything, but you can tell, he's pure class.'

Norbert heard those beautiful words; from someone who knew their way around martial arts, it was all the confirmation he needed.

Geoff had found his level. What Geoff did to Jack and most of the others, Digor did to everyone; his level was way out there.

Later Norbert wrote his notes up. He remembered how

Digor would often refer to the wider process of development in horticultural terms. 'First, we plant a seed, then you must water it and let it grow. Keep tending to it, nurturing, taking care of it, especially in the beginning, through the blossom, and look after it right through to the end.' He could not remember Digor telling the class to strangle the fuck out of it, which was what Geoff had done tonight in practice. Norbert laughed and shook his head. Thankfully there were no casualties, no broken bones – only bruised egos. He made a mental point not to take Geoff back again.

That was the basic set-up of the class.

Chapter 28

Domino effect

He couldn't quite believe it. Were his eyes deceiving him? Was it the same car? Norbert was on the usual off-road route home from training late one evening and there it was, the very same racy black Merc that had sent him scrambling into the air just a few weeks ago. The number plate, triggered from somewhere in the deep recess of memory, brought back to vivid life the moment Norbert saw it parked on the roadside. *What to do ... shall I just press the buzzers of the two or more possible houses it's parked outside and have it out with the bastard? Don't get mad, get even.* Keys in his outstretched hand, he followed the gentle cultured contours of the body, meandering along from the rear to the front, digging deeper at the point where he had collided. He looked back and couldn't see any scratch – it was dark. He dismounted his bike and in the next instant, overcome with temptation he leapt onto the car's bonnet in a squat jump. The metal folded beneath his crushing feet, the car alarm wailed, dogs were barking; he'd never had so much fun. He pedalled off, surging into the night.

He never saw the car parked there again, and a short while later received redress via the solicitor with a payout sufficient to cover the cost of his new bike and repairs to the old one with a little left over for good measure. The police had let him down, but his hungry, money-grabbing no-win, no-fee solicitor had thankfully come good.

The next couple of years passed by in a semblance of normality. Norbert was back and forth with work that had expanded at breakneck speed. From one machine they had ballooned and gained four, spaced over an extra three industrial units, more staff, more rent, and some legendary parties. Norbert was nervous about the whole shebang; everyone was earning well. Experience had taught him some invaluable lessons, one of which was that when something was good and plentiful it seldom lasted forever; Premiership footballers, please note. He took out redundancy cover; he needed the security of the job now more than ever since buying the family house. All the money he had made from the investments had gone into the house, the furniture, the car. It went so quickly.

Family life was good, and Nikki was a constant reminder of real love. His little girl was at an age of innocence and fun. Norbert made up silly games, building bridges from sofa cushions. 'If you fall, the crocodiles will swallow you up.'

'Again, Daddy, do it again.'

He cherished the moments they played in her little undiluted world.

Training was going well; everything was going swimmingly, and then he got a phone call from his workmate Gibbo who was working on the opposite shift. 'Bomber,' he said, 'the firm's gone under. You gotta come in and collect your bits ASAP.'

In an instant, the gravity of the situation sent his brain scrambling, searching for solutions. 'What if I just fuck off, go to Thailand, be a beach bum?' Nikki and his little girl dissipated his dream.

Two days later and the formal letter arrived in the post. It was 1 August 2002 when the great ship that was Caspian Graphics Limited ceased sailing because of insolvency. Geoffrey Chaucer supposedly said 'All good things must come to an end.' The bastard was right, but why now, Norbert cursed, just as things were so delicately poised? Divorce, prison, and now redundancy. This one knocked the stuffing out of him.

But Norbert never yielded from a fight. Besides, he had a couple of tricks up his sleeve.

The redundancy payment could make him some more easy money once he put it to work in his spread betting account. The result? He blew the full account. Half lasted a couple of weeks, and the next tranche went in a couple more months. Was that progress? The more desperate and leveraged the positions he took, the more easily they turned to dust. He had sleepless nights, twisting and turning, grinding his teeth; what a disaster. Ten thousand pounds went down the drain until he reached the painful conclusion that you cannot make money when you are under financial constraints. Fuck. He was redundant and struggling to get by. This was not the time to go big-game hunting.

The mortgage protection meant he wasn't about to lose everything just yet. Nikki tried her best to comfort and console. 'Things will turn out alright,' she said, and he had to believe that she was right. He had better shake the dust off and get proactive about the future. The first port of call would be the job centre, and an appointment was made. It was a fine day, which for the summers of late seemed to be a rarity. On the way he had the same gut feeling of nervousness and anticipation as he'd had on that fateful day he last walked to court. Once inside, he waited, his eyes shifting around the floor, looking around at the scruffy misfits and other unfortunates; it was a bleak picture. A smart bearded gentleman with small-rimmed glasses ushered him over to a desk. He commented on how long Norbert had been working and paying into the system.

Norbert signed on for Jobseeker's allowance, and together they looked for any print jobs, of which there were precisely zero. 'I want you to next think about what else you could do and we'll start a new search in two weeks at your next appointment,' the adviser said. Once the redundancy cover kicked in, plus the Jobseeker's and council tax relief, Norbert was gobsmacked to discover he was coming out ahead. He was faced with a real conundrum: if he was going to accept one of the theoretical other jobs that he was told to think about, he would lose the benefits and in one fell swoop it would put him in a far worse position financially. This was serious; everyone has a breaking point, and losing the house to the bank was his.

Another game of cat and mouse with the system, then;

twelve months to avoid menial low-paid work and use the year's redundancy cover to retrain and find something else – a job paying enough so they could all stay in the house they loved. He just wasn't sure what to do. It was a faint hope that he could get something in the print industry; a new digital era signalled that those glory days were well and truly numbered.

The next appointment rolled around with the same gentleman, only this time he was a little less concerned – quite po-faced. Norbert tried delicately to explain the Catch 22 of him taking a low-paid job and losing out all round. The man understood perfectly, but this was how it had to be; raising his tone, he said, 'You can always get a smaller house.' The battle had begun; he had inadvertently laid his cards on the table. The aim was clear – it was a numbers game. They wanted people in work and the consequences – losing a lot – didn't matter.

The man asked, 'What about a driving job?'

Norbert drew his sword and took a swipe. 'I'm on a four-year ban following a conviction for drink-driving.' This spanner in the works immediately killed off about three quarters of the so-called jobs that the assistant was suggesting for Norbert.

Norbert went in for the kill. 'I've been thinking a lot about what you said on our last meeting, about thinking of doing something different from the print.' Norbert watched his tormentor's body language reflect positivity, the way he sat upright and leaned forward ever so slightly in hopeful anticipation. 'I've decided I would like to be a dentist. They seem to do alright and as far as I can tell seem immune from recession.'

Mr Jobcentre's eyes rolled towards the tiled squares of the bland ceiling above as he let out an exasperated sigh. He bit back, 'Look, I meant something you could do immediately.' This was the official end to their love-in; the appointment ended with neither happy with the outcome.

Money was tight, and Norbert approached Digor to ask if he might pay a little less than the normal £60 a month. He was still getting there, even if it wasn't as regularly as before.

Digor told him to pay nothing. 'You can start paying again when you find yourself a job,' he told Norbert. Well, he already respected him more than you could imagine as a person of moral values and integrity, but now, wow, he was taken aback by his generosity and his estimation of the man grew some more. It gave Norbert a massive boost. At this stage he was like a sponge trying to soak up all the information and his wing chun was blossoming, developing at speed. Norbert had cast off the awkwardness of a beginner and was now trusting how the techniques worked. He simply couldn't get enough. This juncture of his life, when he couldn't afford to pay Digor any money, was when Digor spent the most time with Norbert since he'd started, showering more techniques on him.

Things were on an egg timer. The grains of sand only had so long before they ran out. He needed a job and a decent income; the mortgage protection only covered him for a year and that was flying by. Part of the Jobseeker's deal was to attend a short getting back to work course where Norbert discovered they actively discouraged you from applying for any jobs in the papers; apparently, you had little chance of getting one of those! He was glad he didn't listen, because a short while later he was offered an interview with British Gas who he had written to after seeing their ad in the local paper. There was a vacancy in London.

With just three months of his year's sabbatical left to run, he embarked on a new career as a gas engineer. It was April 2004, his driving ban had recently been successfully appealed, and he was back in employment – in the nick of time judging by how stretched their finances had become. The pot was nearly dry and never was it noticed more than when a bestie of his announced he was getting married in Majorca and would dearly love Norbert and Nikki to be there to celebrate the special occasion. They made it, just about scraping the money together, and while sitting at Mr B's wedding reception in the most secluded seductive hillside retreat with a cold beer and friends all around, Norbert could momentarily forget about his financial woes and party.

Chapter 29

Back on the merry go round

Norbert was given a small van, tools, a uniform, and a survivable starting wage that would increase after training. College was in Erith, a vast industrial hub. It was not a sight for sore eyes, and bloody difficult to get to from Ashford because of the usually congested spew of traffic around the M25. The twelve-week course was intensive, with a ton of rules and regulations to learn as you might reasonably expect when working with gas-fuelled appliances. The group he was thrown together with was a very likeable mix; they all got along. But there's always one, isn't there? We need to talk about Kevin.

Physically there was nothing untoward. He looked like an ordinary Joe – well, he passed the interviews, so someone saw promise in him. It was upstairs between his ears that set him apart. As the training progressed, each student was given a beast of a task – to complete a long but necessary paper, evidence of all work that had been carried out. Everyone was fretting about it. Mark the tutor made matters worse by continually reminding them of its importance. 'Kev,' he would say, 'we need to see more evidence on your written assignment, like yesterday.' As time moved on, everyone made a special effort to get it done, because it contributed towards the end qualification.

Sitting next to Kevin in the canteen one day, Norbert couldn't help himself. *A little wind-up maybe, wouldn't hurt.* 'Mark's getting stressed about your assignment, Kev.'

'Can you tell?'

'You gonna do it?'

'Nope.'

'Shit, mate, you not worried they'll kick you off the course?'

'Norbert, they wouldn't have the balls. Think about it, all the money they spend on our training.'

'I never looked at it like that,' said Norbert. Absolutely no chance of winding Kev up; he just didn't give a shit.

Kev's stance spread through the rest of the group like wildfire; it naturally agitated everyone who had spent hours swotting away at the damned thing. He was making a mockery of it all, and his one-man defiance started a bit of a running joke. It was said within the group, indeed bets were made, that Kev would turn out to be a serial killer once let loose in customers' homes.

Another of the guys, Christian, was young and built like a brick shithouse. A fast wit, he also had some experience in this line of work so was good to get close to. He helped Norbert out a lot; he was a genuinely nice fella and they talked about martial arts. He told Norbert how he practised Ju-Jitsu and Norbert told of his endeavours with wing chun.

'My teacher Ross practises wing chun. Tell you what, why don't you come along to one of our classes?'

'Can't do any harm, you're on,' said Norbert.

They met in a car park a few days later somewhere near Swanley in Kent. Norbert followed Christian into a small complex of outbuildings that formed part of a larger centre, a multipurpose training base for many other classes. It had that old tuck shop feel about it. Modern it was not, but these no-frill types of places seemed to have a more honest gutsy feel about them and they often revealed a better standard.

Low rafters strutted out along the entire ceiling, making it feel even more intimate, increasing the usual dank, stale smell that hung in the air from sweat-laden gis. Ross, the teacher, was kneeling on the foam mats explaining a ground hold as Christian and Norbert joined them on the dojo. He was smaller than expected, but the rest of the group was not; there were some fucking giants in here. Ross stood to demonstrate a throw and then asked people to partner up; it was like a game of musical chairs. People quickly paired off, leaving Norbert with a huge young man mountain.

'Looks like it's us,' he murmured, and Norbert smiled back. *Fuck knows how I'm going to get him air bound.* 'Seeing as how I'm the newbie, why don't you go first?' Norbert requested.

'Sure thing.' The lad took Norbert's arm and collar as he swept in, hoisting Norbert with considerable ease. *This is going to be a long fall down to the ground, I better make a good fist of my breakfall,* Norbert reminded himself mid-air.

The next thing, there was a loud snapping sound as Norbert's right trailing leg crashed into one of the low roof beams. It hit with such force that numbness and fuzziness came over him instantly as he slumped to the floor like a lead balloon. The entire class stopped. Ross rushed over, yelling at the guy, 'What have I told you? In the bloody gaps, not underneath the rafters – in the bloody gaps.' Norbert was convinced he had broken his leg; however, his ankle had taken the impact. Ross, Christian, and this now sheepish-looking moron helped Norbert back to the changing room. They sat him down and got him a bag of ice to hold to the swelling. His Ju-Jitsu adventure had lasted all of five minutes.

Norbert sat forlornly in the changing rooms, cursing that fucking idiot. Once the class finished, Norbert hobbled back out to his van with Christian and a sincerely disconcerted Ross who offered his apology once more and shook Norbert's hand.

'Christian tells me you practise wing chun – who is your teacher?' he asked. This was a standard probing question that cut right to the chase.

'Larry Blake.' It drew a blank, but given how Larry had gone underground, it was not a surprise. Maybe it gave a little window into Ross's wing chun; Norbert needed to know.

'Can we touch hands?' Norbert asked, and in the next seconds, they were rolling sticky hands in the car park. The pain from his ankle was excruciating if he tried to place his full weight on it, so he just tried to balance and shift most of his structure onto the other side. They rolled arms, but the tempo was all wrong – too fast, there was no substance; this was surface wing chun. Norbert wanted to step inside and test it, except he couldn't; it was farcical. This wasn't going to be the scene in *The Karate Kid* when the youngster fights on with his leg injury. Norbert was too hindered and unable to engage in a spar.

They shook hands again and said their goodbyes. They never met again. After a couple of days off work, Norbert returned to British Gas training with his bandaged limb just about intact, to a smiling Christian who still couldn't believe his unluck. Norbert sensibly declined any further offer to go back for some more, but Christian left Norbert with a small nugget of praise. 'Ross said you have excellent hands – your wing chun seems strong.' It was a kind gesture, but Norbert thought he was just saving face in that time-honoured Chinese way. Norbert was too embarrassed to tell Digor of his venture out into this other world.

The gas training was nearing its end, but not before one last act of petulance from Kevin sealed its place in Norbert's heart forever. For one fortuitous event was taking place and putting everyone on edge. The powers that be had selected his group for a promotional film of British Gas's gold-standard training programme. The cameras would capture the CEO in a meet-and-greet showcase finale. The set-up comprised constructed bays that mimicked the living rooms and kitchens of the nation. If asked, you were to explain in simple terms what you were doing. 'And, boys and girls,' Mark, their tutor, said, 'let's see you tomorrow looking your best – early night so you can be bright and bushy-tailed for the morning. Fist pumping, comrades, let's make the company proud.'

Norbert was as nervous as hell, his tools laid out neatly on the royal blue sheet next to the gas fire he was servicing. The bright lights from the camera crew were moving down the galley towards him. Instinct told him that the silver-haired CEO would stop in his bay. The big cheese did just that, stepping forward, smiling, firmly shaking Norbert's hand. 'Tell me, young man, are you enjoying the training?'

'Excellent,' Norbert replied, 'they are really looking after us.' There were more smiles all around and then the suits were gone. He got a thumbs up from Mark, who was at the back of the cortege. As Norbert's heartbeat settled back to normal, his eyes focused directly across on Kevin's bay. There, curled up on the floor in front of the fire in a foetal position, fast asleep, lay Kevin, hungover from the night before, his ass hanging out of his pants, shirt a crumpled mess, and hair looking like he had been dragged through a hedge backwards.

Norbert knew when he was in the presence of something special. And this was. He could only marvel at this omnipotence. Never in a million years would he have the audacity to pull something like that. Few people could; it was an almost spiritual existence, like a tai chi expert elevating their being to another plane; with everything that was going on, it was astounding. All hail Kevin, King Yogi, he who lived by the axiom of getting as much as you can for doing as little as you can.

Norbert was let loose, out on his own, once the gas training had finished. With a laptop to download the day's jobs, he went bustling off around South East London, house to house, servicing boilers. It was busy and relentless and he realised pretty quickly what it was all about – it was a numbers game. Without actually coming out and saying it, they wanted you to do as many calls as possible in the quickest time. The call centres were under pressure from customers, and managers were under scrutiny to improve their figures. It all boiled down to a frenetic rush. Some engineers cut corners; experience had taught them what they could get away with. Norbert couldn't, he was too nice – he wasn't Kevin. He had to sleep at night; the jobs took him longer than most.

It was a real eye-opener into other people's lives; some customers were obliging, grateful and decent. Some places were a filthy, disgusting mess.

Five long days a week in London was killing him; he had been used to working on shift for three days for the best part of twenty years. This was hurting; he missed Nikki and the girls. An overworked mule, with no light at the end of the tunnel, he was desperate for a break. Something had to give.

He had applied to do the Knowledge, to become a London

Licensed Taxi Driver, just before gas training, but because of his previous convictions for drink-driving he never thought he had a chance. One day, after another bout of tearing his ass around the local estates and houses, Nikki called earlier than usual. She had a letter from the Public Carriage Office regarding his application. 'Would you like me to open it and read it to you?' she asked.

'Yes,' he replied earnestly, 'put me out of my misery.'

'"Dear Mr Jennings,"' it started, '"it is with pleasure that we ..."' She didn't have to finish the rest – he was euphoric.

'Yes,' he growled, 'fucking yes.' He knew that a way out lay ahead, another chance beckoned him. Every moment it made more and more sense. He could be his own boss, work the hours around his family, and wouldn't be pushed around by number-crunching managers.

Maybe he'd get to see Digor more regularly. He couldn't wait to get started.

Chapter 30

Manor House station to Gibson Square

Norbert acquired a red scooter, parting with £600; his pal threw in some waterproofs and a crash helmet for good measure. Learner plates affixed, it was time to twist and go. He rode the bike back from Chislehurst to his mum's flat in Bermondsey. His maiden voyage was a total shock to the system. The unfamiliarity of his head crammed inside a crash helmet and the suffocating compression were difficult to get used to, but it was the exposure to the cars, white van men, and lorries that appeared to want to blast their way past that freaked him out. One false move and he would die, so his mind bent into sharpness – staying alive mode, full concentration required.

On Mum's estate was a row of sheds. Somewhere between the pop-up crack dens and makeshift dumps of rubbish, there were remarkably a couple still intact. In the far corner hung a black wooden door, the corner severed like it had been the victim of a shark bite. Norbert gambled that any local beady-eyed thief might overlook it. He stored his scooter there and the next afternoon made his way over to the nearest local knowledge school and purchased his first set of runs. Excited and keen with the novelty, he secured the route to the clipboard on the front of the bike and made his way to the starting point of his very first run. He had done no preparation; he just thought he would crack on with it, learn it as he went. He paused at the side of the road outside the main entrance to Manor House Tube station. With an intake of breath and a quick lifesaver check over his shoulder, off he went, leaving on the left as the run stated. His learning of the acclaimed Knowledge had begun.

Blue-book run number one: Manor House station to Gibson Square. He rode along Green Lanes looking for the right turn into Highbury New Park. The light was fading and onward he rode, looking for the turn. Shop after shop, turning after turning, but no Highbury New Park. The road was a brute; it seemed to go on forever, especially if you were heading in the wrong fucking direction, as Norbert was. Norbert wasted two hours sodding around. Eventually, he completed the run and called it a night.

'How did it go, son?' Mum asked.

'Oh, fine, Mum. I'm tired – I need a lie down.' He slumped onto his bed with a searing headache, disbelief raging around his squashed head.

After such an inauspicious start it didn't get any easier. There was one word better than all the rest to describe doing the Knowledge: it's vulgar, Shakespeare loved using it, it starts with a C and ends with a T, and here's why. Once a run was completed, you had to read and recite it repeatedly every day, forcing the run begrudgingly into your memory. At first, it was not so bad, but after adding every new run, of which there were hundreds, the act of calling them became a living torture. The relentless number of streets and places soon snowballed to become an avalanche of information. Norbert hated it with a passion.

Norbert was making slow progress. Holding down the gas job at the same time was stressful enough. He was mostly too tired for anything else, and his training was put on hold.

His first appearance at the carriage office soon came around.

He was a bag of nerves, sitting in the waiting room. The scent of fear and dread hung in the air like a death knell. He had sweaty palms and fidgeted uncomfortably, praying for something he would know. There were four questions to answer; you had to identify the first arrival point and then the destination and be able verbally to navigate a path between them. Simples. Another guy was sitting opposite, chomping down his nails like a beaver. It was all very intense. The other guy broke the silence. 'First appearance?' he asked.

'Yes, you?' replied Norbert.

'Second.'

'How are you getting on?'

'Yeah, I passed my first one – big stuff they asked, stations and hotels. Thought I'd be a bit more used to it this time. It's horrible.'

'Mr Jennings,' a voice called out, interrupting them.

'Good luck,' the man said.

Norbert winked. His heartbeat was supercharged as he followed the examiner along the corridor to a small room. It was Christmas of 2006. *This could be a blinding Christmas prezzie if it goes well,* Norbert thought.

'Take a seat, Mr Jennings,' the examiner said. He gave the shortest smile and sat behind his desk with a map to his side. 'Okay,' he said, 'let's see how we go.' And then he began. 'Porchester Hall?'

What the fuck? That's not big. Norbert was expecting a mainline train station. 'Oh, sorry, sir,' Norbert replied, 'not sure about that one.'

The examiner looked back, clearly not impressed. 'Kensington Gardens Square?' he asked next, and again Norbert drew a blank.

'Try this – "Central Park Hotel,"' the examiner said.

Norbert saw nothing. He trembled softly at first, then became more agitated and bemused by his lack of knowledge. He fell apart and the shaking intensified. Every point the examiner asked of him was a round of *Blankety Blank*, and each time his nerves increased to the point where they shredded. He must have been asked eight, nine, maybe ten questions, all the time clinging to the faintest hope of knowing one of them.

Exasperated, the examiner asked, 'Woodchester Square?'

Somewhere in the back of Norbert's mind was a memory of this little square in the backstreets of W2 where he was now being put to the sword. Norbert, a nervous gibbering wreck, was trying to unscramble his thoughts to call a route from there to his destination: South Kensington station.

'Leave by Cirencester Street, right onto Harrow Road,' he mumbled, and then he ran into a wall. It all finally caught up; he could see nothing, and his mind filled with the blackness of thought. Desperately trying to link up a blue-book run to finish the call, he tied himself in knots. It was a bumbling mess, his first test, and he could not finish the run. He had failed miserably.

The next three runs were okay in the sense that he knew most of the bigger points asked and he called them off alright. When you make a hash of things you sometimes relax, and that was what happened. However, the damage had been done; the examiner duly marked his card with a fail, grade D; so much for any late Christmas present. Norbert walked out of there, tail between his legs.

Sitting on the train journey home, depressed, he promised himself to never be that unprepared again; he had to dig in and get serious. There were fifty-six days until his next appearance; the fight had begun.

Long, exhausting years lay ahead; going out on the scooter in the freezing cold at silly o'clock to some far-flung part of London, he may as well have been in bloody Kathmandu, so alien were some areas he was having to familiarise himself with. He looked for points, obscure shops, bistros and embassies, buildings, pubs, nightspots, and other gems that might take the examiner's fancy. The big stuff, police stations, train stations, hotels, theatres, hospitals were taken care of in the early appearances; towards the end you had to get out there and try to learn pretty much anything of interest, which included some extraordinarily insignificant points. That was the Knowledge, being kept in a state of learning where you felt that it was almost impossible to absorb any more information. It seemed never-ending, and all the time was the constant need to call those runs. They formed the bedrock of one's knowledge. They were a poisoned chalice, but essential. All this while holding down a full-time job.

Eventually, he progressed through the appearances; they

became shorter, every fifty-six days, then every twenty-eight, and last every twenty-one days. The pressure and strain of his circumstances just added to the weight of the situation. It was intense. It forced everything to play second fiddle, while getting to a place of such selfish endeavour. He lived, breathed, talked, and walked the Knowledge to the point of obsession. He tried two or three schools before settling in with some other students, and together they collectively pulled each other through. Having the support of his family was crucial. His mind seldom focused on anything else. There was little time for anything else, but there was a brief respite from the unlikeliest of quarters.

They were struggling by with money and every time the phone bill came in, Norbert had to have a go at Nikki who was regularly phoning into every damn daytime quiz, the sort where they have a dumb question and you have absolutely no chance of winning. On the phone bill they glared out a pound or more a time; it was stupid and costing a small fortune. Except this one time.

Nikki came rushing up the stairs excitedly. 'Norbert, I think I've won.'

'Won, won what?'

'I answered correctly that it was the Chinese New Year of the dog. They'd picked me out with two other entries and told me to wait by the phone.'

'The cruel bastards, we've won nothing,' Norbert said, 'otherwise they would have already told us.'

A few moments later the phone rang. Norbert looked at Nikki's face of disbelief. 'No, no, I can't believe it,' she exclaimed, 'oh, we really could do with a holiday – my partner's doing the Knowledge and it's all been very strained.' They were stunned; they had won a three-week trip to China, all expenses paid. That evening a recording of the phone call was broadcast at the end of the local news. You could hear Nikki whooping with delight, live on the television.

'Three weeks, love, that's a long time to be away,' said Norbert. He was thinking about the Knowledge, losing momentum. Nikki was thinking about leaving the girls.

Nikki said, 'I know, it's a real shame. What are we going to do?'

'We don't have the money to take them,' Norbert said.

'Besides, you can't just drag them out of school,' Nikki reminded Norbert.

They called the holiday promotion company the next morning who let them trade China for a shorter break to Cancun, Mexico. Norbert was gutted, but the upside was a much-needed break to look forward to, and the chance to relax and have a drink or two.

Their first night out abroad they got chatting to some Scottish lads in the hotel bar; by the end of the night, both Nikki and Norbert were a drunken mess. He collapsed on the floor of their sumptuous suite in a crumpled heap wearing a hooped Celtic football shirt. She was bent over the toilet, praying to her god. They spent the rest of the holiday purely, for health reasons, trying to avoid the Scottish contingent who drank hard like that every night – professionals.

It was not all relaxation. Norbert had to take those bloody runs with him and so every afternoon for a couple of hours he left Nikki sunbathing by the pool or on the white powder sands with the warm soft breeze and the gentle lapping of the waves, while he went through the monotony of study back at the room. The holiday was cut short by the intervention of Hurricane Dean, perhaps a blessing in disguise. Much to her relief, it got Nikki out of a planned mini-adventure Norbert had booked – swimming with sharks.

He didn't think it possible, but somehow (and there is scientific evidence to support this), his brain had swelled; the mass of information stuck, and he could now call off a route practically anywhere in London without thinking.

The sacrifice and dedication worked. On his return he passed the final appearances. Nigh on three and a bit long, impossibly tough years later, by the summer of 2008 he had passed the Knowledge and received his coveted green badge.

Chapter 31

Work the cash machine

Now passed out as a taxi driver, Norbert rented his first cab from a local garage. With an incredible turning circle, it felt like an oversized dodgem car to drive. Nervous but keen to earn, he took a deep breath and reminded himself that this was what he had busted his balls for. He pushed the button on the meter and a bright orange glow illuminated the near vicinity, telling everyone he was now for hire. Nearing London Bridge, an elderly man raised his arm in Norbert's direction and, as he slowed down, fumbling with the passenger side window, the man leaned forward and bluntly asked for Harley Street. This was his first job, and all the routes were dancing around his brain. *Which one to take, oh panic, just fucking drive and be careful,* he told himself.

When they reached the destination, Norbert, not wanting to unleash a thousand curses on himself, congratulated the gentleman and informed him he was in luck – it was a tradition for newly trained taxi drivers to offer their first fare free. The man smiled and offered a lagniappe, a fiver. It would have been bad karma to refuse. Norbert was off and running in the cash machine. Any fear and trepidation were overridden by the need to make some money. On that first shift, he stayed out for eight hours before going back to Mum's, eager to count the takings. Times were good, and there was a seemingly endless supply of passengers to be transported around. Ah, the good old days.

He was also testing the water to see which shift was best to work, but when evening fell, he headed home, eight to nine o'clock. The mood and atmosphere turned after that, spurred on by alcohol, from calm to edgy it was tangible and spooky. His bestie Pat, another cabbie, said, 'Bomber, all the best work is late at night: the thirty, forty-quid jobs.' So gradually he stayed out a bit later, each night a bit braver. Pat was right, the takings went up accordingly. By Friday, nearing the end of his first week, Norbert was feeling quite pleased with himself. It had been a good first week. Lots of near panics, but with the nous of experience, he knew it would get easier.

Waiting at a red light on a busy junction heading back to the West End, around midnight, the rear passenger door suddenly opened. A guy jumped in and said two words, 'London Street.' This guy was big, bald, with an air of menace about him. He looked like something out of one of those American gaoler films. The cheeky fucker had not hailed Norbert, he had just opened the door and sat right in. Survival instincts kicked in. Norbert smiled back and said, 'London Street it is then.' The guy didn't say a word the entire journey; he just stared intently in Norbert's direction. *Spooky.* Norbert suspected there might be a problem.

A few minutes later they were heading up Sussex Gardens, the road that crossed London Street, which was one way from the opposite end. Norbert stopped and hit the meter. The fare showed £7 something, and the big guy spoke at last. 'You should have known it was a one way.' With that, he opened the door, heaved himself out and made off, giving Norbert no chance of redeeming the situation. The passenger door was left open, and Norbert watched horrified as the man turned and spat a flying gob, spraying the back of his cab. He turned and walked away. Norbert's pulse sky-rocketed; adrenalin pumping, he couldn't take his eyes off him, but the guy never turned around to check back on the situation.

Norbert spun a U-turn, forgetting about the door; luckily the cab's motion cleverly closed it for him. He bunged his money bag under the central console and got out of the cab, locking it remotely as he crossed the road in hasty pursuit. His eyes were fixed on the big lunk who was casually walking along with not a care in the world. Norbert had never started a fight in his entire life, but the sheer arrogance riled him.

Good wolf in Norbert's head spoke first: *Ask him for the money.* Bad wolf interrupted this line of thought: *He doesn't want to give you any money. Do him, teach him a fucking lesson.* Then, suddenly, amongst the throngs of people that were busying about on a Friday evening around bustling Paddington, the man made a right turn down a quiet alleyway. Norbert looked; no one else was around, no CCTV cameras. He was thirty yards behind when he started to run, closing in fast but softly on the hard pavement. When Norbert was close enough he jumped into a right turning kick, landing it slap bang in the middle of the lurch's right leg directly behind the knee. The force took his quarry face down to the pavement, where he let out a panicked scream.

Norbert didn't know whether the force into the ground broke anything, but knee onto concrete, he would feel that later. He stood back as the bewildered man came to his senses and turned. They looked again into each other's eyes; he went for Norbert. Being a little woozy, he was way too slow. Norbert reeled off a fast snap punch straight into his bloated face.

'You're taking a fucking liberty, mate,' Norbert said, 'have that, and if you want there's more where that came from.' Norbert was venting but he was done, bad wolf happyish. Good wolf intervened; there was no need to go into overkill mode, he had made his point. Norbert turned and walked away with the same cockiness he had earlier witnessed, except he was ready, aware of any change in energy, just in case; there was a lot more in his war chest ready to come back out if needed.

Back at the taxi he was still feeling pumped; he needed to calm down. Not wanting to worry Nikki, he called his cabby mate Patrick. He also did a bit of training and had had more than his fair share of altercations over the years.

'Fuck me, 'Pat said, 'I took two weeks to have my first tear up. Well done, it only took you four days.'

It was a fast learning curve. Norbert could not carry on like that, having fights with every piss-taker. Any more of those and he would lose his badge and the livelihood he had worked so hard to get, plus he might eventually pick someone to come undone with. Being involved with martial arts taught him what other people could do, not to take too many unnecessary chances. This time, however, he had stood up for his principles.

At the end of the first week, he discovered three things. One was to lock the doors late at night so you were less likely to be mugged off; two, the money was better working nights, albeit with the added grief that came as part of the package. And three, his wing chun had worked. Bills and financial responsibilities came first, which meant for now Norbert couldn't afford to get back to class with Digor.

Chapter 32

Change is in the air

Norbert was not the only one dealing with change. Larry Blake had vacated the church hall for training. The gentrification of Greenwich had taken hold, and it was now a fully-fledged playground for the yummy mummies with their oversized four-by-fours, and the rise of smart coffee shops, bookstores, and artisan fairs had seen commercial rents skyrocket.

Larry had been busy making some instructional videos. The idea had come from one of his first wave of students; Yasir was a quiet, introspective black Muslim, who now lived in America. Norbert had seen him in England once or twice but knew little about him. He had moaned to Larry that it was really hard to find any quality wing chun instruction stateside and suggested Larry fill the void. Larry grasped the idea fully, putting together the first of what turned out to be a trilogy, showcasing his ideas and interpretations of wing chun. Using many of his students, there was an enormous amount of detail in them to keep both novices and experienced practitioners happy, and the devil was in the detail. They sold around the world with very positive feedback. People appreciated what they saw, and Larry duly received recognition for it.

Larry liked Yasir a lot. He looked at him like a brother and he was becoming drawn to the world of Islam. As Yasir himself said to Larry, 'You behave and live life already like someone of faith. It would be a natural step to convert and join the path to Islam.' It wasn't rushed. Yasir introduced him first to an Imam who encouraged Larry to read the Koran. Larry was looking for something to fill a gap he felt he had in his life, and slowly he was reassured. The books covered everything; he had found all the answers he had been searching for. The similarities between this new-found faith and his martial arts were powerful. Both came from having good structure and balance as a person, one from outstanding teachers, the other from good strong parents. Islam guided him. He embraced it into his life.

From that point on, his martial arts changed in the sense that Allah now drove it from the soul; it became directed as an expression of his faith. Digor moved across the borough to set up teaching in a building next to a local mosque. In the name of Allah, the most gracious, the most merciful, he was free to worship, train and teach. He made it his full-time career, and his skills in wing chun took off exponentially again.

It had been a couple of years since Norbert had trained with Larry. Money was tight but Norbert figured he could squeeze in a night or two at the new school. They had kept in touch by phone. Norbert walked up the narrow shabby stairs. It felt just like all those years ago when he took those initial first tentative steps, walking into the unknown. There were a couple of guys in there already who he didn't recognise.

'Can I help you?' one of them said.

'Oh yes, I was looking for Larry.'

'Haider?' he replied.

'Yes,' Norbert answered, a little lost; he didn't know he'd changed his name.

'He'll be along shortly.'

Norbert went through some warm-ups with the rest of the class. *Where are my old classmates? Where's the musketeers?* Oh, it had all changed; his heart sank.

And then the familiar deep-toned voice of Larry, Digor or Haider (take your pick)! His voice and laughter preceded him, echoing along the corridors until there he was, standing in front of Norbert, looking resplendent in his robes, and bearded! He marched straight up and embraced Norbert in front of everyone. It was a warm public show of affection, and it lifted Norbert's spirits. Digor was later joined in class by Gilly, his trusted lieutenant, but as far as Norbert's seniors went, that was it. Gilly was a wily older student and now he was helping Digor supervise the class. He didn't have an ounce of fat on him but boy, was there some firepower stored in those arms of his. Norbert always enjoyed their training sessions together.

Digor's wing chun hadn't stood still; it was continuing to evolve and develop and it showed. This was different alright, and right from the off the training had changed. Drills had gone, replaced by new ones that had the intensity turned right up on full. Gilly recorded a lot of footage, in class and in seminars, collaborating with Digor. It all added up to a ton of information. YouTube was taking off and opening up the world at large, and now Digor was at the forefront of the widespread appeal of martial arts. Every post that went on was greeted by a myriad of positive responses from people all over the globe; seeing Digor perform for the first time, they were blown away like the rest. He was known in Norway, Australia, even America. The responses were overwhelmingly positive, and Gilly put up more and more posts, promoting Digor and his ethos. The class was full, mostly of brothers from the mosque. Digor was loving his new-found faith and with God on his side perhaps he really was unbeatable.

Norbert drove home; he was happy, happy for Digor. But he was sad, too. He liked the old party, music and bev, fun Digor. He passed Jay's shop where once he bought fishing socks, jeans, and Dr Martens boots. It had closed down, replaced by a Halal establishment. Above the shop the old faded billboard still hung – a young man in jeans looking out to beyond; maybe there was a hint of suspicion in his eyes, maybe it was a sign of the times.

Chapter 33

Bastards

The finances were just about straightening out, and Norbert was juggling family, work, and training.

Ninjas, those clandestine, stealth-like assassins, were less honourable than the samurai. When you sneak around in numbers terrorising poor souls, it's unsurprising you end up with a bad name. So it should have come as no surprise when some unscrupulous shits called Fanny Mae and Freddy fucking Mac ran into trouble, underwriting ninja (no income, no job, no assets, no way to pay them back) mortgages. They were symptomatic of a much wider financial ticking timebomb. When Wall Street and the banks were trading high-risk sub-prime toxic mortgages, it was only a matter of time until they dumped the buck on the unsuspecting, gullible public. The taxpayer. It was a gigantic game of pass the parcel.

What ensued was a deteriorating housing market and the inevitable cyclical rise in mortgage defaults. It got worse, a bunch worse. Without liquidity, a financial meltdown snowballed and spawned a global credit crunch. The scale of bank losses was unfathomable. The contamination spread far and wide; Europe and, in particular, the UK had been buying into the toxicity – pension funds, local councils – and the contagion caught everyone one way or another. So-called experts agreed that if the housing market collapsed further, the consequences for the banks and subsequent recession could bring down the entire financial system like a pack of cards. In their wisdom, they bailed out Fanny and Freddy to the tune of some 250 billion and counting.

There is a saying – if Wall Street sneezes, we all catch a cold. What followed was a period of prolonged low growth and rising unemployment, highlighting the major problems, particularly in some Eurozone countries like Ireland, Spain, and Greece, which saw overinflated housing prices crash and a run on the banks. *Quick, get your money and hide it under the floorboards!* Messrs Bush and Brown intervened with quantitative easing, or printing more money; it revived the economy and put it back into action.

The Queen asked, 'If the problems are so big, why did nobody see it coming?' To which the reply should have been, 'Because, ma'am, everyone was too fucking greedy to stop. The snouts in the trough were insatiable.'

And in times of hardship, who can forget the immortal words of the politicians when they claim we are all in it together? It's difficult to bend your head around that one when you learn of them smashing the gravy train of the after-dinner speech circuit, or passing top corporate jobs around like sweets. Consumer spending was reined in, which meant fewer hands raised in the air hailing taxi cabs. Norbert was shafted.

There was no way he could afford to give up working lates and return to class. Norbert settled on a compromise – a private lesson with Digor. Once a week, for one hour, he could have the spoils all to himself. However, one hour a week, even with one of the finest teachers, was never going to be sufficient.

Chapter 34

Sarnie

Maybe he was about to get a break. This particular morning had started well. Making love to Nikki was always a good start to the day. Norbert was taking a shower and Nikki was downstairs fixing something to eat. By the time she returned he was dressed in casual jeans and a T-shirt. They sat up on the bed and he marvels at her and her culinary skills. It was only a bacon sandwich, but everything about it exuded excellence. Crisp bacon and fresh bread buttered to its extremities, made with care. Nikki cared.

'Look what I've got,' she said. 'It was wedged in the letter box.' She handed Norbert a flyer.

Normally their Jack-Chi cross Rufus would have torn it to shreds – he had serious little-man syndrome – but with the aroma of bacon in the air it had escaped his attention. Norbert read the bold letters: '"New wing chun class". Oh wow, thanks, babe. I'll give them a call.' He scoffed his sandwich, itching to get on the phone.

Norbert called and said, 'Hi, I've just seen the flyer about the new class and I can't tell you how glad I am to find someone in my neck of the woods who does wing chun.'

Steve introduced himself and informed Norbert he was part of a big academy. 'Have you got any experience?' he asked.

Norbert couldn't blurt out the answer quickly enough. 'Yeah, I've been training with Larry Blake in London for the last eight years.'

Steve asked for Norbert's address and ended the call.

Nikki said, 'How did that go, any promise?'

'Well, yes, he's coming round to see me for a chat.'

'Okay, when?' Nikki asked.

'Like now,' Norbert said.

'Really, that's keen.'

Five minutes later the bell rang and the dog went nuts. Norbert opened the door; using his leg he wedged the gap because Rufus was chomping to get at the stranger. Steve was of a similar build and similar age to Nobert so it was looking hopeful. Norbert ushered him round to the quiet of the back garden. He told him that he was stuck in no-man's-land, unable to get to class, and showed a couple of little moves around the wooden dummy he had in his garden as he was talking, all very casually because he wanted Steve to see he wasn't bullshitting. Steve said this was a new class for beginners.

'Look,' Norbert said, 'I won't step on anyone's toes. I'm willing to learn under your instruction and if I can help in any small way, I would be more than happy to. I have been lucky to find an exceptional teacher. I'm just in need of some practice.'

Steve said, 'Sorry, pal, it's beginners only.'

Ouch. What a kick in the teeth. Then, to add insult to injury, Steve began bigging up his teacher. 'He's the world champion!'

Norbert never even knew that there was a world contest in wing chun. It was all slipping away fast. In one last desperate ploy, Norbert guided Steve's arms, saying, 'Let's have a little feel if you wouldn't mind.' He was trying to get him to roll hands, to engage in a spar. Norbert thought, *Maybe he will come to his senses, see that I'm no threat, and welcome me into the fold.* He couldn't have been more wrong.

Steve was critical of Norbert's structure. 'This is out, this is wrong, we do it this way . . .' and so on. Did he want to fight, did he have a point to prove?

He wasn't having any of it, refusing to engage further.

Norbert watched him leave, utterly disappointed, scratching his head in puzzlement. Later that night Norbert left a message and sent an email, an olive branch, with a suggestion to hook up if he ever changed his mind. There was nothing, no reply. *How rude, how odd.*

Next lesson Norbert told Digor.

Digor laughed. 'There's no way he's gonna let you join the class, Norbert. He won't want you to undermine him, especially in front of his students.'

'But I told him, I'm no threat.'

'You are, Norbert, to him, you are.'

They got into some fighting. At the end, Norbert's limbs were aching and his head was ready to explode with all the information that he was receiving. Positioning, structure, the correct path were all done at a quick pace, and thrown in were brief blasts of free play where Digor would destroy him. He was glad the hour was up if only to give his body a break. He needed to wind down; he had a shift to work in the taxi.

Digor had some advice. 'Norbert, the best thing you can do if you're looking for practice is to find some students yourself, teach them.'

'I dunno, Digor. I mean, I'm not sure if I'm good enough for that, yet.'

'Norbert, you're ready – besides, you don't have much choice, do you?'

'Well, I'll think about it. I'll see you next week. Thanks, Digor.'

Chapter 35

Stepping up

Norbert was in no mood to leave Digor's teaching, still wanting security beneath his powerful wings. Teaching would be a big step into the unknown. He realised that once you open your doors and invite the world in, you don't know who will show up, perhaps to test you. Norbert had been taught self-control, but from his experience he knew there were plenty of poor attitudes and inflated egos out there in the big world, and any of them could come through the doors. Yet a couple of days later he made a firm decision, and for him that was something.

Norbert handwrote some small simple cards, which read: 'Wing chun class – learn self-defence'. He added a line about a free lesson to entice people in and left a mobile number on the bottom. Taking them round to the local shops, he paid for a couple of months of window space on their shop fronts. All he had to do now was wait for any prospective clientele to come out of the shadows. While the weather was warm, he could temporarily teach in the back garden.

Over the next few days, he searched for a more suitable venue. After a couple of scouting trips he found a small mission hall just up the road, St Francis of Assisi; it looked like one of those gospel churches found in Deep South USA. It reminded him of *The Little House on the Prairie*, with its white-clad exterior exaggerated by the lush green of the surrounding fields, a tiny cross on one end of the pitched roof. Inside was spacious, and outside there was parking for a few cars. It was perfect. He met the caretaker across the road who showed Norbert where he kept the key and how to use the old-fashioned heater. It was one of those old coin-operated jobbies.

Norbert was expecting his phone to ring off the hook after his advertising, but there was nothing, not a single enquiry. Same for the next day and the next. On the fourth day, just when he had all but given up, a guy called and asked about the class. He seemed keen and was duly invited to the hall. This was to be Norbert's first official class.

Next Monday evening rolled around, and Norbert opened up a little early, paid the £5 fee for one hour across the road to the caretaker and got settled inside, waiting for his new student to arrive. As seven o'clock came, tutting to himself about late showers, he started his usual warm-up routine of stretches. The small clock on the white wall was a permanent reminder and Norbert kept checking it – five past, ten past – even by quarter past the hour he still had not given up hope on the guy. Eventually, he faced the bleeding obvious; the call had been a false dawn, a waster. Perhaps he was interested and had a late change of heart, who knows; for now, it was just Norbert in this quiet lonely space. Seeing as how he had paid for it, though, he thought he may as well use it. He trained on his own, going through tons of drills, shadow sparring, channelling his disappointment; he worked his socks off for an hour.

Driving home, the irony was not lost on him. Just up the road was that fucking Wing Chun Academy that had blanked him, probably full of people, and here he was struggling to get a single person. He seriously considered going in there uninvited. He reasoned that if he challenged the teacher to a fight or spar and won then just like in those old Chinese kung fu films, he would lead all the students out of there like the pied piper. He was dejected; he didn't have the character to go out troublemaking.

'Hi, love,' Nikki said when he got back. 'How did it go?' She looked up at Norbert's face; nothing more needed to be said. Nikki gave him a hug. 'You'll get there, you always do.'

After one call and one no-show, remarkably the cards came good. Or rather it was time that worked, having the patience to wait a little longer. First one student came then another. The heart-lifting thing was that once they saw him perform, they brought along mates. He had doubled the class organically.

It was an odd mix. One of them, Abu, actually knew more of the wing chun forms than Norbert; he was also focused on judo, on a mission to achieve a black belt. *This could work out well for both of us,* Norbert thought. When they got into the nitty-gritty of using the forms to fight with, though, Abu was a little lost. Norbert could tell he could fight; it was the improbable scenario that he had never been shown the depth of the forms he had. They were empty of substance. This was where Norbert came in, to fill the gaps; there he was teaching and the students seemed suitably impressed. Maybe he was ready after all.

Almost a month in, Abu had to let it go when work relocated him. Norbert never saw him again, and any hopes of incorporating some judo groundwork into the proceedings vanished with his exit. His sidekick Pete also quit. Norbert wasn't that sad to see him go; they hadn't got off to a flying start. When Norbert was introduced, Pete was smoking a fag. Norbert watched him casually throw it onto the drive. Stuff like that was alien to Norbert; he struggled to understand why people displayed such a lack of common decency and respect.

His and Abu's departure coincided with an awful incident in the summer of 2010 when Raoul Moat went on a killing spree. It was all over the news.

Nikki joked, 'Funny, isn't it?'

'What is?' Norbert asked.

'How alike Pete is to Raoul Moat! Do you think they are one and the same?'

Norbert had to laugh. He loved the way Nikki's mind worked. Maybe Norbert had a lucky escape. But back at his class, the numbers had dwindled to two, which soon became one after another lad left and followed his heart into kick-boxing.

It wasn't just his inability to form and keep a class that was giving Norbert some concern – his cash flow was also stuck in the slow lane. With the success he'd had previously in getting on board the technology boom, he had never given up on his passion for investing. But his next financial break was more elusive, always just out of reach; by God, Norbert was busy trying to swim instead of treading water.

Chapter 36

A good walk spoiled

Due to Nikki's claustrophobia and hence intense fear of being trapped, confined in the tube of an aeroplane, many family holidays for Norbert and the girls were spent trying to make the most of wet summers in England's south-west. Except for a year when Norbert bagged a short golfing holiday to Myrtle Beach, a city and holiday resort on South Carolina's Atlantic coast. Out of a motley crew of Scottish and English participants, he proved to be, and this was no easy task, the worst player on the entire break. The great time had off the golf course made the pill a bit easier to swallow – great banter, some fantastic nights out, and some hilarious moments.

It was nonsensical; one of the lads, Harry, seemed just to do it for Norbert's amusement. After returning from their daily trips to the shops for snacks, he would expertly screech the tyres of the rental car around the corners of every turn in the multistorey hotel parking lot. That was a helluva lot of loud streets of San Francisco action; it could be heard a mile away and made Norbert nearly wet himself every time. The look on other people's faces who didn't know what the hell was going on was priceless. Real uncontrollable giggles in the belly, Norbert eagerly waited for his afternoon fix.

Once back on terra firma in Blighty, Norbert decided on some golf lessons to work out where his golf game was going wrong once and for all. The local golf pro, Howard had a fine coaching pedigree; he knew his onions. Apparently, Norbert had a hip sway that was destroying his shots. It wasn't just on the dance floor that it roared to life, or was that a stone in his shoe? Anyway, despite different drills, it could not be exorcised; it was still there in him, silently lurking ready and randomly raising its ugly head at the worse opportune times – a hard pull left, slice right, or the dreaded shank. Howard might not have helped his sway, despite all the best intentions in the world, but he let Norbert put up a martial arts flyer in the changing rooms, and lo and behold, a few days later he had some more students in the fold of wing chun training.

There was a young lad, Anthony, a skinny, very shy, polite boy who had found Norbert's class after an episode when he was set upon by some boisterous out-of-townies. He was a bit fragile at fourteen when he first tried a class, but Norbert was a sucker for anyone who had been bullied.

'I saw a green woodpecker this morning when I was running, they oscillate up and down. I swear it was following me,' Anthony said. Norbert adored Anthony's innocence.

Anthony would soon hit that teenage growth spurt.

It all came together in Norbert's regular class, every Monday evening at the local mission hall. Training had a habit of ebb and flow; Norbert was riding high, immersed in his martial arts again, teaching to enthusiastic people and gaining a deeper level of understanding and respect for the art. It was evidence as to how far he had come on his journey. There were times he thought he would never get it right, and here he was enjoying the moment and responsibility of teaching. His conscience was clear; he believed in the whole ethos and approach of wing chun, especially following one more bizarre incident.

He nearly crashed his cab when he saw it – a large PVC banner that wrapped itself around a fence corner at the end of his road. 'New Wing Chun Class – free lesson'. Norbert pulled over to the side of the road and scribbled down the number on one of his taxi receipts. For fuck's sake, from years of barren wilderness with no one to practise with in Ashford, nothing, zilch, to finding himself now in the fucking epicentre of wing chun land. He could have been in Hong Kong; classes were sprouting up and spreading like wildfire. There was the so-called Wing Chun Academy to the north of the town, where the instructor blanked him on joining. And now this new class had settled literally on his doorstep; he felt a little hemmed in. Visions ran through his head of this new teacher coming down with his students for some sort of showdown. Everybody was kung fu fighting.

Later he called the mobile number for this new class. Ted introduced himself and explained in a soft, calm voice that he was starting a new class. They chatted and Norbert invited him around for a meet, wanting to check out the competition. Who knows, maybe their classes could merge into one school, both instructing with different approaches – maybe that would work? Norbert had the same approach last time, though, with the academy guy, and look where that got him. Self-doubt was kicking in again. *Shit, perhaps this new teacher will just steal my students.*

Ted called round in quick time; Norbert wasn't the only one anxious about things. Norbert ushered him into the familiarity of the back garden as he had with the previous teacher. After a little small talk, Norbert asked if he wanted to roll hands, playtime.

'I don't know any sticky hands,' Ted said, straight-faced, 'my teacher told me I didn't need it.'

For Norbert, this was like a kickboxer saying before a fight 'I can only punch, no one has shown me how to kick'. Or a boxer who says 'I haven't been shown any footwork'. It's daft, empty of substance, and ridiculous.

'Well, what if someone does this?' Norbert said as he slowly aimed a palm to his face. Ted blocked. Norbert then countered with a locking move, which had Ted tied up with nowhere to go. There was a momentary pause before the penny dropped.

'Would you teach me?' Ted asked. And that was that.

Norbert gave him his number, class details, and invited him and his students along to his class. Norbert never heard a thing. A short while later, Ted's class must have folded; the banner was removed, not by Norbert, and he was gone. In their brief chat, Ted had mentioned his dream of going to China to find proper kung fu – become the prodigal son.

Norbert could not believe Ted's naivety or plain stupidity;

here was he, willing and able to show him, fill in the pieces for him and get him to a higher level, and after his humiliating display, one might think he would be keen to balance out his martial arts. But no. A fool like that would be parted from all his money and given crumbs. Norbert couldn't believe how some had such contempt for the art to take people's hard-earned money by masquerading as a teacher. He beat the shit out of his wooden dummy, imagining it was Ted.

Chapter 37

Suburbsville

Norbert's class had some consistency, and together they all improved. Teacher was proud. Over the years the small group bonded. Seeing Anthony develop into a young man full of confidence especially sat well with Norbert; he learned organically all about the young man's life, his family, and particularly his sister.

Rebecca, with dark long flowing hair, completed the picture-postcard family, with mum Sally and dad Phil still sprightly and smart in their late fifties. Home for them was the affluent town of Tenterden in the weald of Kent, comfortable and secure. Rebecca had a boyfriend, Timothy, or Timmy as everyone called him. They were serious and like some first loves, thought they would stay together forever. Mum and Dad didn't approve of their relationship at first; fifteen was so very young, and they didn't want their daughter to grow up into adulthood too fast. But they were smart enough to know that if they interfered or tried to discourage it, Becky might push them away. Timmy was welcomed into the family with open arms.

It can work in different ways when siblings are similarly aged; either they'll forge different paths and different friends or, like Anthony and Rebecca, the circle intertwined. They shared friends and acquaintances through school and continued the same theme after leaving when new worlds opened up. Social occasions when all were together made a large group. Meeting up at one of the many local pubs or restaurants in town was an opportunity to gossip and enjoy the safety and closeness of each other; they had a strong bond. Each time they met, it cemented their unit a bit tighter.

Timmy was besotted with Becky, but not enough to go

shopping with her on Saturdays; working overtime got him excused, and that was not to be understated. The last ordeal still stung; Rebecca had made for the changing rooms with armfuls of clothes. Timmy circled, looking for somewhere to rest. The curtain swished open; she was dressed in black.

'What do you think, Timmy?'

'Wow, you look amazing,' he said.

'Hold that thought.' She disappeared back into the black hole of the cubicle. Re-emerging five years later, sorry five minutes, she was now draped in pretty florals.

'Which one do you prefer?'

'I like them both. The floral one suits your make-up, but the black one matches those shoes.'

'Forget the shoes, Tim.' Rebecca tutted.

'Hun, you gotta go with what you feel most comfortable in.'

Nice try, but it wasn't the answer she wanted. She returned them both and continued looking for something even better. It was not uncommon to have one last panic buy, picking up something on a fleeting whim on the way out of the store. The exit was so tantalisingly close that Timmy could almost breathe the outside air into his nostrils; he felt faint, but inside he was weeping.

Rebecca always looked great to him, whatever she wore. Nine times out of ten she would wear one of her 'go-to' dresses, the ones that hung in her wardrobe on standby, after deciding that she no longer liked the clothes she bought earlier in the day – they would have to be exchanged next week. Any takers . . .?

Chapter 38

Surf's up

B ack in Londinium, Norbert worked some ass-numbing long shifts in the taxi and by the time he got back to Mum's place, he was cream-crackered, knackered. That weary, drained feeling after a long drive became a part of life for Norbert. The need to unwind from all the myriad maps and routes buzzing about his head, and the city traffic, brought stress that only those unfortunates who experienced it could understand. A quick read of the papers started the unwinding process, but like watching the news, it would mostly be full of depressing stories. Besides, he was up to speed with current affairs, having the radio as a constant companion where regular samey news bulletins were steadily drip-fed all day long.

YouTube was kicking off; it had started a few years before, but it was getting more and more attention now. Norbert would pass the time and try to rebalance with some kung fu action, from outer space to the mobile, tap-tapping his fingers. It was probably the least conducive thing to do before bedtime, exposing one's retinas to digital streaming with its false bright lights and psyche responses. But hey ho.

He went fishing, looking for the dragon-slaying masters of kung fu. Was it just confined to the movies? It appeared so; he couldn't find anything of substance, not a morsel. There were plenty of rehearsed drills, tame displays of the forms, but no fighting displays of any substance using wing chun. Of all the hyperbole that came with the territory of kung fu, he might have reasonably expected a small offering of wonderful quality fighting.

One guy was kitted out in a long black gown, eastern looking, long black hair in a ponytail. He was knocking his students – actors would be nearer the truth – all around the floor, spinning them around in weird fake magnetic force fields, propelling them away with the slightest of touches. Some were somersaulting through the air in acrobatic displays that wouldn't be out of place in a circus. Bruce Lee's famous inch punch, knocking a guy back into a chair, had nothing on this. Incredulous, he had to laugh at such fraudulence. One word in the comment box summed it up – 'Really!' How deeply embarrassing.

He surfed on. Lots of movie clips, dubbed highlights. No, Norbert was thirsty for real, not fake. More shit. Kung fu v kickboxer, karate v boxing, wing chun v wing chun, all ill-matched, one-sided affairs. He was hoping to find something with a bit of quality about it, not a fucking teacher beating a useless student – two fighters, real, warts and all, preferably with one fighting back, not rolling over and having his tummy tickled. Wing chun with its rough edges. He had that sinking feeling once again that something was not right. Desperately seeking Susan.

Worse still, like a dark cloud following him around, there was no shortage of UFC, MMA, and Brazilian Ju-Jitsu protagonists fighting like lions. A part of him was beginning to seriously dislike Ju-Jitsu and probably for all the wrong reasons. To begin with, from the very first time he ever tried anything close to fighting when he was a youngster, it was judo that held a position close to his heart. Plus, the previous encounters had done nothing to build any bridges; more to the point, both experiences had left a foul taste in his mouth about all things Ju-Jitsu. Was it full of dumb overzealous nutters? However, there was one overriding emotion that was blurring his vision and filling up inside him – jealousy.

When he started out learning wing chun, it still had that air of mystique about it. It had kudos. Kung fu was like magic, you couldn't understand how it worked, but the illusion amazed you. *The Water Margin*, *Kung Fu*, *Enter the Dragon*. It had, in Norbert's mind, put itself up there on a pedestal. And he like most bought into it until the make-believe cast into reality.

Things were changing. There was a time when kung fu was never questioned. Now if it was to get to the top in an argument about which was best it would have to get there on merit, and that was making things decidedly uncomfortable. Norbert could see trouble ahead. He knew that good kung fu was out there. Larry was the shining light closer to home, but there had to be others, surely. But finding any evidence of it was proving difficult. In the harsh glare of public scrutiny, it was letting itself down; who was going to champion the art?

He found himself watching the inevitable footage of animals messing around. Surfing the net does that, leading one down a warren of blind alleys, dead ends, and circles. You could waste an eternity, always looking for something better, click, closer, click, change, click, next. All done with a quick swipe, looking for that perfect fit in an age of instant gratification. He was expecting the usual cat and dog fighting stuff, dumb dog, smart cat, Tom and Jerry, and as cute and funny as nature can be, that wouldn't hold his gaze for long.

Until he happened upon the honey badger. Badgers look cute and cuddly, but they weren't something he was too familiar with. There was the time Norbert remembered as a kid being taken to a delightful place on Dartmoor called Badger's Holt while holidaying in Devon. He couldn't remember seeing any badgers though, as nice as it was. He'd never seen one in the wild. Then there was Badger in *Breaking Bad*, which was probably about the extent of his connection with the black and white creatures.

But this clip about the honey badger hooked him right in. There it was strutting around on the wild plains of Africa, seemingly without a care in the world. It was black and white, but not like the striped visual long-snouted docile ones we are used to seeing on wildlife posters, more like a cross between a punk rocker and a pit bull. This guy was menacing, busy snaffling around all the honey it could maraud from a hive, despite being stung many times. The footage was narrated by a camp-sounding very excitable man, the theme being that the honey badger doesn't give a shit. Sure enough, it goes around eating practically anything it can get its strong claws on. It has a penchant for snakes; the clip shows HB passing out from the venom it has ingested and then waking to carry on eating the dead snake. This got the commentator very excited. HB takes on anything in its path; having a tough thick skin that is very loose enables it to absorb many attacks. A ferociously powerful bite and the ability to secrete potent stink bombs adds more weaponry to the arsenal, giving it an extremely effective fight plan. Lions, hyenas, humans, it will take them all on; this is one tough cookie, listed in the Guinness Book of Records as one of the most fearless animals.

It reminded him of bloody MMA fighters, with their utter disdain for whatever is in their path. It was getting him down, forlorn. Night after night he kept looking. *I know the ocean is vast, but it can't be that real masters only exist locked behind iron curtains or closed doors, in tiny secretive pockets of China, sworn to secrecy of the innermost teachings in some faraway mystical sacred temple, only ever to surface in times of duals to the death with rivals. Hello, step forward anyone, hello.*

What about this? Norbert's heart missed a beat – was this real wing chun in America? *Please be it,* he wished as his fingers hovered and clicked. A few seconds in and it unfolded with the telltale signs, following or chasing hands, no technique, poor wing chun again. He only had to glance at the comments to realise his worst fears. Where once kung fu was feted, now the onliners were seeing straight through this tosh. 'Anyone from MMA would eat these guys for breakfast.' Mr Anon from stateside was right. The knocking was relentless. Norbert was desperate for something to stem the flow, hold back the floodgates, because those cocky MMA bastards wanted to rule the world, a world full of honey badgers. Who in their right mind wanted that?

Chapter 39

Warriors come out to play, ay

It was time for Norbert to become a keyboard warrior, a cyber equaliser. To tell the friendly folks online that not all wing chun was shit, level things out a tad, champion Larry, what could go wrong? It was late, another evening shift was over with no dramas, which was always a blessing. He was hungry and needed a snack; the world wide web could wait a little longer. After too many biscuits, he washed the last one away with a large glug of cold orange squash and was primed.

First, he aimed stateside, right into the home of the MMA community. He was reading from one of the popular sites, the supposed global authority on mixed martial arts, giving audience to the question, 'Does wing chun work?' The following post grabbed his attention:

'So, because Donnie Yen looked cool in the *Ip Man* movies, every kid around the block suddenly thinks wing chun is a good fighting style, despite the fact that even the elite wing chun fighters (like Stephen Falkner) lose at the blink of an eye whenever they're in an MMA match. Wing chun simply doesn't work and that should be clear to anyone who isn't stark-raving mad. Yet, some people refuse to accept the truths that MMA has brought to the table and they still insist on wing chun being some kind of ultimate killer art. It's as daft as those who refuse science and stick to their old pagan beliefs of the world being flat. Sometimes the truth hurts, but if you're grown-up, man, then stop wanking to Asian martial arts movies like that, it's as far from real fighting as anything gets, no matter how extreme it looks. I used to like tae kwon do. That's a martial art best suited for fighting against old women, just like wing chun. But I got over it. It sucks. Why can't adult men just move on from their shitty arts instead of having gay feelings for a set of moves that serves absolutely no purpose in either dancing or fighting? Fuck wing chun. I respect *Ip Man*, I like the movies, but it has brainwashed the retards into thinking that they can get fighting superpowers without even doing any fighting at all.'

Fuck wing chun, retards, the slight bit of homophobia ... go for it, mate. Obviously, this guy is no fan of wing chun. Norbert was spitting feathers. There were tons of threads in the forum section. He skipped over anything not mentioning wing chun; he had enough on his plate without having to deal with other styles and their battle for supremacy. He found another post from someone who had a laughing gorilla set as his profile picture. That should have given the game away:

'Wing chun does work, my Aunt Mable used it the other day to handbag some poor old biddy who tried to push their way past her in the bus queue. I was there, I saw it with my own eyes.'

'That's a good one, dude,' someone replied. A few others gave it the thumbs up. Norbert scanned through some of the usernames. He liked 'kiss-my-axe'. It was clear that whoever tried to defend wing chun would be in for ridicule, made to stand in the middle while the honey badgers baited, circled and pulled their petty-rival pants down.

'Put up or shut up,' another honey badger tormentor posted. And of course, they couldn't.

What's the fucking point. No honey badger is going to change their opinion, especially one as angry and flippant as that first guy. An hour flew by; Norbert was busting for a pee. He sat down like a girl, laughing to himself. 'Aunt fucking Mable.' He squeezed and held for his Kegel exercise, counted, got to two and gave up. He went to bed not knowing whether to laugh or cry.

Chapter 40

Masterclass

Norbert brushed himself off, knuckled down, and went about his business. It was not easy, given the sorry state of the capital's roads. 'Every journey matters', Transport for London, the sorry body in charge of managing things, would tell you. Tell that to the disabled people who want to get somewhere without running the gauntlet of frustration on the bus or train, the businessman late for a meeting, the commuter who wants to make that train, or the holidaymaker who needs to be on that flight, and what about the ambulance urgently on its way to save someone's life? All were stuck in the poisonous glut of traffic, a consequence of those making the decisions and their abject failure to see the bleeding obvious right in front of their eyes. Uncoordinated roadworks coupled with stupid changes, until the only thing that moved was a Boris bike. TFL regularly sent out surveys asking for an opinion on how they were doing. Is there anything we could improve on, they say?

It was supposed to be a normal working day's shift – 11 May 2017. The London taxi trade was slowly being dragged kicking and screaming into the twenty-first century by offering punters the choice to pay by credit card. Cabs were fitted with a payment device in the back. Norbert was waiting for the transaction to process of a punter who was late, and stress levels were rising.

'I'm going to miss my train,' the passenger said.

'Look it's not my fault.' Norbert was desperately willing the bastard machine to connect with some outer space signal and spit a receipt out, to free them both from the state of suspension, but the computer said no. Tick-tock, tick-tock, the train was about to leave the station. Norbert hurriedly scribbled his banking details down on a receipt and slid it through the small hole in the partition. 'Look, go and get your train. Send me a bank transfer, mate, please?'

'Will do, thanks, cabby.' The passenger sprinted off with seconds remaining.

Exasperated by the bloody thing, Norbert decided enough was enough and had the media company strip the damn thing out. He booked back in with another company, and luckily, they squeezed him in for the next morning. Funny how they moved mountains when it was entirely for their benefit. It meant he unexpectedly had the rest of the day off.

Not wanting to waste the time, he made for Digor's class. It was still light when Norbert arrived. Pushing the aluminium door open he entered and climbed the stairs. The carpet looked worn. Norbert heard the familiar deep tone of Digor's voice echoing around the thin walls. His stride gained a little impetus. Upstairs, the regulars were joined by a small contingent that had come over from Greece, for a few days of intensive training. Norbert was greeted with the same warmth that he had become accustomed to over the years; it never let him down.

There was no time for small talk – straight into the thick of it this evening. When Digor picked you out in class, it was your time. First out, Norbert wasn't required to do much. Digor was explaining some basics and how you learn to this new group. Norbert felt a little rusty, to say the least. It was not performing like a seal, clap clap, get a fish, but he still wanted to be good, meaning following the path, pulling out the right techniques for the right moment. If you did the movements would flow, try to wing it or pick the wrong techniques, then it would all grind to a halt. Norbert was not match fit, and he felt it. Anyhow, on with the class. The next demonstration, Digor bloody nearly broke Norbert's arm. *A little over-exuberant tonight, Digor.* This was shaping up to be one of those nights.

The regulars were used to it, and the new visitors were treated to a full-on display. Round the class Digor went, moving through everyone for a little play, tuning in to their nuances and levels, bringing their wing chun to life. Midway through the class, Digor stopped and explained that he and a few of the brothers would go to the mosque next door to pray. It gave everyone else a chance to catch their breath, let the mind pause, and try to ingest some information. Ten minutes later he was back, searching everyone out, going around the class one by one, twenty-five, maybe thirty students, feeding them lines, drills, lots of fighting.

When it was Norbert's turn again, he pulled out some nice techniques, but it just wasn't that great – slightly out here and there. In the full glare at the centre with everyone looking he couldn't hide what would come out when exposed to Digor's octopus arms and speed of movement. The session was getting more physical; the heat was being turned up. This time around with the seniors, Digor upped his game. Norbert's turn again, and Digor caught him off balance, deploying a move that had Norbert's spine transverse away from its natural curve. Held totally in his power, it was sobering how quickly Norbert was overcome and nullified. Norbert was trying, they were all trying to fight back.

Anything goes in or out of wing chun. Everyone was taking a beating tonight, measured, thankfully. It hurt. When the attacks came around again, Digor hit Norbert all over the place, from one side of the gym to the other. He cornered him and Norbert thought he saw a move as Digor switched his horse stance behind him. Norbert bar armed his chest and tried to tip him backwards. Digor had other plans and grabbed Norbert's head and twisted it. Norbert released immediately. He loosened, Norbert regained his composure, and they went again, almost an identical move, but this time Norbert thwarted it momentarily by holding Digor's arm. He felt a knee hit his chest and fell to the floor. He was startled but not surprised; it was familiar territory for Norbert when they sparred. Digor offered Norbert a hand up and they went again. This time he trapped Norbert's arm and palmed his head in a manner that contorted Norbert's limbs like they were on a rack. It ended with Norbert's face sprawled against the mirror near the corner wall, much to the amusement of the rest of the class.

Norbert hadn't a clue what was going on between them that night, but it was a masterclass for everybody present. When you are the one in the storm's eye, it is all automatic. You can't remember the details like those looking on, it's much of a blur. In an hour, Norbert was beaten remorselessly. He could have had his arm and back broken. What reality, sometimes fierce, but it was always with control and humility. God knows how it might feel for real – you would not want to go there.

Before Norbert left, he caught up with some of the others, one of them Charlie, a likeable fella who had a bit of pedigree with arm wrestling; his arms still bulged out of his T-shirts.

'Digor's magical,' he said, looking on spellbound.

'Maybe we should call him Paul Daniels then,' said Norbert.

'More like Houdini,' Charlie said.

Norbert left with the same Ready-Brek glow as always. When he got home, he checked his bank statement online to see if the passenger from earlier that day was a gentleman and had done the decent thing.

Chapter 41

Q & A

Norbert may have been let down by the last passenger with a lower moral compass but from that last lesson with Digor he's positively buoyed. A few days later and he's ready for another crack at the online community.

He found a question-and-answer-type website and signed up, ready to put his two-pennorth in. Rather than start with a full-on 'my style is better than yours', Norbert decided to change tack slightly; he didn't want to attract any psycho honey badgers, so he put out a simple question: Why does wing chun struggle in MMA?

One of the first responders was a guy called Pete, who gave a withering assessment of the state of play:

'When Bruce Lee had his first fights, all he knew was wing chun. He very quickly realised that wing chun has some excellent points and some glaring holes that needed to be remedied. Unfortunately, wing chun has evolved little, and there is a cult of 'keeping it Hong Kong' and glorifying the past despite the evidence that the 1950s Hong Kong rooftop street-fighting heroes weren't that good. Other martial arts evolved, wing chun didn't. It's not helped by some Chinese society stuff around respecting and never questioning your elders. Also, when kung fu first came to the West it was acceptable to teach literal nonsense to white people and save the good stuff for the Chinese. As a result, there are a bunch of idiots running around claiming to have the 'one real true authentic wing chun' and they argue endlessly about it on forums.

'There is some very good wing chun around, but the best people I've ever seen are guys who train in garages, not the kind who get on the cover of magazines. Wing chun overestimates the importance of chi sao (touch sensitivity), has no wrestling, and has completely incorrect groundwork. Also, wing chun only has one punch, the straight blast. It is more effective on the street than in MMA since it is a relatively weak but fast punch, like a jab. On the street, this will cut people up, but when I did wing chun I didn't knock many people out. This is all compounded because wing chun spends too much time fighting against itself, petty bickering about who's teacher is best instead of testing it out. When they hit other styles they fail miserably because they have been raised on a diet of "this is the best style ever you are unbeatable". One last point. I've never met an in-shape chunner. Skinny fat, dad bod, no cardio people don't fare well in real fights.'

This guy knows his stuff. Norbert posted back: 'You make some excellent points, Pete. I think even if you believe the system to be limited, doesn't it still come down to the skill of the practitioner? Unfortunately, few people get to the level where they can use it effectively against a skilled fighter. Here's one who has – Larry Blake. You won't find him in any magazines, but trust me, his level of wing chun is astonishing, he's the spoiler. A pioneer who after forty years is showing the way. Larry's is a selfless quest with no fanfare. It's a shame more people don't know about it, not least to shine a light on the charlatans but mostly to answer back by saying 'Look, world, not all wing chun is shit.' It's a very lonely place where I bang my drum.'

Pete responded: 'I've met good kung fu. I have good kung fu. Good kung fu exists; it's just uncommon in wing chun. Have you ever seen your teacher fight a world-class opponent? First time I tried it I realised I was like a weekend golfer at the PGA.'

It was a fair point; Norbert had to concede that the answer was *no*. They jousted some more. Pete explained about fighting in Bangkok, a hub for past and present champions, belts, and titles galore. Norbert couldn't match that, not even close. The last time he sparred at Larry's class was against Alan, a fat sod whose only belt was a lattice one holding his jeans up. Norbert felt the mood lighten a little, but still he probed on a deep level.

Norbert posted again: 'Pete, whoever comes to our school or attends one of Larry's seminars is invited to spar. It's not like the days of old when one teacher would seek another out to challenge. And it's not the same as turning up at another dojo to spar and tap out. I get your apprehension; I get the bullshit. But I know a good fighter when I see one.'

Pete came back: 'I've seen good wing chun. I know it exists. I've also seen flat-out fraudulent wing chun on every corner of the globe. Good wing chun is so rare as to be unicorn spotting. Also, if your teacher does not spar regularly with world-class opposition, he by definition cannot be that good. I taught kung fu for over a decade, and I can easily spar my students one after the other, beating them twenty in a row. I can also knock out dummies on the street like it's a movie. I've done it a hundred times. It's exactly like a good weekend golfer beating his buddies. Anyone decent can. Beating up your students is easy. Beating up world-class opposition … not so much. There is so much ego in the world of wing chun they don't fight with each other anymore for fear of letting down their lineage. Unless you fight against very high-level opposition regularly, you cannot be good. Period.'

Fucking hell, is this guy a one-man wrecking machine, a hundred bloody fist fights – that's some attitude you got there, Pete. Norbert was tapping away at his keyboard.

He replied: 'So we agree on the same principle, but disagree with how we rubber-stamp our levels. In your world, you have to spar with other world-class fighters, and in mine, you can't, which in your words means you can't be top level. I am suggesting you can. Some people find their way.'

Pete posted: 'Can't? Why not? I've sparred against world-class opposition a dozen times in three countries over the last year. They welcomed me like a long-lost friend in every gym I walked into. You could too! To take one of a hundred examples, this is one trainer at a gym I train at in Phuket when I need a break. Fifty dollars gets you his time for an hour, or you can go to the morning sparring session and get a few minutes sparring with him when it's your turn. What you think is "impossible" really means "unwilling to test for real how good my ego thinks I am". When I used to travel the world visiting kung fu gyms, I got all kinds of snaky looks and ego-proving games. Boxers, wrestlers, sambo, submission wrestlers, catch wrestlers … would rather train with you and learn a few things than protect their ego.'

Norbert replied: 'OMG, feels like I am banging my head against the wall here. What I can't concede is that the only way to get to a high level is to test your fighting on a mat.

'When you ask if my teacher has fought any world-class fighters, the answer was no, but with a big fuck-off *but*. But he has fought those in front of him in America, Europe, and Hong Kong and fared very well. Black belts in karate and Ju-Jitsu do not maketh a world-class fighter, but if you can deal with what's in front of you, well that's a good start. When someone says you have to test it on a mat, I say you do not. When someone says you have to be ripped and an elite athlete to be effective, I say you do not. Real fights are like a ticking time bomb when it explodes, kneeling on a mat, trying to get a good grip on a collar, wouldn't an opponent just punch you in the face?

'In a ring you can get away with it but on a street, you might not. A suicide shoot could take you down, but it might just get your neck twisted. A foot stamp won't bounce off concrete like a spongey mat, imagine that. Outside the ring, all bets are off. I invite you to YouTube Larry Blake, and perhaps you can make up your mind if it's real or if wing chun could work away from the ring or mat.'

Pete's last contribution: 'How good someone is, is a question of how good a fighter they can beat. It's that simple and not arguable. When someone claims to be good but has never fought anyone good … that is a ludicrous claim. No different from a weekend golfer claiming to be better than Tiger Woods.'

And that was that. Norbert questioned himself. *Is Pete stubborn or am I naïve? Larry never claimed to be anything, it's me putting his stuff forward as a shining example of wing chun. Did Pete ever check out Larry's wing chun to see if it lived up to the proper stuff he had seen, who knows?*

And then, out of nowhere, came a punch into the sides of Norbert's ribs from a guy in Austin, Texas called Brad. 'Public Service Announcement: Wing chun does not work anywhere, in the cage or on the street, unless that person knows zero about fighting, is disabled, drunk, etc., I'll fight your wing chun lead instructor.'

Norbert couldn't type it out fast enough: '*Cunt, absolute.*' He sent the two words before there was any chance of a change of heart.

For crying out loud, not only was Norbert getting no bloody nearer knowing whether someone with a high level of martial arts like his man Larry with his Wing Chun could ever match the fiery honey badgers outside the octagon, but worse, it seemed as if things were descending to a level where he was potentially inviting a bunch of trouble to his teacher's door. He imagined the scenario:

'Hi, are you Larry Blake?'

'Yes.'

'I've come here to fight you.'

'Okay, why?'

'Well, I've seen your student Norbert's posts and I think you're all full of shit.'

Norbert had backed himself into a corner. Eulogising and attempting to rebalance the debate would not make a difference to anything. Some days passed, and a comment came up on his phone. He half expected to be banned, but ...

'Hi there, you must be new seeing as this is your first post. This thread has been done to death a million times. You're going to receive the following things: 1. A flame war 2. Dishonest answers 3. Some war stories.

'You're also going to hear these arguments: Wing chun doesn't work because it's TMA (traditional martial arts) and TMAs aren't practical for modern-day fighting. Wing chun doesn't work because they don't spar properly and practise complicated and inefficient moves without knowing whether they work on a person.'

But then there was this little carrot: 'Wing chun can work if you know how to apply it effectively and it's the person, not the art.'

OMG, this is what I was trying to say before I threw my toys out of the pram. At last. Norbert sighed. He responded with a heartfelt *thank you*; he also realised this was about as good as it was going to get – one lonely voice supporting his notion in a set of honey badgers. Norbert was ready to throw in the towel.

Chapter 42

Snakes and ladders

It's a fact of life that any taxi driver, whether renting or buying their own cab, will spend a fair amount of their precious time in a garage staring at the walls, wondering how the fuck they chose that particular career path.

Old boy George was the local Arthur Daley. He had a small Portakabin office at the back of the local taxi pit stop near London Bridge. There he bought and sold cabs, adding his £200 commission fee on either side of the deals. Tired of renting, Norbert knocked on the door and stepped inside.

George was sitting behind a desk, his flowing silver hair creeping 'neath a smart dark herringbone cap. He was wearing gold-rimmed spectacles and smiled a perfect set of gnashers. 'Yes, young man, how can I be of assistance?' George lowered his supine palm towards a stripped-out taxi seat.

Norbert duly sat down. 'I'm looking to buy,' he said.

'Nuff said, son. I'll put you in a cracking cab.'

They went through the formalities and sure enough, within a week, George called. 'I've not seen it yet, but they told me it's immaculate. £25,500 but I know they'll take twenty-five bags,' George said.

Norbert was boosted by George's enthusiasm; they arranged to meet over on the east side of London at a respected Turkish-owned garage where he was given the full red-carpet treatment.

Erkan, one of the sons, showed Norbert around. 'My dad built this place up from scratch,' he told Norbert. 'He passed away almost two years ago now. Look at these photos – you know, all the local garages closed and they lined the streets as a mark of respect when the funeral cortege passed through here.'

Norbert looked at the framed pictures, bowled over. 'Wow, I can see how much he was loved. Sorry for your loss, Erkan.'

'Life goes on, man.'

'Yep, it sure does,' Norbert said.

Erkan showed Norbert the black taxi in question. 'Take it for a spin,' he said.

Norbert got in and turned the key; another mechanic gave him a generous thumbs up while nodding at the cab, which Norbert drove around the corner to a quieter street. He stopped. *Should I pop the bonnet and have a look? Ah, what's the point? I couldn't tell if anything was amiss – bloody hell, I just about manage to fill the screen wash*. Instead, he left the noisy workhorse of an engine rattling away and got out. Away from all the eyes, he had a walk around the taxi, inspecting the bodywork. There were a lot of digs and nicks, but nothing major.

Norbert made his way back. 'Will you take twenty-five?'

Erkan looked to the side, blew out some air from his cheeks and quickly offered his hand to shake. Norbert was in, hook, line and sinker, and left as the proud owner of one of London's famous iconic black taxis. George left with two hundred smackeroos wedged in his back pocket. Everyone was happy.

Two weeks later, niggle after niggle saw Norbert returning to the garage like a boomerang.

'Don't worry, man, bring it back in and we'll sort it,' said Erkan. Yet it was feeling like Groundhog Day. Norbert threw some more money at it for a new tyre after one had inextricably peeled a layer off in the middle like a golf divot. He was driving on the motorway at the time; the loud *thump, thump, thump* nearly scared him to death.

Summer had arrived; it was getting hotter each day. Norbert was sitting in traffic when the air-conditioning decided to stop giving its cool relief.

That's it, I've had enough. That fucker Erkan can give me my money back, he thought, just as an oncoming vehicle passed his rear and turned right through the traffic. The driver completely misjudged it, clipping the back end of Norbert's near side with the faintest of touches. *I don't fucking believe it – this car is cursed.* The other driver got out, full of apologies. On inspection, the rear light to Norbert's car had split and a small hole had appeared out of the casing, a scuff mark tracing the path. It was all minor; Norbert was angrier about the air-con than this bump. Details were exchanged. No whiplash claims here, but seeing as someone else would be paying, he booked the repair in at his local taxi garage.

He dropped the vehicle off later that afternoon. It was Thursday; he was resigned to the fact that his week had prematurely been cut short. He was just about to walk out the door when a stubble-chinned mechanic in oil-stained overalls called out.

'Excuse me, Norbert, can I have a word?'

Norbert stopped and turned. 'Sure, what's up?'

'Come with me a minute.'

Norbert followed the mechanic round to the back workshop where two other guys were standing by Norbert's taxi, pointing, smiling, yes, definitely smiling, and scratching their heads with puzzled looks on their faces. 'We never thought we'd see this car on the road again,' one said.

'What do you know that I don't?' Norbert asked.

'Follow me.' Stubble man led him to a small back office. A few clicks later, he pulled up computer details of past jobs. An image of Norbert's taxi flashed across the screen. He could see the mangled wreckage from a fucking great smack up the rear.

'We quoted on the repair, which we gave as £5,000, but wait for it, £18,000 labour. A new chassis, complete strip, and refit. It was written off by the insurers. We never got the job and we thought it was heading for the scrap dealer. You can imagine how surprised we all were when you brought it in here.' He took Norbert back to the car and opened the rear passenger door, peeled away a floor mat and caressed his hand over the carpet floor like a skilled surgeon looking for an abnormality.

'Here,' he said, 'it's still there, feel this.'

Norbert leaned in and found a bump in the floor, revealing

the remnants of a twisted chassis that had never been repaired.

'Cunts – I knew it. I've had nothing but trouble with this cab from the first moment.'

'In this state, it's probably illegal to be on the road,' the other mechanic said.

'What can I do? Norbert asks.

'Back it, get your money back,' they all agreed.

Norbert was on the phone instantly. Erkan, the unscrupulous snake, point blank refused to accept any responsibility.

Chapter 43

Not tonight, Josephine

Next day, Norbert was driving the blasted thing home; he was on the hands-free to the legal eagle at the London Taxi Drivers Association; 'We're here for our members', their website proudly boasts. Norbert dared not even think about the possibility that if there had been an accident, the vehicle he was driving would be found to be unroadworthy, illegal.

'Thanks for getting back to me, Oliver. This vehicle, it's a fucking deathtrap – I drive my girl to school in it. This bastard could break in two at any time – what the fuck am I going to do?' asked Norbert.

'Look, Norbert, you need to try and calm down,' Oliver said. 'I've spoken to Erkan. He tells me he bought the taxi in good faith.'

'Faith and Erkan don't belong in the same sentence, Oliver!'

'There's not a lot we can do if he's willing to fix it.'

'Where do I stand legally?'

'I would strongly advise against going down that route – it will cost you a heap of money. At least give him a chance to put it right. Look, we've never had anything like this, it's uncharted water for us. Call me back and let me know how Erkan gets on with the repair.'

Norbert hung up. *Great, just fucking great, woop de fucking doo.*

He called the old boy, George. 'You told me it was immaculate, George. Your words.'

'I never said that, son. I hadn't even seen it until we met over the East. I gave it the once over and it all looked dandy,' George said. He was back-pedalling faster than a pedalo heading for Niagara Falls. 'I've been buying and selling taxis for more years than I care to remember, and I've never had anything like this happen to me.'

'Yeah, well, that's what everyone is saying. The thing is, and I can't get my head around this, but Erkan has shit on his doorstep. He has fucked me over. We're in the same fucking trade, for God's sake.' Norbert let that sink in; he was so fucking angry he ended the call.

He went through it all again with Nikki, every minute detail. She didn't know what to say as they cuddled in the corner of the sofa. Rufus was on to Norbert's energy and curled up beside him. Norbert held Nikki tight, his other hand stroking Rufus's ginger-fox-coloured head. And Norbert started to cry. Nikki rubbed his back tenderly and wiped his tears. Norbert didn't want to move.

'Come on, let's go and pick up our kid – she'll be well excited to see you. I'll drive.'

'You're going to have to because that bastard taxi on our drive ain't going nowhere for now until I sort this shit-pile out.'

They headed for the school through the villages, Norbert watching people going about their routines. *I wonder how many of them are vexed like me.*

Late on Friday afternoon, he left Nikki and the girls outside in the garden and headed inside to make some more calls. Rufus followed him hoping for a biscuit. Out of desperation, Norbert tried the police, who swiftly reminded him it was a civil matter. What irony. Next, he thumbed through the local directory to the listing for solicitors. Leaping out at him like a gazelle on springs came the name 'Storm Catchers Law'. He had to call them.

'I'm sorry, I can't get to the phone right now, please leave a message and I'll get straight back.' Norbert left a heartbroken, half-hearted message and persevered with more calls.

The same response came back every time. 'Oh, we're sorry, we don't deal with motor offences.' The afternoon had rolled into early evening; he paced around his front room, not knowing which way to turn. He wanted to cry again; he wanted to beat the shit out of Erkan.

Norbert dragged himself to the kitchen where Nikki had prepared a feast fit for a king. As hard as he tried to focus on the gang, Norbert's mind was elsewhere; he had to force himself to eat. He wasn't hungry; he was not hangry, he was just fed up. It soon became clear that Norbert's problem was going to take a while to fix, and no one felt the urgency as keenly as Norbert. He couldn't be more pissed if he was tanked on alcohol.

In bed Norbert and Nikki kissed. Norbert thought it was a goodnight kiss, but Nikki had other ideas. She stayed there, her tongue probing, and Norbert let it into his mouth. Her breathing deepened; he couldn't help himself getting aroused. They made love, but it was cut short; like a balloon deflating, he couldn't keep it up.

'I'm so sorry, Nik. I just can't get that bastard out of my head. I—'

'You can't let him eat you up, Norbert. Nothing should come between us.'

'I know, you're right. I just need some time for this, to figure it out. It's not just the money. This is a real setback for me, us.'

Nikki turned away, head on the pillow. Norbert stroked her head, kneaded her temple, which sometimes got rid of her constant headaches. After a few minutes she stopped him and squeezed his hand, clenching it three times – code for *I love you*.

The last thing that Nikki would ever do was add to Norbert's headfuck, but she unwittingly had. Everything was working against him, and it began to take a toll. The next couple of days, while the girls attended school and Nikki held down her part-time job helping adults with acquired brain injuries, Norbert barely lifted himself off the sofa.

There was another thing driving him mad: the endless shit they put out on the box in the name of daytime TV. Jeremy Kyle aside, it was comforting watching people more fucked up than himself. He was doing no training, taking no exercise; he was just waiting for the phone to ring, looking for answers. He had to find something before he went out of his troubled mind.

Chapter 44

John Graham Chambers rules

The art of pugilism, the uncluttered simplicity of a one-on-one fight, appealed to Norbert's inner fighter. He loved to watch a good scrap. And the heavyweight division was where it was at. He could have only been seven or eight, but somewhere in his psyche, Norbert remembered Grandad Fred watching some characters on the TV. There was the black guy with the electric shock, gravity-defying silver hair who talked a lot. Then there was Muhammad Ali, who also talked a lot. Fred eulogised about him, full of admiration. 'That, boy, is the best fighter in the world, and he will need to be if he is to beat him.' Fred pointed at the man mountain that was George Foreman.

Too young at the time to be caught up in the fever of the 'rumble in the jungle', or indeed to know much about the other heavyweight kings locked in the most ferocious era, Norbert's appetite had however been whetted. Those bad boys resonated. He came back to them, watching all the fights of yesteryear, to appreciate them the second time around and to have that connection, however fleeting, with Nan and Grandad. The heavyweight guys would not buzz around the ring constantly as the flyweights or bantamweights did, kites dancing on the breeze. Standing toe-to-toe slugfests – that got Norbert's juices flowing. He hunted down all the fights and documentaries he could and binged like never before.

Mirror, mirror, on the wall, who's the baddest of them all? No one epitomised the dark side more than Iron Mike Tyson. It was easy to see why, witnessing a young Tyson working the punchbag, which quivered and buckled under the power of his punches. Destroying all before him, he was a wrecking ball, not just in the ring. Bounding through life, he had lost his guiding light, D'Amato, his trainer and mentor, and now he was struggling. His tribulations, like those of Princess Diana, were being played out in the full glare of the media spotlight.

After the life story, Norbert YouTubed Mike's greatest knockouts. Fucking incredible. Then for some balance he watched one of his less successful bouts. It was only a couple of years ago when Tyson had fought Lennox Lewis, and Norbert remembered it like it was yesterday, how he had yearned for Tyson to get back to his formidable best, to thrash the lackadaisical big-talking Lewis and show some of his former greatness.

He watched the fight again – showtime: the build-up intensified and the excitement energised Norbert. He came alive at the spectacle. And in it all, he could not take his eyes away from Tyson, the enigma, the menace of Iron Mike. He got it, the demeanour. He was his fucking idol, the way he did away with fanfare and his eagerness for battle, to get it on. The commentator bellowed into the mic, 'Let's get ready to rumble.' The baying crowds cheered, and the throngs of people inside the ring cleared, leaving the referee and the two gladiators. They stared each other down, Lewis already standing out of his corner, an early statement of intent.

The fight began. Two and a half minutes in and Lewis, in the first proper exchange, threw and landed an uppercut. Where was the Tyson explosion? Tyson looked slightly cumbersome. Lots of clinching from both fighters. Tyson held the middle of the ring but Lewis held his ground, picking Tyson off with jabs and uppercuts, leaning in on him, wearing him down at every clinch. Where was the speed and footwork from Mike? As the fight progressed, it was clear how he looked like a shadow of his former self! Round three and there were some flashes from Tyson, but Lewis, gaining in confidence, was picking him off easily with his long-reaching left jab. He had the measure of Tyson, who was now cut and bleeding, a wounded animal. Round four and Tyson crumbled from a punch and more leaning from the lurching Lewis.

The realisation that Tyson's best was behind him hit home. Norbert was saddened and angered by the spectacle, again.

Tyson was finished, but still, Lewis hadn't the courage to get in the mix and finish it, just more messing around. Lewis punched and leaned and wore Mike down. Tyson to his credit was soaking it all up; he had nothing left to give of his own, but he never backed away. He stood there like target practice for Lewis, round after round, and in the eighth round he fell to his knees, but the fight continued. *'Someone should have stopped the fucking fight,'* Norbert yelled. It had gone way past comfortable viewing, watching his man beaten down until Lewis landed an enormous right; knockdown – and the game was all over.

Norbert watched Lewis gloat in the victory, proclaiming himself the best fighter on the planet. Norbert had had quite enough of this – the whole affair, the fight, the pre-match antics, and the sorry conclusion left an unpleasant taste in the mouth.

Nikki would be home soon; he'd take the car and do the school run, grab everyone fish and chips – he hadn't eaten all day. *It's the least I can do.*

Nikki stayed home and showered. Norbert drove, but he couldn't shake the feeling that he was being mugged off. It was agitating him; he was irked at Erkan and now boxing was doing the same as more and more recent fights fell short of their build-up and hype. Boxing was a victim of its earlier success. Norbert wished he had a time machine to take him back before the tide turned. To a time when he never had to drive a taxi, to a time when the prawn sandwich brigade had been thoroughly spoiled during the heydays of the seventies, or the eighties stateside with the fabulous four, or in the UK with the irrepressible greats of super middleweights. Those generations bludgeoned a trail, setting the bar ridiculously high.

He wanted to go to a place in that simpler world. Then he saw his little girl skipping out from the playground and all his troubles suddenly didn't seem as bad.

Chapter 45

Shaken like a snow globe

Next day Norbert was back on it like a car bonnet – the fighting, that is. He'd broken the seal and now he was looking deep into the well. After the disappointment of watching Tyson washed up and beaten by Lennox Lewis, there was a new kid on the block for fighting matters. He came across the rerun quite by chance. Much lauded on Sky was a heavyweight Grand Prix event that took place in the national outdoor stadium of Tokyo, Japan. The showcase became known as the Pride Shockwave Dynamite event, and it was a huge draw. Such was the widespread popularity of wrestling in Japan, the arena packed 71,000 vociferous excitable fans ringside ready to watch the spectacle unfold. There would be five fights, not winner takes all format, more like a five-course meal, a taster menu.

Norbert was hoping for some proper action. Intrigued and stirred he had butterflies in his stomach as the build-up began. It was a beautiful evening in Tokyo. The opening ceremony of fireworks spectacularly blasted into the evening sky. A flame lit by the torchbearers Antonio Inoki and Helio Gracie heralded the start like an Olympic ceremony. Norbert told himself to settle down. He had been wound up like a key before on the premise of tough talk, fanciful promotions, and then let down many times with boxing, but this felt different. These guys all had one thing in common: they had come to fight.

First, up the axe murderer. They pitted him in a middleweight contest against an MMA debutant from Japan. The referee called them in and Silva the axe murderer was right in the face of Iwasaki. The New Zealand haka had nothing on this intimidation. Norbert's heart was beating fast;

the adrenalin was building, and he was sitting on his sofa leaning forward. Despite home crowd advantage, the karate expert was overcome by the axe murderer, who was smashing shots into his face as they fell to the canvas. He tried to choke him out, but somehow Iwasaki wriggled out and just as he was climbing to his feet, was felled by a kick to the face that David Beckham would be proud of. Silva ploughed back in, landing a barrage of punches to the head and face of the bewildered Iwasaki before the referee intervened and stopped the fight after a minute and fourteen seconds.

Norbert couldn't believe it. He was open-mouthed, stunned. Unbelievable – he had found his fix, and this was just the hors d'oeuvres. The next courses came thick and fast, delivering more fights – a mixture of wrestling, brawling, and the infamous ground and pound. Blood spills, kicks to the head, knees to the body, submissions, chokes, and elbows, these guys brought it all to the table in full-on style. It was as close to real fighting as he could get; Norbert was in genuine shock, feeling voyeuristic like it shouldn't be allowed, but here it was in amazing colourful animation – raw, primitive fighting stripped of unnecessary distractions.

And then this happened.

Bob Sapp was a former American football player who was creating quite a stir in the professional heavyweight championships in Japan. He became the first African-American to win the international wrestling Grand Prix. This hulk of a man was a big celebrity in Japan, where he was crushing the Japanese pro fighters like a steamroller flattening tarmac. When he stepped up to fight the 140-pounds-lighter Antonio Rodrigo Nogueira, aka the Big Nog, or Minotauro, it was a classic power versus technique play. The chest-thumping Sapp rushed in and, of course, the Nog tried to shoot him down to the ground. Sapp folded his mighty arms around Nogueira and hoisted him in the air. He dive-bombed him back to the ground head first in a sickening move that could have killed him outright. The Nog survived to face a barrage of blows to his face. He was hanging on for dear life, desperately trying to find a technique to stop that colossus, who threw him around like a rag doll every time the Nog attempted to lock him down. They wrestled and fought and the Nog went on miraculously to win after Sapp ran out of gas. It was an incredible display of heart, real David v Goliath. Minotauro, body of a man and head and tail of a bull – quite.

When Norbert witnessed Sapp pick his opponent up and try to slam the neck of Nogueira into the canvas, he knew that was a defining moment; it could not have been more brutal, to end the fight in a way that could easily have crippled someone for life. Once privy to that, seeing the battle lines drawn, there really is no going back. The cards were shown, and although they were fighting within the confines of some rules, they were flimsiest at best.

In that one piece of treachery most foul, Norbert knew in his heart his martial arts, the world in which he belonged would soon be under attack. Because after such an ultimate test, everything else in contrast looked fake. That reality was as close as he could get to the very essence of fighting. Compared to the tripe the lazy boxing promoters had fed him of late, this was like dining on caviar and champagne. Norbert was stirred by the emotional ride – shaken to the core. He needed to see no more to be convinced. Yet his eyes and heart never left the action until the last gladiators finished.

Chapter 46

Ladies and gentlemen, I give you the Gracie family

The amount of snow in an avalanche will vary based upon many factors, but it can be such an enormous amount as to bury the terrain at the bottom of the slope in dozens of feet of snow. When deadly avalanches occur, the moving snow can reach over eighty miles per hour. Many unfortunate thrill-seeking skiers have found themselves trapped within these walls of snow. While it's possible to dig out of such avalanches, not everyone will escape. If you get tossed about by an avalanche and find yourself buried, you might not have a genuine sense of which way is up and which way is down. An avalanche can start with a trickle.

It was just after midday on a Tuesday when Norbert found them, properly found them. It ain't gonna take long if you are looking into the formative years of MMA. Like them, loathe them, question them, worship them – you simply cannot deny them. Unquestionably the greatest and most important family in the development of martial arts ever. It was a bold claim, but delving into the official Gracie story, this was what they did, what Norbert learned:

In the early 1900s, Japan, somewhat tired of trying to conquer lands with military force, was focused on a more peaceful approach to expansion. That wouldn't last long, would it?

Anyhow, their sights were focused on Brazil, a country rich in minerals, metals, and precious commodities, something the Japanese desperately sought. A contingent was sent to Para in north-eastern Brazil to help facilitate the setting up of a colony. Mitsuyo Maeda was a part of that early wave, and he also happened to be a judo expert. There he met Gastao Gracie, a local political figure who used his influence to help Maeda and the incoming Japanese.

In return for Gastao's help, Maeda offered to teach Gastao's son Carlos. This was a big deal. Similar to the Chinese mistrust of Westerners, Japan considered it a crime to teach non-Japanese. Nevertheless, Maeda took it upon himself to teach Carlos; never in his wildest dreams did he imagine how this kid would have such an impact on things to come.

Carlos trained with Maeda, aka Count Coma, from the age of fifteen until he was twenty-one. Carlos soaked up everything he saw, right until Maeda left and returned to Japan. This was a catalyst for the next stage. Carlos seized this new-found freedom and pushed on, developing his art outside any confines. At first, he taught others from his house; this turned out to be so popular he soon opened a school – the first Brazilian academy in the world. Carlos teamed up with his younger, weaker-framed brother, Helio. Their different approaches came together seamlessly, combining the aggressive attacking style of Carlos with the technical genius of Helio, who it seems was adept at using the leverages and body mechanics to full effect.

Together they crafted judo and submission grappling into Ju-Jitsu, turning their art into something quite extraordinary, proving it to all and sundry with their infamous Gracie challenge. Carlos ran an ad in the local paper declaring, 'If you want a broken arm or rib, contact Carlos Gracie at this number'. The people came, and he fought them all. He fought in public events and entered many boxing events, eventually becoming the Brazilian national champion, taking on champions of other styles with considerable success.

The Gracie challenge: let's think about that for a moment. Was Carlos's ego out of control? Was he mad?

Brazil was and still is a country associated with poverty and crime. This rough climate could not be a more fertile breeding ground for gangs and fighters, a hotbed for those ready to come out of the woodwork and test themselves for bragging rights. It was a clever move designed to highlight the academy and prove beyond question he could walk the walk. It was part of the Gracie way, and Helio was very much cut from the same cloth.

How the hell did Carlos and Helio win so many challenge fights against far bigger and stronger opponents? The answer lies in their effective game plan, which as so often with masterstrokes of genius came from the simplest of ideas. Using their new revolutionary style of Ju-Jitsu, they tipped fighting upside down, literally. They took the fight down to the floor.

They had techniques to dumbfound; it was a game of rock, paper, scissors. They had an answer for every scenario. Scissors: in an instant they would cut a big strong puncher down, shooting in, taking them out of their comfort zone to the ground. There, with the opponent flailing about like a fish out of water, the groundwork experts wrapped them up like paper to win the battle. Genius, absolute genius, and brave, stupidly sometimes. When they were under attack, they changed into objects of hard rock, impenetrable, able to withstand ferocious bursts. They knew they would take hits often, allowing their opponents to gain the dominant position, waiting for their time, like Ali on the ropes against the formidable Foreman, waiting, knowing the time for victory would come. And did it come?

Helio was fast becoming a national celebrity and, having conquered all of Brazil, he raised the bar; he looked towards the homeland of Ju-Jitsu, challenging the masters of Japan. Japan ordered Masahiko Kimura, widely regarded as the best exponent of Ju-Jitsu ever, and his understudy Kato to fight for the integrity and honour of Japan.

Helio beat Kato, setting up a mouth-watering match with the numero uno. It was huge, the first time a Ju-Jitsu championship fight had been held outside Japan. The stakes were high on so many levels; at the very least, both were fighting for their national pride, and on a personal level, Kimura wanted to right the wrong done to Kato in his defeat. Japan could not afford to contemplate losing this match; if Kimura lost, the Japanese embassy informed him, he would not be welcome back. No pressure then.

To the famous Maracana in front of tens of thousands, including the Brazilian president and the entire press corps of Brazil and Japan.

On one side the stronger, younger Kimura had openly suggested Helio would not last three minutes, and on the other side, the Gracies had brought in a coffin for the expectant Kimura to be dragged out in. They set the fight for two rounds of ten minutes; something had to give.

As it was, it turned out a one-sided affair. Kimura threw Helio around like a rag doll, but these were the Gracie rules – you could not win by a takedown. The softer mat cushioned the falls, allowing Helio to fight on. Kimura then took it to the floor. Helio survived for a while until after about thirteen minutes, exhausted, he succumbed to a shoulder lock. Carlos threw in the towel after Helio refused to tap out. Fighting Kimura forced the Japanese style to show its hand, and now the cat was out of the bag.

Chapter 47

To all-beef patties

In 1954, following the Korean War, America was in the grip of a recession. The federal reserve had exacerbated the situation by raising interest rates. It must have dumbfounded salesman Ray Krok that during these times of austerity, the McDonald brothers were ordering shedloads of his multi-mix machines for their milkshakes. Until then, the American food empire was at the behest of the diner and there was little regularity or consistency between them from one street to the next, let alone from state to state. Curiosity made Ray go and take a look. He saw for himself how people couldn't get enough of the brothers' regular fries, burgers, and shakes. He also knew right there and then that he wanted to be a part of their journey. In 1955, he founded McDonald's System, Inc., a predecessor of the McDonald's Corporation, and six years later bought the exclusive rights to the McDonald's name. By 1958, McDonald's had sold its hundred millionth hamburger, and the rest is history.

As the years rolled on, Carlos retreated into a world of medicine, meditation, and spiritual learning. By the time he reached old age, he had married three times and had an incredible twenty-one children. Helio himself only had nine. Therein reveals another ingredient of their success. They mostly lived together, and there's a sense of real family ethics and a very healthy moral code of living, and of course fighting. They produced a continual line of fighters, all with the same inbuilt qualities, which set them up on a springboard to put their individual stamp on history when their time came.

From this stable of thoroughbreds, it was Rorian Gracie

178

who answered the clarion call to chase his dream and vision to showcase his family's Ju-Jitsu to the world. He was the first to conquer America. He was joined in Southern California by some of his brothers, and together they set their style of fighting apart in dramatic style. Upping the ante of the family's famous Gracie challenge to $100,000 thrust them all into the spotlight. The challengers came and were undone. The Gracies had by now been smothering opponents and killing the fight for many years.

Rorian teamed up with slick salesman Art Davie and John Milius, a Hollywood director, and together they formulated a plan: a pay-per-view event to showcase Gracie Ju-Jitsu. They presented their ideas to a couple of networks who turned them down flat. Art sent a fax to the head of programming at Semaphore Entertainment Group: 'You are going to see a 400-pound sumo wrestler fighting a 200-pound kickboxer. You can turn off the sound and every young guy between fifteen and thirty is going to know what this is all about. You don't even *need* sound.' It worked. SEG stuck their necks out and bought into it. Once the finance was in place, they hand-picked a venue. The McNichols Sports Arena in Denver, Colorado, was chosen because of its lack of governing boxing laws, and a date was set: 12 November 1993. The format was a limited rules mixed fighting competition, winner takes all. A tweak of the name, and the Ultimate Fighting Championship was born.

Now all they needed was some fighters to make up the card. That proved harder than they had imagined. Befuddled by the lack of rules, Chuck Norris declined. James 'Bonecrusher' Smith followed suit, also turning them down. Eventually they filled the card with a hand-picked selection of fighters from a range of disciplines.

Perhaps Rorian's masterstroke was who he selected to represent the Gracie family. By all accounts, Rickson was the strongest fighter in the family by a country mile. Nevertheless, Rorian chose Royce Gracie, one of the youngest and smallest. It was possibly the most important fight in their entire history and they didn't even select their best fighter.

It was self-belief or arrogance. If Royce lost, the decision could backfire spectacularly, undoing years of progression for the family. However, the play of the moment epitomised the confidence the Gracies had, that their Ju-Jitsu, despite size disadvantage, was superior to anything else. They put everything on the line, culling black belts for fun.

Chapter 48

Fight night

An eight-man gladiator competition, winner takes all. The rules: no time limits, no biting, no gouging – that just about covered it.

In the first fight, sumo wrestler Teila Tuli, in beautifully exotic colourful shorts, took on a tall skinny action-man-type Dutchman, savate champ Gerard Gordeau. In the opening exchange, the sumo guy charged like a bull across the octagon ring, Gordeau punching Tuli's face while retreating. The bull kept on charging forward, and such was his momentum that when Gordeau pulled out of the way, Tuli lost his footing and fell to the floor. The giant was down and unguarded, whereupon he was met with a roundhouse mule kick to the face. Teeth fragments flew into the air. The partisan crowd had never seen anything quite like it. That was it – it was all over. The referee called an end to the first match; a bloodied, stunned Tuli could not continue, much to everyone's disappointment.

Next up were two big fuck-off kickboxers. The fight started and they traded blows, Frazier getting in close with some real telling knees to the body and some vicious uppercuts, pulling the hair of Rosier and keeping the fight in close. Both fighters landed some heavy blows. There was lots of grappling, and it was clear they had no wrestling or ground techniques. Frazier could have finished Rosier in a choke if he'd known how. Instead, both fighters exhausted, it got a bit scrappy; it briefly looks like a pantomime until Frazier ran out of gas, all spent. This allowed Rosier to finish the fight with some hard punching and elbows crushing down on Frazier. He went to the ground in a heap. Kevin Rosier smelled victory and went in for the kill, landing some almighty crushing blows and foot stamps down to the head. Frazier's corner threw in the towel. Wow, five minutes of hell; the crowd were loving it, the bloodthirsty bastards.

Back to the other half of the contest. The lightest fighter on the card, Royce Gracie, was led out in a chain of family and trainers, linked in one unifying conga procession as he made his way to the centre stage. All the years of work from Carlos and Helio culminated in this one defining moment. In the other corner was Art Jimmerson, a professional boxer weighing in at slightly more than Royce. Unusually wearing only one glove on his left hand, Jimmerson's game was speed and rapid punching skills honed through years of sparring fellow fighters in the gym and working on fast combinations on the bag.

But Royce wasn't using that script. After a cautious start and a lot of sizing up, Royce threw out the opening gambit of a leg kick to distract his opponent. He seized his moment to shoot in, wrapping his opponent's legs and taking the prime fighter to the ground where the game plan began. Jimmerson was on his back – wearing only one glove hindered him. It was only a matter of seconds before he tapped out. The crowd was disappointed; they wanted to see a fight. There was no fight per se, not a single punch had been thrown; for all his years of experience, the boxer was nullified and despatched with consummate ease.

The last quarter-final fight pitted Ken Shamrock, a 220-pound mean-looking shootfighter from the tough Japanese circuit, against Patrick Smith, a tae kwon do expert from Colorado. Both fighters looked in incredible shape and could adapt to a ground fight. It looked like a mouth-watering prospect. They both went to the ground but looked comfortable. Ken Shamrock got a foot lock on and after a momentary struggle, Pat Smith was forced to tap out. Smith losing was a bit humiliating for him. With so much ego and adrenalin pumping he had more to give and wanted to continue the fight, but for him, the fight was over. This set up a semi-final against Royce.

Back to the other semi. Kevin Rosier was fighting Gordeau.

It was a destruction; Rosier still hadn't recovered from the first fight, which had just about sapped the life out of him; the much fitter Gordeau seized this advantage and used it to his best ability, raining in punches and some wicked kicks to the joints. Rosier was felled, and the end came quickly; the towel was thrown in amidst the barrage of blows. Gordeau looked the real deal.

Ken Shamrock stared Royce down in the next semi, but Royce looked focused. This looked like another great matchup with Shamrock already displaying his prowess on the ground; it could be a genuine test for the Gracie fighter. After the usual stamp down from Royce, they were straight onto the floor. They got up to their feet and back down again, manoeuvring for control. Looking in, you could not call it at this stage; they both looked adept. But somehow it was all in Royce's plan; he was never pressured, had it all under control, and eventually Shamrock tapped out, much to his disgust. Another ego has run away; Shamrock wanted to continue fighting to give a fuller account of himself, but like the others, it was too little, too late. Superior Ju-Jitsu triumphed again.

The crowd was not enamoured by it; where was the traditional stand-up fighting? To the victor, the spoils, and to the loser, a humbling lesson that their fighting system was lacking.

The curtain call for Royce was the final. Gerard Gordeau v Royce Gracie. Rorian set the stage with a brief speech and a presentation honouring Helio with a commemorative plaque, recognising his achievements, and giving thanks. Rorian could feasibly have passed as a double for the suave Tom Selleck (Magnum) in his prime. Some of the crowd were booing; they didn't give a damn about history or protocol. They came to see blood. Despite some reticence from the impatient crowd, though, it was a nice touch. The Gracie family in unison were all behind Royce, Rickson behind him in the human train massaging his shoulders on the way to the centre stage.

Now the only ones left in the ring aside from the referee were the two prizefighters. And what a prize, $50,000 up for grabs, but it was clear that what was more important than money, or the title of UFC champion, was the honour of the family. The Gracies were up against yet another karate champion; would it be the same old story? Stalking around in the ring, out came the inevitable foot stamp and shoot from Royce. Down and then up again, Royce clinched in, throwing some headbutts where he could, Gordeau trying to make it difficult, but they went down once more.

The petulant crowd was booing because they understood nothing about this style or the technique involved; no one did apart from the Gracies. They wanted to see a stand-up fight, not grown men cuddling on the floor, but the fight had been killed. Gerard already had a bad reputation as a brawler and scrapper, so it was no surprise when he gave Royce a little bite so when, a minute or two later, Royce got him in a hold and Gordeau tapped out, you can see Royce choking him out longer than normal protocol might allow.

Gracie Ju-Jitsu hit the stratosphere and the fighting world was left with no choice but to acknowledge their triumph. What people saw was fighting, not how they perceived it was done, but how the Gracies did it; they had entered the casino and stacked all the chips in their favour. They knew their effective game plan worked, honed by previous generations, and now so did everybody else.

That first UFC had 86,000 pay-per-view buys and unleashed a juggernaut of a monster in the realms of fighting. The secret was out; Ju-Jitsu reigned supreme. The king was dead; long live the king. MMA was the new birth, and Ju-Jitsu the prodigal son, leading the way forward into a golden era for the Gracies. A tsunami of fighters would emerge out of the shadows who didn't much care for pretence or tradition; for better or worse, nothing in the professional fighting world would ever be the same again.

Chapter 49

Superman

It was now Wednesday. Norbert had spent the last four days on and off devouring anything about fighting he could find – he was obsessed – reading, watching, searching endlessly. He gained a lot of knowledge, but he was still unsure where he was at, in everything.

His mobile phone rang and startled him; he didn't get many calls. Mr William Harrison of Storm Catchers introduced himself and apologised for not getting back sooner.

'I took the other half away for a few days to the West Country,' he said. 'Now, I want you to tell me exactly what's happened, Norbert.'

Norbert repeated the same story for the umpteenth time. He could hear William shifting things around, office noises, and then there was a brief moment of silence.

'Don't worry,' said William. 'I specialise in motor cases. In fact, I've just helped someone in a similar situation to yours to get all their money back.'

'No fu— no way, William.' Norbert held back on the swearing instinctively; he didn't want to give the wrong impression. The sense of relief was palpable. Norbert's fist was clenched.

'I'd be delighted to take this case on, but please just call me Bill,' William said.

Bill asked for all the information to be sent to him, and he went to work like a drill sergeant.

After the call Norbert ran into the garden followed by Rufus. Norbert was turning and twisting until he fell to the floor in a fit of laughter, Rufus licking his face, play-fighting. Norbert lay on his back and hoisted Rufus into the air. 'Yes, you little beauty,' he yelled, Yes.' He rushed inside to call

185

Nikki. 'We're going to be alright, love, things will work out.'

'Bomber, let's not get carried away just yet – we can celebrate when it's over.'

'Baby, we're celebrating tonight – I'm gonna be so rude to you later ...' Norbert, it seemed, had gotten his verve back.

Bill followed the normal protocol, but Erkan predictably did not. Erkan ignored all the letters Storm Catchers sent out, basically dragging his heels, denying any responsibility through the whole legal process. Bill now had him firmly in his sights and instigated a court case after, as he put it, all the Ts had been crossed and the Is dotted. When the hearing came round, Erkan didn't show and judgement was quickly awarded to Norbert. There was now just the small matter of getting some money back for Norbert.

Cue for a crack team of High Court enforcement officers, very much like the ones seen on TV reality documentaries.

'It's amazing what the threat of seizure of goods does to focus the mind,' Bill said. 'The thing is, Norbert, it's a family-owned business and either his brothers are in on it or, as I suspect, when they discover they're about to be closed down ...'

'They would be well pissed. I bet his dad is turning in his grave,' said Norbert.

'Exactly, wouldn't you know it? Erkan soon found all the money that he supposedly never had. So you can expect your first instalment tomorrow. The rest will follow in a few days.'

'I knew you was going to come good Bill, I just knew.'

'To listen to you now after that first voicemail you left me, the difference is telling – you're like a new man. You're a good guy, Norbert, and you and Nikki deserve a break. Glad to have been of assistance. Ah, sorry, old chap, call on the other line ...'

Norbert had a card made depicting Superman with the name *Bill* emblazoned across the superhero's chest. It winged its way to the offices of Storm Catchers. William loved it.

Chapter 50

Sticks and stones may break my bones

B ack to normality, which meant back to work. Norbert was able to buy a brand-new taxi. First trip he made was to the Southwark pit stop to see old boy George. George, to be fair, apologised for missing the previous damage, and glad to be rid of the whole tawdry business, he gave his finder's fee back. Now it was Norbert's turn to trouser the £200 wedge.

Norbert's class was ticking along at a slow canter, but he needed fresh blood to inject a bit of life, to stop it all from stagnating. He got proactive and ran some ads on two fronts. One in the local supermarket after convincing the seriously miserable customer service lady that his class was a non-profit organisation; considering renting the hall and the lack of numbers, he was on safe ground there. She relented and gave him a spot on the coveted noticeboard. The other went in the local paper over the Christmas period.

It read something along the lines of: 'Self-defence, traditional wing chun, for beginners and improvers of any systems (that means you MMA bastards)'. He swallowed that last thought and left his number to call with the time and location of the class. The net had been cast far and wide. He paid around £100 for it to run for two weeks. It seemed the best way forward.

A week later. 'Not one fucking enquiry, Nikki, not one,' he said.

'Give it time, darling,', she said.

'I mean, God knows what the footfall is walking in and out of Tesco's, and what about all the people who've eaten and drunk too much? *Kung Fu Panda* and *Karate Kid* were showing on Christmas telly. If that doesn't get the juices flowing, nothing will.'

Nikki laughed, 'If it's meant to be, it will be, don't stress.' She rubbed Norbert's shoulders, just where he liked it.

His resolve was severely tested, but he never wavered. Online, too, he was getting into more and more spats with the keyboard warriors and however much he tried to tip the balance of power back in favour of good old wing chun by trying to get across his point of relevance, the sense of knocking was relentless. All traditional martial arts were now fair game. Karate, Ju-Jitsu (not the Brazilian type, of course), aikido, judo, hapkido, capoeira, krav maga, tai chi, and Uncle Tom Cobbley and all. Whether they were standalone systems, spin-offs, or hybrids, if they had any connection with the past, they were dismissed as second rate.

Especially kung fu. It was the season to expose fake masters to ridicule. The likes of Shaolin monk, and he was one of the better examples. At first glance, things looked promising; there he was, standing proud in the ring in his silky robes, defying his opponents. Years of training and study passed down from older, wiser generations. Absorbing punches using his mental strength, qi energy, blows that would fell people twice his size. Until wham, someone knocked the stupid showboating bastard out cold.

To be fair, on the evidence he was seeing out there in cyberland, the naysayers had every right to expose kung fu as out of touch – endless clips of so-called masters of TMAs getting their asses handed to them by the marauding honey badgers, who certainly didn't give a fuck about history or protocol. Louder and more vocal came forth the criticism, UFC Joe Rogan, calling it straight on the so-called bullshido (bullshit, fake, no-touch) martial arts.

Norbert closed his laptop; he'd had it a little over three years, and still used the protective packaging cloth that covered the keyboard; he enjoyed the silent close. His mind was rarely quiet. It had to be out there, the Bermuda Triangle of martial arts. A vacuum between the bullshido and the UFC fighters, a place where real kung fu of pure technique existed. Norbert's problem was there was only one person who knew about applying it, being true to himself: Digor.

Would he have to wait for the rest of the world to catch up? He wasn't saying his teacher was best, hell no. He was just hoping for something to prove him right, hoping it would be wing chun.

Norbert did a lot of hoping and sometimes had to concede that there are only two hopes; *Bob* was sadly dead, but *no fucking* was very much alive in his little world.

Chapter 51

Camera, lights, action

Out of the blue, Norbert got a call on his mobile. 'Hi, I've seen your ads and all, wanted to know if I can come down and have a look at the class, do some sparring.'

'Yes, of course,' he replied. *Blimey, the ads actually worked.* 'What's your name?'

'Great, I'll see you Monday, looking forward to it,' he said, and the phone cut dead. Private number, call details withheld. How very fucking weird. Scared the bejesus out of him, and he bottled it all up inside. Monday's lesson rolled around and he was struggling to keep his concentration, kept looking over his shoulder expecting someone to walk in. By the end of the session, he was a near wreck. The other guys, a sum total of two, possibly sensed the apprehension but said nothing. He'd been expecting the worse, but nothing; no one came, and he returned to normal, whatever that meant.

Looking at his nails, he made a mental note, *I must cut them sometime this week, the pinkies and hooves.* Sizing them back put a little spring in one's step; it felt lighter and he could bound around like a little Bambi. But he never did. The thought just ran away.

At Norbert's class the following week he was talking to Anthony. He set up the laptop to play some music, and it filled the small hall with noise and nullified the quietness of the gathering. 'Just me and you tonight, mate. Had a text from the other two guys that they can't make it.' They came or not as a pair.

Then out of the corner of his eyes, he saw two guys walk in.

'How d'ya feel about a bit of a spar then, fella?' The one talking was walking towards him in a confrontational manner, arms splayed wide.

Norbert was stunned, no time for anything, fight or flight. Then the words came tripping out of his mouth before taking any time to think about a measured response. 'Go for it,' Norbert said. Adrenalin was coursing through him like a surging electric current; all the training in the world and he was way off the radar with this, on automatic pilot mode. He didn't know them, didn't recognise them, and one of them was closing towards Norbert. He was of a similar size, six foot tallish, perhaps more muscular. Yes, definitely more muscular. Even under a grey hoodie, Norbert noticed his physique. *Shit, he's big, powerful looking.* Norbert stepped up to the plate, and with one defiant gesture he called it on. 'He's not involved,' he said, pointing at a bewildered Anthony. *If I can't save myself, I might as well save Anthony.*

'Neither is he,' the motherfucker said, pointing at his comrade who had a fucking phone on a stick, ready to film the ensuing action.

'All ready, Russell, mate,' the accomplice said.

They met, and when the distance was close enough, Norbert threw out a kick that missed. *Great fucking start.* Russell came in and in the blink of an eye ducked under Norbert's arms. Pouncing forwards he grabbed Norbert's waist, trapping Norbert's left arm. Russell's arms were wrapped around Norbert who missed the hit. *This bastard fights, surprise, surprise, Brazilian Ju-Jitsu, are we destined for the floor?* Crouching in and Russell picked Norbert up, turning him elevated like a kettlebell swung in the air. Norbert instinctively tried to grab hold of Russell's head with his left arm, but his balance was gone. He was tipped over the brute's right shoulder in a fireman's carry. Norbert was momentarily lying horizontally in his clutches; he was then tipped up with all the ease in the world and dumped down on his back.

'Nice move, Russell,' phone stick man said.

Norbert crashed to the floor. It didn't hurt like he thought it might; he was still alive and fighting – and he still had the bastard's head. He tried to sit up, but he was getting nowhere. Russell's knees were straddled wide on the floor for support. Norbert couldn't budge him, and he was bloody trying.

Norbert's legs were flailing in the air, and he desperately tried locking up Russell's right arm with them, but Norbert was cradled like a baby in a mother's arms. They rocked about but Norbert couldn't hold him tight that way for much longer; his strength was sapping fast. Russell freed one of his arms and got Norbert in a side mount, wrapping his left arm around Norbert's head. Norbert tried hitting him back with his right but couldn't get any purchase. Norbert was still on his back, which was hurting. Now Russell was free and in a dominant position.

Maybe I'll bite the bastard on his shoulder. But Norbert did not.

Russell was all over him like a fucking rash, side controlling him with his weight dispersed all over Norbert, pinning him down. Legs stabilising his frame, he may as well have been sitting in his favourite armchair, TV remote control in one hand and a beer in the other. Norbert was powerless. He was rolled onto his side like a helpless turtle, expecting the punches to come raining in, but they never came. Norbert's legs rocked side to side, trying to unlock himself, to wriggle free, but Russell's structure was super tight, airtight, impossible to wrestle out of.

Norbert found his head next to Russell's, locked tight like prop scrums. He managed to trap one of Russell's arms in his legs. It lent him a fraction of a second to nowhere. Norbert turned away but Russell was all over him; he had Norbert's right arm and pulled himself in, straddling Norbert. Norbert was briefly on all fours as Russell, lightning quick, switched from one side to the other, rolling across Norbert's back. Using his chest and superior body strength to keep him still and pinned down, he simply got Norbert in a rear-naked choke and put him to the sword.

Norbert tapped out, and Russell released him in a gentlemanly manner. Norbert was slaughtered, and his fighting world fell apart at the seams.

'No hard feelings, mukka,' Russell said.

Mukka, fucker.

As quickly as these guys had appeared, they were gone.

And yet they were not smiling, laughing, or congratulating each other. It was very businesslike, chalking up another fighting win, like missionaries on a quest to settle matters using their challenges to snuff out any competition or quieten down any loudmouth cyber twat that couldn't see the wood through the trees. Job done, next?

Norbert sat on the floor, back against the wall, trying to fully understand what the hell just happened. Completely outfought, outmanoeuvred, outwitted. He thought it was annihilation.

Young Anthony spoke. 'You cut his face – he had a lightning-bolt of blood running down his neck, did you see it?'

'No, how the hell did that happen?' Then it dawned on Norbert: he hadn't cut his nails. 'How long did that last?' he asked.

'Two minutes,' Anthony said.

'Fuck, it felt much longer.'

'I thought you did well – you could tell he didn't want to stand up and fight.'

'Yeah, but seriously, mate, I had no answer for the floor fight. Something's not right. That shouldn't have happened. I fluffed my lines. I'm not sure I can continue with things the way they are. It could have been a lot worse. Perhaps he's done me a big favour.'

The realisation that what Norbert thought he had was not enough rained down like a ton of bricks. Norbert had suffered the embarrassment of getting beat up before, but this felt different. An epiphany. All those years, was it all a waste? Soon he would be YouTube famous, and he cringed at the thought. Just another embarrassing display confirming the TMAs as bullshido, ineffective against the all-conquering honey badgers. It seemed appropriate to call time on his class.

Chapter 52

Churches and mosques

Or, for the sake of equality or not wanting to upset anyone in this day and age, mosques and churches. But of course, someone will be upset, impossible to avoid, particularly with those religious types who are so easily offended. The only thing religions seem to agree on is that they can't agree on anything. Having different gods does that; it changes one's perspective. And even when they have the same god, the detail becomes the difference and religious beliefs part company. Was Jesus the Son of God or the messenger of God? The answer decides what camp one belongs to – two different camps, two different books, two different paths, one positively thriving while the other fights for survival.

Larry Blake chose Islam and held his class next to the local mosque. Norbert was always going to be brushing shoulders with Muslims and overlapping into their lives somewhat. One time, on his way to Digor's for a private lesson and after driving around the tiny roads looking for a parking space, he was met by a sea of people, men and boys. Bearded fellows, dressed in their robes, hundreds of them were spilling out from Friday's prayers. It was reminiscent of a foreign land, more Calcutta than Catford, South London. Larry informed him that at Friday prayers there wasn't a spare space in the mosque, everywhere packed out to the rafters, with maybe a thousand people in the main hall and many more spread out in the adjacent buildings. But where were all the women? Norbert naively thought.

On any street in the same towns, be they Catholic, Anglican, Presbyterian, they all painted a rather bleaker picture, attendances in freefall, empty pews. Norbert saw with his own eyes the popularity of Islam. Muslims had more children and a younger demographic; was he witnessing the fastest growing religion? Maybe Britain was on the path to becoming a Muslim state. Norbert sensed his traditional way of life slowly ebbing away. Real life was mirroring the pattern of martial arts, losing ground to the stronger. The squeeze was on.

Norbert's constant restless search for any counterarguments had got him nowhere and now he was living proof. Aside from Nikki and Anthony, he had kept the whole saga to himself; he wasn't ready to face the truth with Digor or Cole until the time felt right. He wasn't in denial; he could see the evidence staring him down. Was it time to embrace MMA, accept that they had bludgeoned their way to the top by brave heart and hardened tight game plans? Even if it didn't look pretty, it worked? Nothing hidden, no secrets, brutal fighters taking in all the best bits of martial arts and spitting out anything ineffective, until what was left didn't conform to or resemble anything close to a specific traditional style.

The UFC and MMA juggernaut thundered out across the globe, seeking new countries, bringing new territories into its fold, spawning new honey badgers ready to continue their dominance at the expense of outdated systems and ill-equipped traditional fighters. TMA's place was becoming narrower. Many were faced with a stark choice: accept their limitations and carry on, or kid themselves all was well. Kung fu in China, Tae kwon do in Korea, Krav Maga in Israel, Japan cradling judo and karate, which was still the most popular martial art in the world. All were looking over their shoulder at Brazil, who borrowed Ju-Jitsu from Japan as a small sparrow and then returned a giant hungry fucking cuckoo.

Those that have any degree of success like Muay Thai, Chinese boxing, and their kin had to accept the truth that without adapting to include groundwork, they are just as ineffective.

Norbert considered the bigger picture, particularly what happened to Conor McGregor, once unbeatable as UFC feather-weight and lightweight champion. McGregor exploded onto the scene. His pay-per-view set box office records. With his Irish roots, cheeky chappie persona, and fiercely loyal fan base he rode the wave. Most of his wins throughout his MMA career came by knockout. And that tells you something right there because when he faced the formidable Russian fighter and master grappler Khabib Nurmagomedov, McGregor was taken down and out.

Khabib, chiselled out of granite, with cauliflower ears that would make a rugby prop proud, fighting with a hard backbone of sambo, judo, and wrestling, was now considered the new boss of the ring. By December 2018 he had chalked up twenty-seven victories with no losses.

He was Muslim too. *Maybe the best fighters are,* Norbert thought, *maybe it's the last ingredient in the cake.* Khabib, Muhammad Ali, Tyson, and Digor were all Muslims. Now Norbert was getting paranoid, like the central figure in Edvard Munch's composition *The Scream*.

In the here and now, Norbert knew most TMAs were no match for MMA; the sheer simplicity of taking a fight to the ground rendered most of them utterly useless. Equally, the honey badgers dismissed those styles that have a bias only to groundwork; you have to have a strong stand-up top game as well. To succeed, your game plan had to have three levels – top, middle, and bottom. Top, where you stand up and fight like a kickboxer, looking for head or neck areas. Middle ground where you are close, looking to strike but covering your vital middle organs. Bottom is the floor, the realms of submission, chokes and holds. All levels need to be covered in your fighting that can not only survive but flow seamlessly from one to the other; this is the reality of MMA.

Against this full arsenal, TMAs as entire systems looked weak or at worse bloody dangerous in the big scheme of things. It wasn't just kids who could be convinced they can fight because they had a nice new coloured belt; many adults lived in a superficial notion, a false sense of security from their blinkered fighting experience. In reality, the truth will out. It did with Norbert.

What was left was no fake, no trickery, no smoke or

mirrors, just real fighting. Guys and girls that could scrap anyway you wanted, disregarding tradition; there was a purity about that. And while Norbert and the TMAs scratched their heads wondering why they were losing ground to the honey badgers, the seismic shift will continue until there are none left to slay. Norbert kept half an eye on the internet; he knew it was only a matter of time before his underperforming exploits would be aired.

Norbert saw it coming. Churches and mosques. He got it and was consumed by it. But what was he going to do about it?

Chapter 53

Counting sheep, not quite

For someone with a crushed ego who had spent far too much of his time pissing in the wind with his martial arts training, the answer became obvious. Norbert would have to grow a beard and convert. Considering how his whiskers got wispy when left unshaven, unwilling to resemble anything close to a manly beard, that alone was a big ask.

Back home in Kent, a bit of searching around, and lo and behold, Norbert uncovered a Carlson Gracie fighting school, a five-minute drive away, if that. Norbert phoned and explained the situation. Lowrie, the instructor, agreed on a flat pay-as-you-go fee, £10, which seemed reasonable. He also gave the impression that he couldn't care less about Norbert's previous experiences. When the following Tuesday came around, Norbert kissed his ever-understanding Nikki and with a new gi tucked in his bag, made his way to his first class.

The facility was located in the corner of yet another faceless industrial centre. The gym was filled with bandana-wearing guys heaving and clunking heavy metal weights, and there were powder proteins of every imaginable flavour on the shelves to keep them stoked. An uninterested receptionist pointed Norbert towards the metal staircase in the corner. It led to a large open floor, where it was impossible not to notice the proud banner hung in the centre, showing two mean savage-looking dogs, complete with blood dripping from their ferocious mouths. It set an eclectic tone of intimidation and fight; this most definitely was not a tea and biscuits club. Norbert officially met Lowrie and was pleasantly surprised. First impressions were that he was softly spoken, assured, and purposeful. Norbert filled in a disclaimer form without reading it and he was good to go.

He jogged around the side; there were so many people crowded in there and he marvelled at the size of them. *Looks like a bloody rugby squad.* Soon they were all doing breakfalls, twisting and turning up and down the floor. It was very warm. Lowrie showed a couple of moves on the floor; he made it look simple. Norbert partnered up and gave it a go. Like the game Twister, a couple of wrong positions and he had tied himself up in knots. A couple of tweaks here and there and he got the gist. If he could get a good basic groundwork level in three years, then that should complement his wing chun. That was the initial plan. It was all going okay, and bearing in mind his previous experiences, he was kind of expecting the inevitable spanner in the works.

They were soon on to the grappling; the fun had begun, and just as before, this class delivered the prerequisite shock to the system. Most of these guys were bigger, stronger, and younger. First up was a spotty teenager, possibly still at school, fat and heavy. He just lay on Norbert who found it difficult to move him, expending a lot of energy just to stop himself from being crushed. All Norbert could do was try to survive, not tap out. Norbert's belt had loosened itself on account of not being tied properly. What was left holding his top together was pulled away like a shoelace. Norbert's now flailing lapels were used as a method of crossing and choking him around the neck; as he felt the rush of blood and dizziness overcome all he could do was tap out, *again.*

'Fucking hell, is that allowed?' asked Norbert. Fat boy nodded like the Churchill dog. The timer buzzer sounded and everyone changed partners. He barely had time to catch a breath and he was staring at a face he just about recognised – a severe skinhead and a scar nearly threw him off the scent.

'I don't fucking believe it, Kenny Brown.' Norbert instinctively offered his hand while checking the colour of Kenny's belt – white with no stripes, *Thank goodness.*

'Norbert, this is unreal, I thought it was you.' Kenny fist-pumped.

'Are you still friends with Sanders?' asked Norbert. Even saying that name stuck in his throat.

'Be a bit difficult, he's six feet under, didn't you hear? Killed about two years ago, motorbike accident.'

'No shit, that must have been difficult.'

'Not really, Norbert. I was only friends with him because I was scared of him, scared he might do to me what he did for you and all those others. He was a bad apple.'

Norbert barely had time to get his head around the revelations.

'Let's do this,' Kenny said.

In an instant they were thrashing around on the floor. Norbert fended off the eager attacks and Kenny's attempt to arm-bar him into submission. All of a sudden, for some not so strange reason he found a deep well of energy reserve. And then Norbert found an old judo move to pin Kenny down, who was utterly pissed at being unable to break free. Kenny was wailing like a banshee. Norbert was enjoying this. Other regulars shouted out countermoves for Kenny, but it did no good. Norbert was determined to hang on, as a matter of life and death; he couldn't lose to Kenny, not now, not ever. Norbert found some super-human strength in amongst all the hostility and he scraped over the line, undefeated; it felt like a massive victory.

Norbert was panting hard like a dog. The next rounds were a blur, and the coloured belts tapped him out at will until he was exhausted and barely able to raise his arms. After it finished, everyone shook each other's hands, bowing, with plenty of *ousses* thrown in for good measure. Norbert thanked Lowrie, swerved Kenny, and left for home. He showered and kissed the girls goodnight, but when he finally lay down, although completely knackered, it took him an age to sleep. He couldn't count sheep. Sanders and too many damn honey badgers were dancing about in the moonlight of his mind.

Chapter 54

Spilling the beans

For a few days Norbert was sore and aching all over. At the weekend Nikki, he and the girls had a day out planned. They took a picnic to the grounds of Leeds Castle in Kent. When he finally got the chance he slumped on the grass, looking around at Nikki and the girls playing, without saying a word. It was a beautiful reminder of the important things; nothing came close to this.

It had been weeks since he'd spoken to Digor, who didn't know half of what Norbert had been up to. Norbert was too embarrassed to tell him, plus there was a risk that Digor might see it as disregard for his methods; it was not out of the realms of possibility to imagine him being annoyed at Norbert and his disbelieving. Norbert couldn't bear to spoil their friendship.

Norbert was driving back to London for work on Monday; he knew the motorway and the traffic so well, he could do the journey blindfolded; there was an hour and a half to kill. Somewhat lifted by his trials at the Ju-Jitsu class the previous week, he felt ready to speak about everything that had happened – his beating at the hands of the honey badgers. He used his hands-free to call Cole Williams, his senior and Digor's longest time-served student. He filled Cole in on his latest exploits.

'It's why, after my little spat, I've decided to learn some groundwork,' said Norbert.

'Are you mad?' Cole asked.

'Obviously.'

'Your bones won't thank you for it. You're not young anymore, you're nearly fifty, right?'

'Yeah, and I feel it.' Norbert changed tack. 'You know on

my first night of BJJ, I'm fighting this lad, who it turns out I knew from back in the day, and they're all shouting at him. Telling him, use your hips to lever, do this, do that, all coaching from the sidelines like fucking cornermen. I struggled to get my head around that. You wouldn't get a beginner come into Digor's class and then have any of us shouting out countermoves to beat them.'

'They have no manners.'

'And as for the blue belts, they're on a tear, out to prove themselves – they have no control. One lad, I grabbed his collar with both hands and he lifts me up and slams me flat down on my back.'

'Ouch, could have damaged your spine.'

'Tell me about it, probably explains why there's always some unfortunate soul sitting out the class with an injury.'

'Look, do you think they could do that to Digor?' asked Cole.

'No, I don't. Speaking of Digor, please don't mention this to him.'

'Lucky for you he doesn't watch much YouTube, but if you're out there getting famous, he's probably going to find out sooner or later.'

'Famously beat up, and then disowned by Digor, *woop woop*. Anyway, that's why I always leave the class with mixed feelings. I mean, the instructor and top guys are good, humble even. But you don't start a fight with a fist pump, then search for a grip. Normally one person is trying to bust you up and you have to figure it out from that standpoint.'

'Exactly. Stop trying to solve the world's problems. Get back to the class. Tell Digor, work on the moves that had you beat, get stronger.'

'It's so difficult, with work and all.'

'You have to make time. Get back on board with your private lessons with Digor.'

'Look, I will, soon, I promise. For now, I need some groundwork. My wing chun means nothing in there, nobody is remotely interested. The class is so tight and insular.'

'Some people believed the world was flat. Look, all I'm

saying is that the grass isn't always greener. I know where you're coming from though, most of those guys can't see past their own brilliance. I came across a post on Facebook. I'll send it to you, it'll give you something to smile about.'

'Cheers, Cole, I could do with a laugh right now. You know us mere mortals are not like you and Digor.'

They said their goodbyes. Once back to London, Norbert hit the orange glow taxi meter light and cracked on with work. At the end of the week, Norbert checked his inbox and, sure enough, Cole had sent him the post. A complete indispensable how-to-beat-every-style-of-fighter guide, it ranked right up there with the advice on how to fend off a shark attack (bump them on the nose or shout at them; apparently, they don't like either)! Here it is:

1. How to beat Ninjutsu: start a web search for the console and title you're being attacked on. Look up the cheat code for invincibility. You're now invulnerable against the only kind of ninja that exists.
2. Bodybuilders: bodybuilders are only prepared for a maximum effort of five to fifteen seconds. Circle them and duck in between the area their arms can't touch their sides with until they have a heart attack.
3. Systema: systema was specially designed to defeat complete idiots. If you can tie your shoelaces, you're too smart for it to affect you at all.
4. Japanese Ju-Jitsu: JJJ is BJJ's embarrassing uncle who wears a kilt to every party and is always full of shit. In reality, a JJJ black belt is a half-stripe BJJ white belt. Grab their dress, slam their ass and welcome them to the twenty-first century.
5. Sambo: sambo is what happens when judo gets roid rage. They're a weaponised group of gym spazzes. Sit back, let them screw up a move, and end their whole career.
6. Tae kwon do: tae kwon do is a lot like Santa Claus. You learn it young and ditch it by twelve years old. Grown-ups don't do it so there's no one to beat.

7. Kendo: ask them what their favourite anime is and what they are going to Comicon as. You're now their only friend. Slowly walk away while they nerd out.

8. Sumo: square up with them. Look deeply into their eyes. Tell them chicken nuggets are half price. Watch a 400-pound man sprint away.

9. Capoeira: capoeira is just people who aren't good enough at dancing or martial arts to do either. Tell them that and while they start their stupid dance, walk away and let that destroy their self-worth.

10. Muay Thai: is useless if they can't kick or punch you. So all you have to do is grab a kick, drag them down and humiliate them with white-belt-level Ju-Jitsu.

11. MMA: MMA is abnormally vulnerable to six to twelve elbows and absolutely will not fight anyone they suspect is on steroids.

12. Kung fu: double-check the date and your location. If it's not 3000 BC and you're not on a TV set you're fine. Those are the only places it's ever worked.

13. Krav maga: their entire martial art consists of either a dick kick or an eye poke. So if you can survive a five-year-old attacker then you'll be fine.

14. Boxing: just clinch up with them. You're now free to do absolutely anything you want while they wait for a referee to separate it.

15. Wrestling: let them put you on your back, they will think they've won. Use any basic submission at all. Enjoy the look of shock and horror they make.

16. Tai chi: reach into your pocket and take out your phone. Call the nearest old folks' home. Tell them your grandma is off her meds and hallucinating in the park. Wait for men with sedatives.

17. Aikido: do anything you want to them. Slap their face, pinch their nose, and give them a wet willy. They don't know how to fight at all.

18. Karate: laugh at them and say things like wax on, wax off, hi yah and haduken until they get mad and charge you. Sweep the leg, take their back, and give them a nap.

19. Judo: they talk a big game about hitting you with the world but have no answer for a basic guard pull.
20. Lol. Ju-Jitsu: Make sure you're on the streets; Ju-Jitsu doesn't work there.

Norbert was cracking up; that was the impression he got, that if you had Brazilian Ju-Jitsu, well that was all that mattered. He wasn't sure who the joker was, but a quick look on the associated website introduction revealed this:

'Grappling Mastery effectively combines the best techniques of Brazilian Ju-Jitsu with Greco-Roman wrestling, judo, sambo, and other submission styles such as catch wrestling. To complement our superior grappling, we also teach Bang Muay Thai kick-boxing! It is truly a complete and effective grappling style that will work on the street as well as in tournaments. Grappling Mastery is home to multiple Pan-American, State, and Regional Champions, as well as many other high-level respected competitions! All classes are taught by Gracie Barra Brazilian Ju-Jitsu, second-degree black belt and official Bang Muay Thai coaches.'

There it was, a complete offering, the whole shebang. All the pieces in the jigsaw. Norbert thought about this. *Congratulations to them. Seriously, after what I have been through, if I was starting today in this climate of ground and pound, this would be what I would look for. It would also help if I lived in Florida, where they're based.*

Game set and match.

Chapter 55

Helicopter man

We all seem to want more for less these days, but is it a race to the bottom? There seems to be no end of ride-hailing apps queueing up to muscle in on the taxi trade and offer people cheaper rides. The colossus of Uber, backed by voracious corporations, pushed by soulless politicians who cannot see the long game. But consider this: would you like a disruptor technology to come in backed by a powerful lobbyist machine and almost overnight tear apart your livelihood without you being able to do a single thing about it? Well, by the looks of things, it could come to you perhaps sooner than you imagine.

Cameron and George how-many-jobs Gideon Oliver Osborne were not thinking about the consequences of flooding the streets with thousands more vehicles when they laid down the red carpet for Uber. The number of private hire drivers in London has exploded; the roads have never been more congested; the arteries blocked. Norbert and his ilk are fighting to survive. The population of London can swell to over ten million people on any given day, so it is quite something to pick up someone at random more than once.

The first time the smart casual suited smiling man got in Norbert's taxi was just a normal day of jostling and jousting with the London traffic. Most passengers are stressed and late. He was not. As he sat in the back, he noticed a helicopter above their heads as they crawled along past Trafalgar Square; it was going somewhere it shouldn't.

'Whoever is flying that could get a hefty fine,' he said.

Curious, Norbert asked the obvious. 'Why?'

'I fly helicopters, and I'll tell you for nothing you are meant to strictly adhere to the river when in town, just in case of any emergencies.'

Impressed, Norbert continued the chat; it turned out this slight man of African heritage had a helluva knack for talking and inspiring others as a motivational speaker. He travelled the world and would often use a helicopter. They small-talked some more and the time soon came when Norbert set him down. After scribbling a receipt out, Norbert said, 'I can't let you go without asking for some pearls of wisdom. Come on, tell me how I can improve my life.'

'Well, I can tell you, the sage says, but you won't do it,' he replied with a mischievous grin.

'Go for it,' Norbert tempted.

'You ready?'

'Never been readier,' Norbert said.

'Okay,' he said, 'three little things to make you happier. One, don't watch the news, two, don't read the papers, and three, get rid of your mobile.'

Then he was gone, laughing to himself disappearing through the streets, just another pedestrian in this crowded part of town. Norbert cracked up; it had made his day really, and when he found five minutes back home later, he YouTubed him. There he was in an auditorium, lights on him on stage, this irrepressible bundle of energy holding the paying audience in the palm of his hand, with his slightly madcap witticisms. Norbert shared these nuggets of wisdom with anyone who would listen over the next few days.

Fast forward at least a couple of years. If you are in front with your little orange taxi light on and a bus stops without indicating, you can find yourself temporarily stuck. What you don't want to see is another cab overtake you (they know your light is on, cabbies notice these things), get in front and stop to pick up a passenger that would and should have been yours. There was nothing like it to set Norbert's pulse racing, but when it happened this time, the passenger didn't get in the taxi in front; instead, he walked towards Norbert. The cabby in front had done the decent thing and explained that Norbert was next. *Well done, that man.*

Imagine Norbert's surprise when a face appeared at the passenger window and he recognised him instantly, although he'd long forgotten his name. They set off for some swanky restaurant in Knightsbridge.

'I remember you,' Norbert said, 'you're the helicopter man.'

'How the hell do you know that I fly helicopters?' he asked.

Norbert reminded him of their past conversation and his keys to making Norbert's life happier.

'Well, what are the chances,' he said. 'Did you do it?'

'Yes,' Norbert proudly answered, explaining further how he was putting his life back in order, getting off the hamster wheel, less stress, and so on. Helicopter man couldn't have been more pleased; he was laughing and excited, so happy to have shared the answers to a better quality of being.

A remarkable, fascinating man. Norbert listened intently and soaked up more of his wise thoughts. He had figured out that not having a pillow made for much better sleep; apparently it took him eight days of hell, tossing and turning before he discovered the Nirvana of sleeps like a baby. Only fate would decide if their paths would cross again. It dawned on Norbert that if you are extremely lucky, you might meet maybe a handful of extraordinary people in your life that have something so unique and compelling, it really can change your world or at the least how you look at things.

Digor and the motivational helicopter man had a lot in common. It was the absolute positivity they exuded; Norbert swore it rubs off on him. What these two also shared was how much they laughed – happy, shiny people as REM sang; Norbert strongly suggests listening and surrounding yourself with people like this if you get the chance. If you find yourself a little lost, become a sheep and follow with no shame.

Chapter 56

Quincy

Being butter-fingered scared Norbert. Sometimes he had awful flashes that he might be at the early onset of Parkinson's. His brother-in-law had made an amazing large porcelain bowl-like ornament; he was an art teacher and Norbert could always expect the unexpected as a present from him. A man and a lady were perched on the edge, their hands clasped together on their laps in deep thought, a ladder descending into the depths, and balls of varying sizes all about its heavy self. It was meant to signify a wishing well of sorts, to inspire your dreams. The dark blue and grey exterior shared colour with magnificent leafy bronze flames. It made for a lovely Christmas gift one year.

And there it stood majestically on the side cabinet until Norbert fluked a pen into it that had to be retrieved. He managed to decapitate one of the figures and as he delved inside to find not only the pen but now the severed head, he snapped the frigging ladder, which broke in three places. A more brittle piece you could not imagine, and he was handling it with all the finesse of a bull in a china shop. He had to gather all the pieces on the kitchen counter, which now resembled a coroner's lab; Norbert's day had become unexpectedly busier. With the help of some strong super glue, some elastic bands, and some amazing balancing skills, he made good the broken pieces. Before Nikki returned home, it was back in its rightful place. He kept a respectful distance from the thing in the future and no one suspected anything.

What started with Norbert discovering the Gracie story as a truly momentous find years later revealed some cracks beneath the surface too. Norbert was doing his usual delving;

he could have been an investigative journalist. He read how some suggested a Gracie conspiracy, manipulated fights, stacking the chips in their favour before rolling the dice and moving the goalposts when it suited them. Maybe, he thought. What was not up for debate though was how they all to a man put themselves on the line. The person who wrote said article may not have liked what they were about, but he could not deny what they did. They were so successful in the early UFC because basically, no one knew how to outsmart their cunning.

Norbert was no fool; he knew every dog has its day, and now the Gracie secret was out, the clock would tick down; it was only a matter of time before the rest caught up and the tide turned.

The family had suffered losses over the years, but because they were few, they could be swept under the carpet, kept away from the radar. The thing is, the family always bounced back with someone else ready to step in and avenge a loss, or a quick rematch to settle the score. They were also shrewd enough to understand the need to evolve their game and continually improve, striving for better; restoring and keeping the family's honour was everything.

So it must have been a bloody nightmare when these two thorns came along: Wallid Ismail began training under his master, the late Carlson Gracie, who took quite a shine to him. Gracie had allowed Ismail to train with his camp, even though Ismail had no money to afford the teaching. Wallid competed in Ju-Jitsu tournaments, becoming champion several times, and defeated four members of the famous Gracie family in competition. Four!

Not to be outdone, came the equally impressive Kazushi Sakuraba, a colourful character who forged his reputation in MMA. He wore masks during his entrance to remind everyone of his pro wrestling ancestry. When he defeated Royler Gracie at the time it was considered near impossible. How he despatched him was more powerful than the victory – the implausibility of Royler powerless on his back beckoning Sakuraba to fight on the floor looked ridiculous. Sakuraba returned the offer by smashing Royler's legs with some vicious mule kicks. You could hear his bone whip-cracking from ringside – the irony of a Gracie looking so out of his comfort zone. The tide turned.

When Sakuraba followed this up with a victory against Royce, he was given the nickname 'Gracie Hunter'. Later he added Renzo and Ryan Gracie, so I think he can join the illustrious party of Gracie beaters.

Could it get more ignominious for any of the Gracie fighters? Yes, if someone trapped them into a stand-up fight. When the only way was to the floor, opponents knew their hand and adapted quickly, neutralising takedowns or, as with five times world strongman champion Mariusz Pudzianowski, flat-out destroying his fight against Rolles Gracie with one gigantic punch before any ground fight could happen.

Despite these hiccups, from that monumental first UFC over the next couple of decades, many practitioners, including Norbert, saw no choice but to come good at BJJ in quick time. This was the greatest backhanded compliment.

Chapter 57

Musing for a bruising

We have no idea whether boxing will ever capture the heady heights of the so-called golden generations of heavyweights or the former middleweight kings of the ring. Who would have believed, after the greats of McEnroe, Borg, Connors, and co, we would be spoiled for years to come by Federer, Nadal, and Djokovic? Maybe when their time has passed, tennis will go through a similar barren period. Similarly, we have no inkling whether the TMAs will survive in their current form.

Where once the Gracies exposed other styles, albeit under their conditions, as ineffective, now they must deal with the hard truth that their way is not the all-conquering way. Even honey badgers can meet their match.

It's not hard to notice that fewer kids are kicking a football on the grass these days; most of them have their heads bowed staring into their phone gods, completely oblivious to the world around them. Unless they're on their bikes, in gangs, wheeling into oncoming traffic, running amok on the streets because they can. Meanwhile, the single police Community Support Officer is giving a ticket to a static car on a lonely street. Maybe it's in our nature to choose the path of least resistance or go with the mainstream, just know there are other paths.

We have to thank MMA for filtering out all the background noise of martial arts. It has done everyone a massive favour. The bullshidos and phoney experts have been weeded out, but a note of caution; don't whitewash everything away because you might just miss a trick.

Now some advice for anyone considering learning to fight. It all comes down to three choices, and I'll rank them by difficulty: the first is by far the simplest and definitely the smartest. Don't fight; use any excuse you can, think on your feet, use diplomacy, run, do whatever it takes to not fight. Call the police, laugh out loud (only joking unless you live in a rich neighbourhood). Talk your way out. Do not shag that man's wife; you get the idea – be pre-emptive.

If you do not want to rely on option one, then maybe the second choice is for you. This is the playing smart card. Looking at the weight of evidence that is stacking up in front of our eyes, the evolvement of MMA into a stand-up and grappling game, my advice is clear. Do not pick sides, have both, and cover all bases. Learn to crossfight. Your body may not thank you for it in years to come, but you will hopefully learn a reasonable fight game that can deal with most scenarios. And before you start mentally putting obstacles in the way like 'What if there's more than one attacker or you're on the dreaded street? What would you do if they had a knife?' Defer to option one. 'What if you can't run, you're backed into a corner, blah blah blah.' *God, you won't give up, will you?* Defer to option one, and if that fails you, all you can do is your best; if it wasn't good enough, it wasn't good enough. Hopefully, if you're still alive, brush yourself down, practise and get better.

The third and perhaps last choice is without doubt the most difficult by a country mile. Not only does it involve giving your chosen system or style a hundred per cent commitment, but it is also trusting and taking a stance. What you are saying is even though I am aware my system is old (unless you're developing a new concept) and everything around me is changing, I believe it is enough. If I learn it to the very best of my ability, I believe it will give me back in full technicolour everything I shall ever need.

Norbert was always going to piss in the wind searching for answers in option two; that's what butterflies do. It's similar to the minefield of religion for him. He doesn't want to commit to something he can't see, nor does he want to give up on something that might just be the way. It's a lazy way of keeping your options open. Is it weak or is it smart? Excuse the pun, but God knows. This lack of focus or commitment is why Norbert's fighting will always be average at best.

Chapter 58

Take away

The echoes of Larry Blake's journey have some startling similarities to the Gracie movement and their ethos. Not least recognising that you need two halves: technical and power. Digor found them through different teachers and then set about developing his school outside the confines of tradition and the Chinese way. The change was metaphoric, and the result was a level beyond most comprehension.

Outstanding fighters hone their skills; they have a continuous strive for perfection, knowing they can never achieve it, but let's be honest here – getting damn close. Find a good teacher, good foundations and plenty of graft, yes, lots of hard work, commitment, and many years of practice, an open, enquiring mind, but one that can find the answers within. Yes, you have to be a good problem solver. Be ready to test and prove yourself and learn from faults and defeats. Those are just some requisites to achieving that elevated position.

Someone once said you can be a jack of all trades and be a great MMA fighter, but the key in a nutshell is you can also be a great fighter if you master one system, and even if it is a so-called traditional martial art, you can be a great fighter. Larry never doubted his wing chun; its fighting model was damn near perfect in his eyes. If you end up on your back being choked out, that's on you, not the system. But be careful, for fuck's sake; don't believe everything you hear, question things, and if you are lucky and find an excellent teacher who leads by example, run with it, swing for the fences.

One last note. If you do get to the top, don't be a cock. Use it for good, affect people around you positively, and teach understanding. Lord knows we need it in this world today. This is what Norbert had and you and everyone should too. The result was as illuminating as the Northern Lights in the sky and why this story had to be shared. Digor emphatically chose which path to take. There is nothing wishy-washy about his choices, which explains in part why his fighting skill is incredible.

Clever people figure this out, you can disagree all you like. Yes, but is he better than an MMA champion? Stop it right now; have you not been paying attention? It doesn't matter. There is always someone better and worse. Are you happy? He is, Norbert sort of is, and that's enough really, honestly. Enjoy the ride and be lucky!

Digor never had a family contingent to walk with him on his journey in the same sense as the Gracies. There was the ever-supporting Cole Williams through the early years especially, and later on many notable exceptional students, but Digor's journey was driven from within. Along the way, his wing chun students became the big family. Some were not affected by the experience and some, like Norbert, were deeply changed, motivated, and rewarded by this man. It was their little secret how good he was – a shining inspiration.

If you can get near the top, can you stay there, maintain your level, always seeking to improve, never staying still? The journey is endless for those like Digor. Particularly in the early years, there were no monies to reward him. His riches came from the thing he loved and what it gave back to him. He loves wing chun, and it appears wing chun loves him back.

Chapter 59

Let's be Frank

Norbert still saw the persistent Anthony and the odd waif and stray at his house for some training on a Monday, invited strictly by word of mouth; his garage had been cleared to make some space. He also rolled with the honey badgers aplenty on a Tuesday. The scheduling interference on precious family time weighed him down with heavy guilt. One had to go. He didn't leave with a heavy heart, but tipped his hat to the teacher Lowrie, and some of the Ju-Jitsu guys with their superb ground techniques. He was approaching the ripe old age of fifty, his bones creaked, and time felt like it was running out, but he knew in his heart he wasn't there yet with the training – and if he was honest any fucking thing else. At times he hated being a Capricorn with a vengeance.

Driving his black taxi was most definitely a love-hate affair. But the strangest thing, even against the odds, was that the job miraculously sometimes worked. He found a way through, saw some interesting people and places, from the urban sprawl to the home counties. Witnessed the randomness of life. From mindless rages of violence, hoodies with knives trying to stab one another, to the sweetest acts of kindness from strangers, driving around looking for someone homeless because a passenger had a food parcel from his unfinished meal he wanted to share. Life was a giant theatre show.

He must have driven past it a thousand times, an old disused-looking warehouse, tucked on a side street close to the Highway in East London. He was finally lured by the large faded billboard offering Muay Thai, MMA, and the obligatory Ju-Jitsu. So, one free Saturday morning, Norbert got up early and popped over there to have a nosey. A few people were going through some moves on the mats. To the right, an

Indian-looking trainer put some boxers through their paces. Norbert sat down and watched for half an hour, chatting to a guy whose gaze never left the area of the ground fighters.

'You not joining in the class?' asked Norbs.

'Nah, I got injured last week,' he said.

That figures.

The boxing trainer came over and they had a little talk. Turned out he was one of the managers and to cut a long story short, he invited Norbert back later for a training session. The offer was gladly accepted. Norbert gloved up and he was standing in the ring with Derek, the trainer, and a girl.

'You're going to give her a little workout. Go easy, throw her some moves, and let her do the rest. Be gentle with her.' Derek winked. And so, they boxed. Turned out she was there for a workout with a wee bit of boxing realism thrown in. Norbert feigned some moves and threw out some soft jabs while she hit the fuck out of him. The gloves felt enormous and provided enough protection to guard his face. Nothing hit home too hard.

When her time was up, she thanked them both and left for the changing rooms after a nice little workout. Possibly feeling a little sorry for Norbert and unimpressed, Derek turned and said, 'Come on, let's have a little go.'

Norbert let Derek throw out some shots, dipping his toes in the water, weighing it up, and then he went for it. They exchanged some shots. Norbert was enjoying this; pleased by the fact he was still standing he was getting more confident by the second. Norbert parried one of the shots and got a nice hit into the trainer's side. He threw some nice body shots in, and at the end, they touched gloves.

'Wow, thanks, I really enjoyed that,' Norbert said.

'My pleasure – you're not bad, you know,' Derek said.

Norbert mulled over it for the rest of the day but decided that boxing, as fun as it was, wouldn't give him what he was looking for. He did the honourable thing and texted Derek a bit later to let him know. 'I enjoyed our little spar today but I don't think I can commit to a regular class at the moment. Thanks again, and good luck, Norbert.'

Later that evening a reply came back. 'I think you broke my ribs.'

Must be a joke. Norbert responded with one of his own. 'Yeah, my nose is a little sore too.' It wasn't, but it could have been; Norbert's nose wasn't the smallest target.

'I'm serious,' Derek retorted, 'I've been to hospital and they tell me I've fractured my ribs.'

Norbert was overcome with terrible guilt. *I mean, for heaven's sake I wasn't punching hard, fifty to sixty per cent max, with big padded gloves.* He offered his sincerest apologies. *Fucking hell, when I try out another class, I either sustain an injury or now it seems cause one.* His attempts at broadening his training spectrum were nothing short of an unmitigated disaster. Norbert stayed away from temptation for a long while until another episode came his way and fell into his lap.

A guy hailed Norbert down outside Rooney's boxing gym, formerly a railway arch beneath London Bridge station. During the subsequent trip across the river to the north side of London, they chatted. It turned out Benjamin was also a fitness and boxing trainer (*here we go again*); he told Norbert all about his previous martial arts experience, which included wing chun. Norbert was interested; they talked about their mutual interest and Benjamin suggested they do some training together. Same time next week.

Norbert tentatively stepped inside the gym for their session. Two fighters looked like they were going hard at it in the ring, while people of all shapes and sizes were busy working the punchbags and going through their routines. Benjamin greeted Norbert and ushered him to a side part of the gym.

'You got no gloves?' Benjamin asked.

'No, I came as I am,' said Norbert.

Apparently, that changed everything. Benjamin looked a little lost; he wasn't sure now what to do with our Norbert.

Norbert grabbed the bull by the horns. 'Why don't I show you some drills, throw me some punches,' he said.

Norbert caught Benjamin's first punch with a cupped palm, same again with the second, at the third he simultaneously put his other palm onto Benjamin's face. It was controlled. Benjamin felt it but in no way did it hurt; it just stopped his flow. Benjamin stopped, froze like a rabbit caught in the headlights. Did Norbert see his lips quivering?

'Why did you hit me in the face?'

'Are you serious? That move was with control. I didn't hit your face, I placed a palm onto it, not a fist.'

There was no going back; he'd lost Benjamin, who went into the mother of all strops, bad wolf bending Norbert's head again. 'Let's do it for real and you'll see the difference.' It was no good, this was going nowhere; they'd finished before they had even started. Benjamin was skulking, not saying anything. The silence was deafening. Norbert made his apologies and left in total disbelief. Had he found the only boxing trainer who didn't want to play fight? Apparently, he had. Was he just full of bullshit? Had he never fought? Was it the no gloves?

Back to work, in the taxi, his head was spinning. Well, what a life. What a journey. What a fucking disaster. Someone hailed him down and his mind was back on track, vigilant to the job in hand.

Later, when he broke from work for a bite to eat, he phoned Nikki. 'How're the girls, how was your day?'

Nikki gave him the full run down; he could listen to her warble forever. It took his busy mind away.

'Did you meet that guy?' she asked.

'OMG, it was a disaster.'

'What now?'

He couldn't even be bothered to tell her. 'I'm done, Nik, seriously. I am never telling anyone I do wing chun again. I'm never going to spar, play or practise with absolutely anyone outside class again. Ever.'

'You've had a good run, Bomber. I'm proud of you. You can hold your head high.'

'I love you so much, Nikki.'

'I love you too.'

'Can't wait to be back home tomorrow.' Norbert ended the call. He could tell Nikki was relieved and so was he; his shoulders already felt lighter.

Chapter 60

Old friends

And that was what he did. Norbert kept his trap shut. As the years marched on, both his and Rufus's head hair turned grey. Both the girls had boys, and Nikki and Norbert were proud grandparents. They would still have their struggles; the eldest grandson was autistic, the youngest would witness his parents break up. Norbert never regretted for a second taking up martial arts.

He still saw Larry for the odd private class, more to enjoy the company of the great man than anything else. Larry was going to the Caribbean more frequently to be close to his mum and dad, so eventually the private lessons petered out, but when they did happen it was always worth the wait. They would laugh about Norbert's ordeal; they would laugh about anything.

From his very first lesson, twenty-plus years had flown by; he was neither content with his level nor upset. From his first visit, the goal was simple; he wanted to fight, to protect his family if need be. And, of course, it's impossible to know if what you have is enough. All you can do is prepare the best you can for any eventuality and do your level best in the circumstances. Let's just say Norbert sleeps better knowing what he has, what Larry has taught him, and if he may be so bold, supposes that Larry is pleased somewhat; he rarely gives out compliments, but Norbert can tell. He has gone from the shy, confused, inept, and extremely novice fighter Larry first met to just another now sculpted by Larry's hands into a more rounded, grounded, and adjusted individual.

But look at the trouble questioning his art and his ability had gotten him. Was all that time wasted venturing out in the wider world? I don't think so, but could it have been better spent? Definitely. Focusing on his training and making what he had better would have been a more productive enquiry. Norbert's search for all-roundness in martial arts had left him arguably no better off than before. But that's him all over, his beef.

He'll always be a butterfly; it's just ingrained in his nature. But he's accepted that poisoned chalice and although the moments come and go, age has dampened the madness down, softened the edges. He tries to be a better man, a good father, a good partner. Around Remembrance Day every year he randomly picks someone for a free ride in the taxi, a squaddie going home late at night, cavalry officers dressed to the nines on an evening out, or last year the Chelsea pensioner returning home. Being kind is our greatest gift. To that end, he'll be eternally grateful for everything Digor has taught him, fighting-wise – he could not have been luckier than to find him. In truth, part of him feels that he has let Digor down, underperformed to his potential. We all have our crosses to bear. More importantly, though, Norbert owes Digor a debt more than he can imagine for the shining example he has been of how to lead one's life trying to be the best you can be. That is the tougher fight.

Invitation

If you got to here without cheating, there's a good chance you finished reading my book. Now what?

Well, first let me tell you something. How I felt when I found out that Fargo's "true story" claim was a lie. Like discovering Jools Holland's Hootenanny show is pre-recorded. It left me feeling a little defrauded, I sighed as yet another example of how gullible I can be slapped me right in the face.

The story you just read is no red herring, it's as real as can be, I should know I was there!

Whether you like it or not, you can't deny it. Would you have done it differently? Are you on a similar journey, starting or finishing? I genuinely would like to know.

Please check out my website, www.bobbyhatton.co.uk. Have a browse, it will bring you up to speed with my next offerings.

Remember at the beginning of the book the customer quality guarantee of clawing some money back. I was deadly serious. Again, check out the website.

Lastly if we are to never connect again, I wish to thank you for purchasing my book. It genuinely means a great deal to me, much more than the £1.89 royalty after costs that I earn as an author per copy.

Yours,
Bobby.

Milton Keynes UK
Ingram Content Group UK Ltd.
UKHW011821231023
431199UK00001B/4